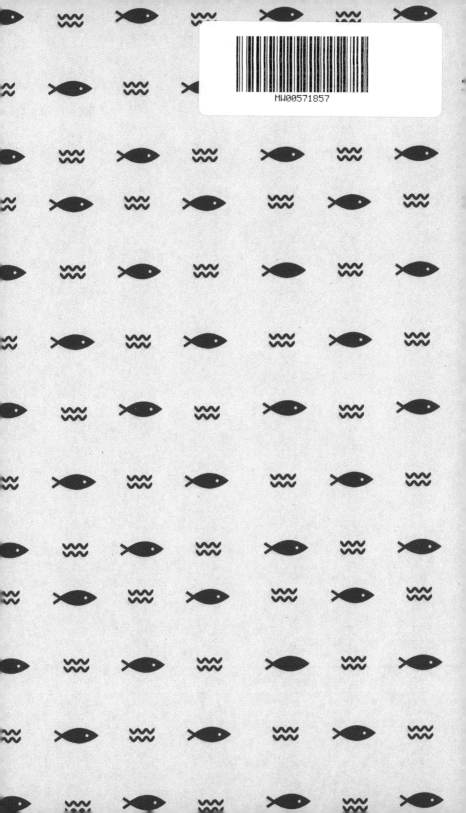

MW00571857

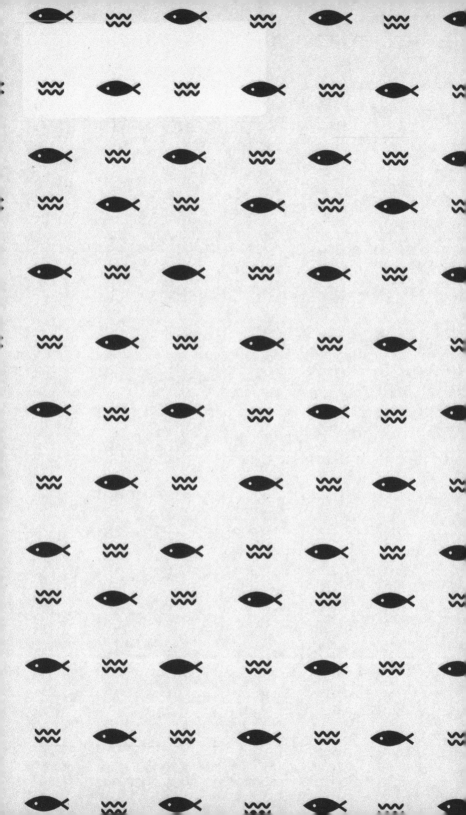

MARLIN
WEEK

Written by
KATHERINE RUSKEY

Artwork by
CAREY CHEN

For my Dad

Ocean City, Maryland
White Marlin Open

If you've ever been so lucky to visit the charming peninsula that we call Ocean City, Maryland, then nothing I am about to describe will surprise you. If you have never had the privilege to visit this quaint town, which settles between the mainland of southern Maryland and the Atlantic Ocean, you are in for a treat. The salty yet beautiful land was actually created by an unforgiving hurricane back in 1933. Its harsh winds and chaotic tides wreaked havoc on train tracks, which connected the southern point of Ocean City across to the majestic lands of Assateague Island. The tracks, since swept away—along with much of the land—created what is now the famous Ocean City Inlet. The narrow inlet now acts as a waterway for boaters and fishermen to cruise from the wide sea of the Atlantic Ocean to the much shallower waters of Assawoman Bay.

For much of the summer, captains and first mates lead their fishing charters from the Ocean City buoy, which smoothly floats over the sea waves just outside of the large rocks of the jetty. And it's right there at that very buoy where the great race that is famously known as The White Marlin Open begins.

Here are the basic tournament rules in a nutshell:

Boats cannot pass the Ocean City Buoy prior to 5 AM on a fishing day.

Lines in no earlier than 8:30 AM and out by 3:30 PM (unless a fish is hooked before the 3:30 PM cut-off time.)

No boat may fish further than 100 nautical miles from the Ocean City Buoy.

Each boat can fish for a maximum of 3 days. Laydays must be reported ahead of time.

Fun fishing is permitted on laydays.

All fish to be weighed must be at the scales at Harbour Island Marina between the times of 4 PM and 9:15 PM (exceptions if there were a drawbridge malfunction).

Rods may not be transferred from angler to angler mid-reeling. No other hands may touch the rod. (Briefly touching the angler to prevent them from falling is permitted.)

In the event of a tie in weight, the fish that is not gaffed will be the winner.

Any anglers to win over $50,000 may be required to take a polygraph test before taking the winnings.

Tournament directors' decisions are final.

On any given year, up to 500 boats register for The White Marlin Open (WMO)—and its popularity is only gaining speed. With a cumulative $10.8 million worth of prize winnings, it's no wonder people flock to "the white marlin capital of the world" for this incredible sight! With that being said, grab a beer, your favorite flip-flops, and let's get hooked!

Tight Lines.

And here is where the lines were dropped...

Last Summer

Sunday
Rob

Rob sat at the bar at Sunset Marina, a cold draft in hand after a long day on the boat. The bar was unusually empty for this time of year. It was the third day of the Marlin tournament and normally, the bar was three people deep. But tonight, there were only a handful of people there. He sat at his normal spot in front of the big screen so that he could enjoy his beer while he watched the Orioles and Red Sox game. The Orioles were down by 2. It was ironic because that was how he felt—down. He and Leanne had a fight last night and he ended up sleeping on his boat, *The Other Woman*. Even more ironic—the fight was over "*the other woman*".

This Summer

Sunday

Captains' Meeting

Category: White Marlin
1st Place: TBD
2nd Place: TBD
3rd Place: TBD

Category: Blue Marlin
1st Place: TBD
2nd Place: TBD
3rd Place: TBD

Category: Tuna
1st Place: TBD
2nd Place: TBD
3rd Place: TBD

FINN

It was the day of the Captains' meeting. All boat captains were required to attend to go over the logistics and common sense basics of The White Marlin Open.
This year, there were over 500 boats entered in the tournament all ranging from seasoned captains to first-timers. Finn saw quite a few people that he knew from fishing there for the last several years. He also saw many new faces he'd never seen before. He saw Brett from *Size Is Everything*, Christian from *She's All I Need*, and Mark from *All Talk*. They grabbed their beers and sat around waiting for the meeting to start. The email said it was starting at 6 pm. It was quarter 'til and there were still several guys making their way in.

This wasn't Finn's first time in the tournament. He'd been involved in the WMO for over ten years now. He started out as a first mate on Rob Hennessey's boat, *The Other Woman*. A lot of what he knows, he learned from him. He owed him a lot.

After several years of learning from Rob, he decided it was time to embark out on his own. He was nervous to tell him, seeing that Rob would need to find another first mate—but he was also excited at the prospect of running his own show. At the end of that fishing season, Finn had asked Rob to stay and have a celebratory beer. He knew that Rob wasn't the type to turn down an opportunity to talk fishing and drink a nice cold one.

Finn ordered two Dogfish Head bottles from Summer, one of the bartenders that had a reoccurring shift, at Sunset Marina. It was then he let Rob have the news.

"I've been doing a lot of thinking," he started. He took a long sip of the hoppy beer to steal some time. "—and I think it's time for me to run my own boat. This is going to be the last year I'm working on *The Other Woman* with you. I owe a lot of what I know and what I've learned from you, Rob. And I can't thank you enough for everything that you've done for me."

Rob was leaning over the bar with his elbows propped up, cupping his own beer bottle. His white visor, which was intended to block the sun from his eyes obviously hadn't done its job. Rob had an intense sunglass tan line on either side of his temples. His sunglasses hung on their Croakies around his neck. He began to nod his head but didn't speak for what felt like several minutes. Finn wasn't sure if Rob was angry, sad, or both. He finally spoke.

Rob patted Finn on his shoulder.

"I'm going to really miss you, Finn. But I completely agree with you. You're ready, and much more ready than I was at your age. I'm proud of you. It's been like having my own son on the boat with me. I've taught you a lot but you've taught me a lot as well. I'm going to miss you, bud." Rob raised his beer toward Finn. "To bigger and better."

"To bigger and better," Finn repeated. They clicked bottles for the last time as Captain and first mate.

And with that, Finn moved on to "bigger and better" when he came across *Weekend Vibes,* a '64 Spencer sportfishing boat. It was a dream! White and tan interior was highlighted with dark brown trim. Two bedrooms, each with its own head, planked on either side of the cabin which led to a good-sized living area equipped with a wet bar and big screen TV. The captain's bridge was donned in brand new Garmin electronics and a view where he would be able to see marlin for miles. She was perfect!

A few years later, *Weekend Vibes* was tied up at Sunset Marina in West Ocean City. Sunset was a hot spot for a majority of fishermen—but a hot spot for a majority of fishermen—but not as hot as Harbour Island Marina on 14th street. Each summer, lines of boats waited to weigh in their award-winning marlins, tunas, and wahoos. Several boats at Sunset Marina and Harbour Island alike entered the WMO. However, several boats fished from other marinas as well. White Marlin Marina and Ocean City's Fishing Center were also popular marinas where great contending boats were kept.

This year, Finn was looking forward to winning. He had been captaining *Weekend Vibes,* for about three years now. He had planned on taking his fiancé, Whitney, on a surprise vacation with some of the winnings. Finn and Whitney had experienced some great losses in the past few years and it was always a challenge to get away with work. They needed a break as much as they deserved it.

He thought about the photo of them that sat on top of their mantle. They were standing side by side on Smathers Beach in Key West. His brown hair curled up from under his ball cap. Whitney's head rested on his shoulder, her shoulder-length brown hair blew in the salty breeze. Both of them were on the verge of sunburn, and Finn sported his sunglasses tan line. By then, he had already bought an engagement ring. They had been dating for less than six months—but he knew. Winning this year's tournament would be life-changing for them.

Snapping back to reality, Finn heard the basic rules of the tournament being outlined. There were five days of available fishing; however, you were only allowed to fish three. Lines were able to go in at 8:30 a.m. and had to be out by 3:30. There were several categories to fish: marlin (blue and white), tuna, and wahoo—among others. The leaderboard was posted each morning and obviously changed throughout the evening as captains, mates, and boats made their way to the weigh-in station at Harbour Island Marina.

As boats come into the docks, people flock to the piers to watch this magnificent event. Million-dollar fish are brought on shore, weighed in, then cut into steaks to either take home or be donated to the Maryland Food Bank. Roughly 2,000 pounds of fish are donated annually by local anglers.

As the emcee of the Captains' meeting finished up with a "Good luck tomorrow, everyone—and tight lines!" guys started heading to their boats for another round. Just as Finn was about to head out, he felt a hand on his back.

"Hey, TJ! It's good to see you, man. Long time." It was TJ Moxley, captain of *Big Distraction*, and his famous dock dog, Marlin. They shook hands and Finn knelt down for a little pow-wow with the pooch.

"Hey, Finn," TJ said as the two shook hands.

"Good to see you."

"How is everything? How's Whitney? Working hard as always?"

"Always. But loving it." Finn felt extremely protective of Whit ever since that first appointment. He didn't want to lie to people about what they were going through, but at the same time, wanted to keep their private lives private.

"Well. I just wanted to stop and say good luck out there. It was good to see you. See you on the dock."

"Thanks, man. Let's try to steer clear of what happened last year. We don't need any of that again," Finn said.

"You're telling me."

The two men shook hands as they walked out of the Captains' meeting, each one of them hungry for the millions of dollars in prize money. And Finn was right. Between the both of them, the chaos that was last year's tournament was nothing they wanted to repeat.

ROB

Rob and Leanne have been married for 28 years. 28 years full of laughing, crying, minuscule arguments, inside jokes, and everything in between. Their most cherished memories however have all revolved around their twin boys, Nate and Josh.

Nate and Josh were identical twins. So identical that only Rob and Leanne are able to tell them apart most of the time. And even from far away, it can sometimes be tricky. Their look is very "surfer-esque." Their tall bodies are tanned from the amount of hours spent in the sun. Widening shoulders and long, lean legs. Their brown hair has wisps of gold from the sun and is a bit longer than Leanne prefers. But she still thinks they look handsome.

In the past few months, Leanne had become more sentimental when it came to the boys. Since they graduated, she missed sitting on the sidelines watching lacrosse matches, soccer games, and baseball. She missed the camaraderie between the other parents that she used to see. She and the other parents for years sat in the freezing cold, biting wind, monsoon downpours, awful scorching heat, and every other weather element you could think of. When it was time for the boys to graduate high school, Leanne, Rob, and the other parents decided they needed to celebrate as well. They all piled into their SUVs full of sports equipment and headed to Fishtales for one last hoorah together.

Nate and Josh were both going to Salisbury University right here on the Eastern Shore for a few reasons. One, they were best friends—there was never talk about them splitting up and heading to different colleges. And two, they both loved the beach here too much to leave, they agreed. Nate decided on a major in sports physical therapy. Nate had always been more into science and how the body works. Josh was more the free spirit, wing-it kind of soul. He had decided to major in business like one of his friends but was still on the fence about what he wanted to do when he finished college.

They were honors students, great athletes, and genuinely nice kids. Rob and Leanne knew that no matter what happened, they'd always have each other.

Both boys had gotten summer jobs in Ocean City at two of the most popular hangouts. Nate busses tables at Ropewalk on 83rd street and Josh snagged a job as a barback at Fishtales on 23rd. Since they were both still 20, the bar scene wasn't quite yet legal for them; even though Rob and Leanne weren't born yesterday. Most of the boys' time was centered around hanging out with friends at the beach, surfing when the swell is just right, and of course, meeting girls. Neither one had a girlfriend that Rob or Leanne knows about, but there had been on-again, off-again faces that Rob recognizes—but their names, he never remembers.

He would ask Leanne their names but she'd been working non-stop ever since the boys' senior year was coming to an end. She worked as a top-of-the-line real estate agent in the Delmarva region. He was extremely proud of her accomplishments and her growing list of upscale clientele. It seemed that as soon as one house sold, two more clients would surface, and she was off again house hunting, showing, wining, and dining.

That left Rob with more time on his hands than he knew what to do with. He would sit around the house and wait for her to come home after eleven just to see her slide off her heels and crawl into bed. A bed where they haven't had sex in over six months. Six months! And every time he tried to initiate or even bring up the topic, she would brush it off with a "headache" or "I'm just so tired. Can we wait until tomorrow?"

What's another three months, he would think, feeling rejected.

• • •

Rob had spotted Finn at a table at the Captains' meeting. He went over to sit down.

"Hey, man. How are you?" Rob greeted Finn with a big bear hug.

"Hey, Rob! You're looking good. Lost a few pounds there?" He and Rob had a running joke that if his wife had seen what he ate down on the docks, she'd have a fit.

The two sat at a table and did a little catching up.

"So, how are the boys doing?"

"Oh, good. Good. They're both working this summer. Josh at Fishtales and Nate at Ropewalk. I'm actually surprised that they split up."

"We love Ropewalk. Their Thai shrimp is one of my favs."

"How's everything going with you? Work? Whit?"

"Work's as busy as ever. And Whitney will be coming down this week for a few days. I'm looking forward to taking her on a nice vacation after I win this year." He laughed and took a sip of his beer as he said this.

Rob's grand laugh echoed.

"Well—you might be staying local for that grand vacation since *I'm* going to be the one winning it all this time."

"That's some wishful thinking. Care to make a little wager on it? Say $500?"

"That's how I know I didn't teach you enough. Make it $1,000." Rob stuck his hand out to seal the deal.

"You're on. Good luck, old man."

• • •

After the Captains' meeting, Rob popped home to the condo to see if anyone was there. Maybe Leanne would be there, even though he knew better. He walked in the door.

"Anyone home?" The kitchen that overlooked the bay was clean. Up to Leanne's standards. The boys were nowhere to be seen and Leanne was not home. *Why did I even get my hopes up?* It was the middle of summer. Of course no one would be home.

He grabbed a beer and sat out on the deck. The sun was a brilliant summer orange color. It felt like it was still 100 degrees outside, even though it was after 8 p.m. Even though Rob preferred that his family were home, he tried to enjoy the quiet. The waves lapped near the piers and the seagulls flew above. It all seemed so peaceful. He tried so hard to relax and take it in. But the truth was, he was missing Leanne something terrible.

He wanted the Leanne back that held his hand over dinner and sat on the deck reading funny memes that she found on social media. Her long brunette hair hanging down past her shoulders and those emerald-green eyes.

Don't get me wrong, he thought. *I am very proud of her—but the money isn't worth not having her here with me.*

It was getting late and Rob was fishing early tomorrow. That meant sleeping on the boat tonight. Tradition.

Walking into the kitchen, he found a piece of paper and a pen. *My Leanne, I miss you! Love, Rob*

LEANNE

Earlier that day, she studied herself in the mirror, first turning right then left, checking all angles. She was extremely happy with what she saw. She had managed to lose a few more pounds that were teetering on the scale all spring. *Must be the long hours*, she thought to herself. Or was it the fact that she actually felt sexy and wanted by someone?

Leanne was one of the top real estate agents on the Delmarva peninsula and was on track to quickly bypass some of her top competition. Business had been extremely profitable for her in the past few months. She had her first multi-million dollar listing that sold in less than a week for more than the asking price due to a last-minute bidding war by clients. Two weeks after that, another huge listing sold for just under the asking price, but with her commission—that's more than some people make in a year.

She felt powerful. She could really get used to this. She could also get used to the unbelievable sex that she'd been having with her new client. He had sought Leanne out of numerous trusted real estate agents in the area. He worked in New York on Wall Street and was looking for a summer place for some quiet time off out of the city. This house he was in the market for would be his third "summer place," just after a cottage in Key West and a "small villa" in Bermuda. Her client was looking for something more secluded, off the beaten path with a direct water view.

"Maybe a cozy little beachside cottage...with no neighbors," he told Leanne during their first meeting. She knew that he was trouble. She knew that she should walk away. She should tell him that she was unable to take him on as a client. Maybe she could make up a lie and say that she was already at her max. But on the other hand, she wanted to take him on. Head on.

JULES

The sun was setting on the bay as Jules was finishing up some last-minute things on her shift on the beach of Assateague Island. The summer months were in full swing and campers were settling in. Vacationers were in and out, campers full of fishing rods, kayaks, and the ever-popular makings for s'mores. Just one more peek over the dunes to make sure things were tidied up and she'd be on her way.

As she approached the top of the dunes, a yellow lab came running up to her! She quickly realized that he or she had just come out of the water from a swim as her pants were now soaked. The dog shook, almost in slow motion, flinging water everywhere including her face and hair. She was furious! Who lets their dog off the leash on a public beach in the middle of summer? What a careless jerk.

Katherine Ruskey

TJ AND MARLIN

After a long day on the dock prepping *Big Distraction* for their first day of the marlin tournament, this was exactly what he wanted. TJ and Marlin took off on a hike down the long beaches of Assateague Island. Looking out over the ocean, TJ could see the light blue Ocean City water tower in the distance. To the right of that, he could make out the outline of the famous inlet rollercoaster that he has to admit has never ridden. Marlin was excellent at playing fetch and loved hurdling himself over the rolling ocean waves to seek out his favorite tennis ball. TJ sat on the warm sand and tossed the ball just beyond the breakers as Marlin dove headfirst after it. They did this about fifty more times.

"Early morning tomorrow, guy. We gotta get heading home. One more and we're heading back. OK?"

Marlin shook his tail; his ears perked up waiting for the launch. Out went the ball and out went Marlin. TJ got up as Marlin led them back down the beach toward the Jeep. The beach was pretty empty on this side—all but a few surfers were left in the water catching the last waves of the day. As they approached the dunes, Marlin took off, leaving TJ much further behind than usual.

"Whoa whoa, Marlin!" he called. He picked up to a slow jog to catch up. As he got closer to the top of the dunes, he realized that Marlin had befriended a park ranger who was now soaked from the knees down from Marlin's greeting.

Great... Now I'm going to get a ticket for having him off the leash. Way to go, bonehead.

"I'm so sorry," he started to explain to the ranger, but then stopped mid-sentence. TJ was speechless. This girl in front of him was simply beautiful. Her long blonde hair was pulled back in a ponytail. Her eyes were the color of off-shore ocean waves. She wore a rangers uniform of dark green khaki shorts and a shirt to match.

"I'm so sorry," he continued. "We were just heading back to the parking lot. He usually doesn't run away like this—ever, really."

He reached down and clipped Marlin's leash to his collar, which had brightly-colored marlins on it. The girl looked at TJ as she stood up.

"It's okay. I mean, it's not really okay. He didn't bother me is what I meant to say. But the rules are that all dogs must be on a leash. There's a lot of other people on the beach and we just have to be safe."

She reached into her back pocket and took out a ticket book. TJ's heart sank.

"I'm really sorry that I have to do this but..."

"Seriously, you don't have to do that. I'll make sure he's on a leash from now on."

"I know you will. But it's park rules," she said.

"We were really just on our way out."

The girl looked at TJ as if contemplating whether this cute guy and his dog really deserved it. "Can I have your name, please?"

His hands were sweaty and he felt a bit tongue-tied.

"I'm TJ," he said, extending his sweaty hand, which also now smelled like a gross tennis ball.

She gently smiled and extended hers back in return.

"Jules," she replied.

"I have to tell you, Jules, Marlin here feels really badly about this. He knows he shouldn't be running off..." Marlin stood next to TJ and looked up at the sound of his name. TJ scratched the back of Marlin's ears.

"I'm sure he does. That's why this ticket is more of a warning." She tore the paper from the book and handed it to TJ.

TJ had never been overly-confident when it came to women. In fact, he was more of the shy and quiet type. So when he felt his heart speeding up at the sight of this girl, whose name he just learned was Jules, he almost didn't recognize himself.

"I understand," he said, shifting his weight in the thick sand of the dunes. "Can Marlin and I show you how badly we feel and take you out sometime?" He straightened his hat, which didn't need straightening. It was always a nervous habit. He knelt down and rubbed Marlin's back. It was almost dry now due to the evening heat.

Jules tried not to smile too hard but this guy was just too cute. She looked down at Marlin with his sandy tennis ball at his side.

"I think I would like that," she replied, smiling. Her ponytail was swaying from the ocean breeze and tiny wisps of hair danced around the frame of her face. She took the warning back from TJ and jotted her number on the back, then handed it back to him.

"You two stay out of trouble. And don't forget to use that leash." TJ took the ticket back. His fingers briefly brushed hers.

Jules turned to go over the dunes toward the parking lot. TJ looked down at the slip of paper. He had a feeling that this was going to be one of the best things that had ever happened to him.

Monday

Category: White Marlin
1st Place: TBD
2nd Place: TBD
3rd Place: TBD

Category: Blue Marlin
1st Place: TBD
2nd Place: TBD
3rd Place: TBD

Category: Tuna
1st Place: TBD
2nd Place: TBD
3rd Place: TBD

TJ AND MARLIN

The next morning, TJ woke up at 3:00 just before his 3:30 alarm was set to go off. The nights before a tournament were usually like that. The anticipation of the day really didn't allow him to sleep but a few hours. He got up, let Marlin out, and made his coffee. Before the Captains' meeting yesterday, he went and took some stuff to the boat which was docked at Sunset Marina. He didn't really need to take much this morning; except for Marlin.

TJ brushed his teeth and threw on his favorite hat with the tears on the bill. He felt that it gave it character. A "Big Distraction" t-shirt, Billabong shorts, and leather flip-flops from K-Coast completed his ensemble. Marlin finished eating his breakfast of Kibble and they were ready to go.

Marlin followed right behind TJ as he locked the door and headed out. It was 3:30 by then. Marlin was used to these early days and enjoyed the brisk morning drives in the Jeep. A short ten-minute drive and the pair arrived and parked. They weren't the first car in the lot. Some people decided to sleep in the boats for convenience. He saw Rob Hennesey's lights on down the dock. Rob owned and captained *The Other Woman*. He was an excellent fisherman and was always one of TJ's friendly competitors.

TJ's first mate, Kyle, was already there prepping rods, lines, and riggers. He would've preferred that all to be done last night but he knew it would get done. After mating for TJ for over three years now, Kyle was one of the best out there and he trusted his judgment and skill.

"Morning, cap," Kyle greeted as TJ stepped on board. Kyle was 24 years old and had just graduated college with a degree in business. He often wondered what he would do with his degree. All he wanted to do was fish. Maybe one day he would own his own charter. He's good for now. He can only imagine what skill set he would have with a few more years of experience under his belt.

"Ready to win?" Kyle asked.

"You bet. Nothing's going to stop us this year! What time did you get here?

"Around 3. Too excited to sleep."

"Same."

"Good morning to you too, Marlin. I didn't forget about you." Kyle reached deep into the pockets of his cargo shorts and pulled out a dog cookie. He kept them on him whenever he worked with TJ, knowing that Marlin would be there, too.

TJ took off his hat and ran his fingers through his brown tousled hair. "Everyone should be here around 4:30. I want to leave by 5 to get where we're going. I think we're going to try the same spot from the bachelor charter, maybe a few miles south of Baltimore Canyon."

Kyle laughed. "Oh yeah, I remember that day. Great fishing day. Hopefully, Monty and his friends can keep their liquor better than the groom and his friends."

"Yeah. What a day. Anyway, I figured we landed some nice-size marlins and that tuna. I want to stick close to there."

During this year's tournament, TJ was hosting Monty Gilmore, 62, a stockbroker from Connecticut. He had invited a bunch of his investment friends to join in on some of the fun. An avid follower of the WMO, Monty had contacted TJ months ago about fishing with his friends on *Big Distraction*. They were excited to fish, had plenty of money to bet, and were hungry for the millions of dollars in winnings—not that any of them needed it. It was more of a guys' trip while their wives stayed home brunching at fancy restaurants, taking barre classes (whatever that was), and drinking champagne while getting Botox.

TJ immediately agreed to host Monty, seeing that he was eager to actually fish. Plus, the idea that the money for the boat and calcutta was chump change to them all. He had a feeling that Monty was footing the bill for it all, but who cared. Let's fish!

As TJ and Kyle wrapped up a few odds and ends on *Big Distraction*, a small wake rocked the large boat. In the dark, he couldn't see anything out on the water but saw the lights of *The Other Woman* heading out. Rob always liked a head start. *I don't blame him.* That's why he's placed in several categories a few times in the past couple of years. Early bird gets the worm. Or the marlin in this case.

Down on the dock, TJ could hear Kyle talking to some voices who he assumed were Monty and his gang. Looking down from the bridge, TJ saw a large man about 6 foot 5, wearing a navy blue polo shirt, khaki shorts, and dock siders. He recognized that to be Monty from the photo attached to his Gmail account. However, this Monty wasn't wearing an expensive Armani suit and tie.

"Morning guys!" TJ greeted them from the bridge. "You ready to do some fishing today?"

"Hell yeah!" yelled a friend from the dock, carrying what looked like a hundred-pound cooler. This guy looked to be about thirty years younger than Monty and didn't really fit the regular stockbroker mold.

TJ climbed down the ladder and extended his hand to Monty.

"Glad you guys made it." TJ introduced himself to all the guys, including the cooler carrier. There was Monty, his best friend Walt—also in his sixties—Sam and Jaque, coworkers of theirs, and then lastly Brendon, the cooler carrier—otherwise known as Monty's youngest son. TJ didn't know the whole story but inferred that Brendon was the odd man out somehow but didn't seem to care. His attire showed more of a laid-back, let's-have-fun vibe while the other four had a relaxed and boat casual time in mind. Either way, TJ didn't care who he fished with. He cared that he was able to boat some fish and win some big money while doing it.

"Kyle will show you the boat and where to put the cooler. I'm going to check a few more things and we're taking off at five sharp. It'll take us about three hours to get where we're going, so relax and enjoy the ride. Lines go in at 8:30, out by 3:30, and hopefully, we'll be heading in with a lot of flags flying."

He knew it was way too early and wanted to wait, but also knew he wouldn't have cell service. He opened his text messages, pulled Marlin's ticket out of his wallet, and tapped in Jules' cell number. It was 4:53 but he couldn't wait one minute longer.

> *Good morning, it's TJ from the beach.*
> *I just wanted to say that I look forward*
> *to seeing you again. I'm fishing all day*
> *and won't have cell service until about*
> *6:30 or so. I'd love to take you out this*
> *week. Is tomorrow too soon?*

Send. His heart had picked up speed as he watched the text jump up. He was ready to slide his phone back into his pocket but stopped suddenly. He was stunned when he saw three little dots come up on his screen indicating Jules was typing. *What was she doing up this early? he thought to himself.*

> *Hey—Good luck today! I'd love to see*
> *you sooner. Is tonight too soon? :)*

Tonight? TJ thought quickly.

*If 8:30 isn't too late, I'll pick you up
then. I just need some time to get
the boat in and weigh the
winning fish :)*

Three dots.

*I'll see you at 8:30. Sunglass emoji.
Go get 'em! Fish and trophy emoji.
Can't wait to see you.
1711 Edgewater Avenue :)*

A huge smirk came across TJ's face as he turned his phone on airplane mode and slid it into a compartment on the dashboard. Well, the only thing that could make this day any better is bringing in that million-dollar marlin.

He called down from the wheel, "Let's go get some fish, boys!" Kyle untied *Big Distraction*, and out of the marina they coasted.

TJ AND MARLIN

Rob slept on *The Other Woman* like he always did the night before fishing the White Marlin Open. It's easier on him because he's already at the marina and he doesn't have a chance of waking Leanne. She'd been killing herself for the past few months making a name for herself in the Delmarva real estate world.

His alarm went off at 3, coffee by 3:05 on the deck while he watched Accuweather on his phone and the weather channel on the TV. North westerly winds at 4 knots coming off the bayside. No rain and 92 degrees. The sun would be shining all day. It was going to be a scorcher again for sure. But the promise of no rain and a calm ocean was music to his ears. Sounds like a day to bring 'em in big.

Rob's mate, Kevin, was a friend of his. He'd been working for Rob for a few years. Kevin was Finn Donahough's replacement once Finn went to captain *Weekend Vibes*. Rob thought of Finn as another son. He's seen Finn grow from a young guy eager to learn knots, rigs, and lines to rigging ballyhoo and boating some monster billfish.

Kevin was good, but he just wasn't Finn. He was due at the boat by 3:30 but would probably show up sooner because that's how Kevin was. The team he was fishing with this year were long-time clients of his. Long enough that they've actually become very good friends. He and Leanne always have dinner with them while they're in town.

Bill Wallace, his wife Sharon along with their two sons, Jeff and Adam, with their wives Jill and Eve all lived in Annapolis. They did everything together. Their families had joined

Rob on a charter about ten years ago. Rob took them out, hammered some fish, filleted it at the pier, and was able to send them home with a cooler full of fresh tuna. Ever since then, Rob and Bill had fished together several other times including the annual Tuna Tournament and The Flounder Pounder. Any excuse to fish, Rob did.

Out of the corner of his eye, Rob saw Kevin pull up in his truck. It was 3:14 on his phone. He could always count on him. As always, Kevin came with his extra-large cup of sweet tea, which he knew tasted like a mouth full of syrupy sugar. He preferred unsweetened himself thanks to Leanne. She had gotten the entire family into unsweet tea among several other healthy foods during her healthy habits kick a few years back. Living in a house full of boys, you would think that soda cans and bags of Nacho Cheese Doritos would be the norm. Not anymore. And they all have Leanne to thank. Maybe.

Leanne was always thinking about what was best for the family. Whether it was health, money, or instilling values. How had he gotten so lucky all those years ago?

"Morning boss," Kevin said as he stepped from the pier to the deck of the boat. "Sleep good?"

"Eh. You know there's always the excitement of the first day. But I can't complain."

"I know what you mean. I told Mya to bring the girls down to the scales tonight. They love coming to see the big boats and fish."

Kevin was a girl dad. And a good one at that. Rob would never know what to do with a daughter—except keep her away from the boys.

"They'll enjoy that. Make sure you bring them on board and take them up top." He pointed up to the bridge.

"I definitely will. Thanks." He walked inside to drop off his backpack. When he reemerged from the cabin, he said, "I prepped everything last night while you were at the Captains' meeting. All the rods are ready to go. Outriggers set, down riggers ready. I know you like things done the night before."

Rob had gotten back to the boat around 9:30 and headed to Teasers for a burger and fries. The bar was packed as always, but he was always able to squeeze himself up to the bar to order food. Luckily, Summer wasn't working. If she had been, he would have taken his food back to the boat and eaten alone. He wanted nothing to do with that clusterfuck again. It almost cost him his marriage last summer.

Just as his thoughts were going awry, he heard a voice.

"Rob! Long time no see!"

Rob's attention snapped back to reality. It was Bill Wallace and his family.

"Bill!" he replied, genuinely happy to see him. Rob stood up and welcomed the family back. Rob held his hand out to help Sharon and the girls on board the boat, kissing Sharon on the cheek. The two boys followed hauling a large white Eagle cooler. From previous charters, he knows that it's full of water and soda since no one in the family drinks. He admires that about them though. Bill doesn't need a beer or a shot of Grey Goose to loosen up. He's happy with his life, and who could blame him? He seems to have it all.

"I hope you guys are ready to win this year. None of that second-place nonsense like a few years back. What do you guys think?"

Sharon spoke first, placing her hands on her hips. "I know I'm ready! This year everyone else is going down. This year is my year for the winning fish."

"Not if I get it first, Mom," Adam said, lifting the cooler onto the deck and handing it to his brother. "Everyone knows you need muscle to reel in that million-dollar marlin. Time to break out the big guns." He flexed to show his impressive biceps while his wife, Eve, stood behind him shaking her head. He loved to see how close the Wallace family was. It made him think of his boys and Leanne. He wanted to be *this* family one day.

"Well, everyone's here. Kevin did a great job prepping everything last night as always. So it's time to head out." He took a look at his watch. 4:45. Leanne would still be asleep. No use in texting her now. He never liked waking her. He'll text her on his way back in. Maybe he'll even invite her down to the boat for a martini.

He climbed up onto the bridge and started the engine. 75 miles offshore would take a few hours to get to. But the bigger the risk, the bigger the reward, and the reward he was going for was big.

◆ ◆ ◆

The Wallace family enjoyed their relaxing boat ride out, about 3 hours from the dock. The girls did a little napping while the men wanted to take in the wide-open waters and share stories from fishing trips over the years.

Checking his watch, he saw it was almost time to drop lines. Kevin was ready for whatever Rob had planned and intended on executing with precision. He and Rob discussed their tactic and Kevin climbed down the ladder and began his work.

Knowing Leanne, he knew she would be in over her head with emails and calls already today. He should've texted earlier.

Rob drove the boat into the area where he had a feeling that they'd get lucky. He'd fished this canyon for years and it never let him down.

"8:30 Kev! Let's get 'em in. It's going to be a good day!" Rob hollered down over the mumbling of the motor.

The sliding door opened. Sharon was the first out.

"Yes! Let's do this!" She clapped with enthusiasm.

"Simmer down there, honey. It's a marathon—not a sprint."

"I know. But this is so exciting! I'm going to catch a fish that's bigger than me." She clapped again.

"Well, that's not terribly difficult," Kevin chimed in. "If I knew that was your goal, we could've just stayed on shore and caught a few flounder," he joked and laughed.

"Oh, she's small—but she's feisty. Don't let her fool you. I've learned that the hard way," Bill proclaimed.

"Dad, do you remember the time when Mom bet you that she could out-ski you in Aspen?" Adam was now outside as well.

"You've been instructed never to speak about that again," he joked with his son. They were the spitting image of each other.

The fish didn't start as early as Rob had hoped for. From 8:30 a.m. to about 11:00 a.m. they'd only gotten a few takes and they didn't meet the 70-inch white marlin requirement. They were out here. Rob just needed to find them.

Zzzzziiiiiii

"He's on the teaser! He's on the teaser!" Rob threw the boat in neutral and watched as the line hissed about a football's length from the back of the boat.

"Get those lines out of the way! Get 'em in! Get 'em in!" This was Rob's favorite part. But he knew with experience that so many things can go wrong between now and getting the fish on board. The adrenaline was through the roof!

"Sharon, sit and take it!" Bill whooped.

"Get her in the chair and strap her in! It's a big one! Hurry up and start reeling!" Rob was dictating from the top.

"Yes, Mom! Reel! Reel! Go! Go!" Her boys and daughters-in-law were cheering her on from behind the fighting chair. Eve had her phone out getting the entire thing on camera.

"Come on! Reel! Reel! Get it, Sharon!" encouraged her daughter-in-law Eve.

Pump, pump, pump, pump, pump. The line slinked

in a little at a time.

"This is exhilarating! I can't believe I'm actually doing this!" Sharon shouted out loud, a huge smile on her face.

"You got it, honey!" Bill encouraged.

Sharon leaned down a little more to get a better grip on the rod. *Quick! Quick! Quick! Go! Go! Go!*

"Left, boss! Left!" Rob steered trying to help keep the lines from going under the boat.

"Keep it! Keep it! Keep it! Go! Go! Bring it in!!" Kevin was just as excited as Sharon. He loved being a mate.

At this pace, it wouldn't be long before the award-winning fish would be boated and ready for Harbour Island.

With Sharon pumping her arms for over 45 minutes, Kevin was finally able to reach down and grab the liter line. It took Kevin all his might to drag the massive white marlin on the deck.

"Wahoooo! Look at that baby! I can't believe it! It's huge!" High fives and photos went all around for the Wallace family, an incredible edge for *The Other Woman*. The 83-pound white marlin was a good start—but Rob knew they would need more.

FINN

It was 4:30 a.m. on Monday morning and Finn had opted not to fish today. He had some business that needed tying up back in Baltimore. Running a construction company was tough but it made it even harder from out of town. He made the three-hour drive at least twice a week to come back and check in on projects, materials, payroll, etc. He never told his crews when he was coming—not that they were unreliable, but it kept them on their "A-game."

Finn had made most of his money flipping houses. He had a good eye for potential and it worked in his favor. He grew up in this business seeing that his dad owned the company before him. He learned everything he knew from him. Around age eight, he learned a flat head from a Phillips screwdriver. By age ten, he knew galvanized vs. stainless steel. And by age fourteen, Finn was being paid under the table for small odds and ends, cleaning up jobs- gutting kitchens, bagging leftover items from auctioned houses, and doing mule work moving junk.

A few years ago, Finn's dad, Jack, had a heart attack that had him in the hospital for about a month. Finn stepped in and had taken over in his dad's absence. And he'd been doing it ever since. Doctors had allowed Jack back to work with the promise of less stress and less responsibility. Jack had agreed that it was time to officially step down and hand the reins over to Finn. Finn didn't have any brothers to share the company with so it only made sense. Obviously, his sisters wouldn't want it. Both Kennedy and Molly were busy raising families of their own. And to be honest, neither one of their husbands knew a hammer from a staple gun. They both worked in finance and stocks.

When he thinks about his older sisters, his heart becomes soft. Kennedy had three kids, two boys, and a girl. Molly has two girls of her own. He loved when the extended family got together. Finn got to be the cool uncle giving, "kitty back rides" as his youngest niece Laurel calls them. The kids also love it when he sneaks them an extra piece of candy. This kind of family time stirs something up inside of him making him long for a family of his own.

He'd had a few long-term relationships that never worked out for one reason or another. And he was never the one-night stand type of guy like some of his buddies. He was looking for companionship. He wanted to buy flowers for his wife every Friday after work, make her coffee in the morning, and surprise her with romantic getaways. And then Whitney walked into his life. Spilling her margarita all over him, he likes to add.

They met on the 4th of July weekend right here in Ocean City. Finn and his friends were out on the boat cruising the bay near the 50 Bridge. After a morning of drinking and taking in the 90-degree heat, Finn and his friends needed a break from the sun. They decided to go grab a bite at Fish Tales. As they were docking, one of Finn's buddies announced, "Bachelorette party on the dock!" His friend Pete was a self-proclaimed ladies' man and often referred to himself as "Party Pete." As they were pulling in, the group of girls decked out in red, white, and blue was boarding one of the floating tiki bars. They were these floating docks shaped in a circle, donned with a grass umbrella awning and a bar and stools in the center. The captain drove you around the bay, played music of your choice, kept the drinks flowing, and kept the party going.

As Finn stepped onto the pier, his feet were greeted with a cold splash of tequila, triple sec, and lime juice.

"Oh my gosh," she said in shock, covering her mouth. She placed her hand on his shoulder. "I am so sorry! It was an accident." She was wearing a jean skirt and a bikini top that resembled the American flag. A crown of red, white, and blue flowers adorned her head along with her wrist and ankle. Her cup was now half-empty with what looked to be a margarita.

She was stunning.

He paused for a second and found himself without words... *Say something*, he thought.

"No, it was my fault. It's fine." It was obviously not his fault.

"Can I get you another drink? I mean, since I spilled yours all over my own feet, it's the least that I can do."

He felt disappointed that she had taken her hand from his shoulder.

"Oh, thank you so much, but we're on our way out. But thank you anyway."

"Well wait a minute. Where are you watching fireworks tonight?"

"I'm not sure yet, but I never miss them." She turned to board the tropical-looking vessel.

"Why don't you give me your number and I'll make sure that you watch them from someplace that you've never seen them from before."

"Come on, Whit!" he heard from the floating tiki.

Finn held his phone out for what seemed like an eternity. At first, she seemed a little hesitant to give her number to a guy she had literally run into. But she caved like he hoped she would. She took the phone and dialed her own number. Her pocket began to quack loudly. She laughed out loud at the sound and handed Finn's phone back. She shrugged her shoulders.

"I'm a huge Jersey Shore fan. No judgment," she called over her shoulder as he watched her climb aboard the tiki. The group of girls giggled and swarmed around her so that she could recap what had just happened.

"Hey, Whitney!" Finn called out. "I'll call you!"

She did a cheers motion toward him. Finn could hear Sir Mix A Lot fading over the water as they floated off. "Unless you got buns, hon!"

WHITNEY

"Oh my God, Whit! That guy was so cute. Who was he?" her friend Isla inquired.

"I'm really not sure what just happened. I spilled my drink all over him and just agreed to go watch fireworks in an undisclosed location. Who am I? That is not like me. It must be the margarita." She looked in her cup and hiccupped. A chorus of laughter and giggles followed.

Never had a more true statement been proclaimed. Whitney was as even-keeled, regimented, and responsible as they came. She graduated at the top of her class at Georgetown with a degree in nursing. She had maintained a 4.0 GPA throughout because anything less was unacceptable. Several hospitals had offered her great positions in the nursing field but she had held out for her dream job at Johns Hopkins University. She didn't have to wait long. About a month after graduation, she was finally offered a position in the ICU and she jumped at the opportunity. She's always wanted to save lives and now she finally had her chance.

"Well, are you going to go out with him? You should! You rarely loosen up and have fun," Isla encouraged.

"I don't know," sighed Whitney. "I mean I don't even know the guy. "What if he's a serial killer or even worse, a Steelers fan..." She cocked her head to the side and raised her eyebrows.

"Oh come on. You never take any risks. It'll be an atypical Whitney move. Take a chance. Go out and have fun!"

"I go out and have fun. I'm just really cautious about going out with perfectly handsome strangers when I just meet them."

"Mmhmm. Let's get a guy's opinion. Hey Marco!" Isla called. "Can we get a guy's opinion on something? Whitney looked confused for a second. She had no clue who her friend was talking to. When she turned around, a clean-shaven, dark-haired man was mixing up a cocktail.

"Your name is Marco? Like Marco Polo?" Whitney asked leaning over the bar—her American flag top showing off perfectly-sized breasts.

"Yep, just like that."

"Girls! Our captain's name today is Marcoooo!" She yelled it like she was in a pool full of young campers. All of the girls including Whitney lifted their cups high in the air, yelled, "Polo!" and cheers-ed toward the captain. By now, Marco Polo was pouring a line of shots in tiny plastic cups. He skillfully finished, and passed the mini cups around to the six girls, keeping one for himself.

"Happy 4th of July! Salut!" he yelled.

"Happy 4th of July!" the choir of girls echoed.

"So Marco, I literally just bumped into this guy on the pier. I spilled my drink all over him. And guess what he did?"

"I'm hoping not ask you out because I was going to," he responded laughing out loud and collecting shot cups.

"He did! He asked for my number and asked me to go watch fireworks with him tonight. What should I do?"

"Don't do it. You'd have a better time with me." Obviously, he was joking as he wore a black gunmetal wedding ring on his left hand.

"From a guy's perspective... Go out with him!" His Latino accent made it sound fun. "What do you have to lose? He clearly liked you enough to ask for your number. It takes a lot of courage to do that; especially in front of all his guy friends. If you said no, he'd never live it down. He took a risk. I had to beg my wife to just go out with me. Just once!" He laughed talking about it.

"How many times did you ask before she said yes?"

"Quite a few times actually." Marco Polo was now steering the tiki north up into the bay. "We were sixteen, very young. She worked in an ice cream parlor. One day I took my little brothers to get a cone after school. They're much younger than I am. Anyway, we walked in and I just knew that she was the girl I wanted to marry. I could feel it right here." He pointed to his heart.

"I didn't have the courage to ask her on the first day. So I took them every day after school for about a week. When I finally got the courage to ask, she said I was nice but she didn't think we should. After that day, I was set on asking her out. I ask the next day and the next. She still said no. My brothers were getting so chubby because of all of the ice cream that I decided to go by myself the next time. I went to place an order at the window. I asked her what her favorite flavor was. She said chocolate. I asked her what time she got off. She told me five and my luck it was 4:55. So I ordered two chocolate cones and met her outside when she came out. I handed her one of the cones and I walked her home. And really that's all she wrote. We got married four years later. Now we have five kids and our first grandchild is on the way." He had turned the tiki around and was now heading south toward the inlet and bridge.

By now, all six girls were crowded around Marco Polo at the tiki bar, listening. "Go out with him," he said, eyes on the water in front of the tiki.

Whitney took a sip of a new margarita that Isla had given her. She smiled, lifted her drink in her hand, and cheers-ed.

"Marcooo!"

"Poloooo!" the remaining voices replied.

The rest of the tiki drive was full of shots, dancing, and even some swimming. The girls had requested to go somewhere they could get in and cool off. Marco Polo pulled close to the sandbar near the over-the-water restaurant, Sneaky Petes. All six girls took their margaritas and mojitos and pranced off the side into ankle-deep water. They posed for a few pics showing off their patriotic leis and beads. First, a selfie followed by a group shot, and lastly, a group shot featuring Marco Polo smack in the middle. Once the pictures were approved by all parties, everyone climbed back on board.

Marco Polo steered the party of girls back to the pier at Fish Tales. All of the girls climbed off single file, careful not to tumble in. Whitney was last off and surprisingly felt herself looking for...oh God. She didn't even know his name!

"Hey, Whitney!" Marco yelled out. "Go out with him. You'll regret it if you don't."

"Thanks for the advice." It was already four o'clock in the afternoon and Whit was ready for a nap. She had never been good at day drinking.

• • •

QUACK! QUACK! QUACK! Whitney was woken up from her midday drinking nap. She didn't recognize the number and went to set down her phone. But suddenly, she realized! She quickly snatched it up remembering it might be *him*. She slid to accept the call.

"Hello?" she answered.

"Hey! How was your tiki ride?" She smiled at the sound of his voice.

"It was really fun. We got back a few hours ago. Everyone's here relaxing and resting their eyes." She looked around sleepily. Isla was on the sofa, passed out covered with a beach towel and the other girls must have gone to the pool.

"Ah- sounds like a good day on the water to me."

"It really was." Still in her jean skirt and bikini top, Whitney went to find a bottle of Tylenol to try and stop an inevitable headache. She slipped out on the deck so she wouldn't wake Isla.

"How was your boat day?" she asked.

"It was nice. I just like being out on the water. Not the

drinking part so much. But it was a nice guy's day. We just got back actually. And I was calling to see if we were still on for fireworks tonight."

Whitney looked out over the ocean. The beach was thinning out as the sun slipped toward the bayside. Their building cast a long shadow on the sand.

"Where were you thinking?" she asked, stretching her long legs out across the lounge chair.

"Have you ever watched them from the ocean?" Finn asked.

"That's where my friends and I were planning on going. We were going to lay a blanket down and sit with the crowds."

He laughed. "I meant have you seen them from the actual ocean? Like from a boat? I'll pick you up from Fish Tales at 8:30?"

Whitney imagined Marco Polo shaking her margarita. *Go out with him.*

"I'll be there."

"Perfect. I'll see you then."

Whitney ended the call and then quickly cursed. *Damn it!* She opened a new text with his number in it.

I'm Whitney by the way
Three dots appeared. She waited while staring at her phone.

I know. Sunglasses emoji
And you are...

Excited to see you tonight.
Upside down smiley face emoji.

She laughed out loud. Three dots...

I'm Finn. It's nice to meet you.

It was later in the evening and Whitney was getting ready for her fireworks date. Her friends didn't mind that she was skipping out on their girls' night. In fact, they encouraged it. Whitney never did anything for herself. It would be good for her.

She showered and dressed in a red tank top and her jean skirt from earlier, and added some red, white, and blue beaded star necklaces. Her long legs were tan with the unavoidable ankle tan lines from her long runs outside. She put on little makeup: mascara, eyeliner, and a little lip gloss. Her hair hung straight at her shoulders. Taking one last glance in the mirror, she added a small glittery star sticker to the top of her left cheek just below her eye.

While her friends were all getting ready to fight for a spot on the beach, she was about to leave for a night she would not likely forget.

Whitney came out of the bedroom and asked, "How do I look? Is it too much? The beads and all?

Isla always looked out for Whitney. They had laughed together, cried together, and everything in between. Isla was the sister that Whitney never had.

"Aww, you look so cute! Perfect for tonight." She placed her hands on Whitney's shoulders. "Have so much fun, and text me if you need anything."

Whitney had already filled the girls in about where Finn was taking her.

"Let us know when you get back in so we know you're safe."

"I will. Love you guys. Have fun!"

"You, too!" Isla kissed Whit on her cheek.

She grabbed her keys, phone, and wallet and headed out the door.

FINN

Finn was already waiting for Whitney as she walked from the parking lots. His boat, a 27-foot Pursuit with twin Yamahas was docked a few slips away from the tikis. He was sitting in the captain's chair holding a Corona in one hand and another drink in the other.

He made sure to run home to shower and change. He had on a red Under Armour T-shirt and khaki shorts. His hair was short, curly, and adorably windblown. He didn't have time to shave and he wasn't wearing any shoes.

When he saw Whitney coming from the pier, a smile instantly took over his face. Her short hair was just touching her shoulders and she was dressed in red, white, and blue. She approached the boat as he came onto the pier to meet her.

"Hi," he said, still holding two drinks.

"Hey." She tucked one side of her hair behind her ear.

Finn almost felt tongue-tied.

"I got you a drink. I figured I owed you one." He handed the drink over.

"Cheers," he said. "To Fourth of July."

"To fireworks," she replied. "So where exactly are we going?"

Finn led Whitney toward the stern and stepped in. He turned around and held out his hand. *"A true gentleman always helps a lady,"* his father always said. He grew up watching his father dote all over his mother. Her hand touched his and they locked eyes. They had both felt it. But neither of them knew how to react. She gently stepped onto the boat, slipping off her flip-flops. She sat down in the chair next to where Finn would be driving. Propping her legs up, she sipped her margarita. She watched as he skillfully untied the boat, put her in gear, and led them out toward Assawoman Bay. He stood at the wheel with one hand while the other still hugged his Corona.

"So I thought it would be nice to have a spot all to ourselves to watch the fireworks. I'm not a fan of huge crowds. We're heading out in the ocean to watch."

Finn had watched the weather and prayed to the ocean gods for no wind so they could anchor up to enjoy the fireworks. He looked down at her sitting beside him. She looked so sexy with her long legs stretched out.

"You're kidding! I've never seen them from the ocean before." She stood up next to him. Her head came just to his broad shoulders.

"I love being out on the water. Especially this time of night. I call it '*the golden hour*.' The sun hits the waves at just the right angle and the sand has an almost warm glow to it."

They could see De Lazy Lizard and their neon palm trees lining the tables begin to glow. They have the best crab dip grilled cheese in Finn's opinion. They passed Sneaky Pete's bar over the top of the water. As the boat slid through the pilings of the Route 50 Bridge, they both looked up to see it peppered with fishermen hoping for a bite.

Assateague Island lay sprawled out to their far two o'clock and the new Ocean City Ferris wheel flashed its rainbow colors over the inlet.

"So, tell me about yourself. What do you do for a living? Are you local?" He wanted to know everything he could about her.

"I actually live in Baltimore. So no, not local. I work as a nurse in the ICU at Johns Hopkins. And I graduated from Georgetown. Go Hoyas!" She made a little arm movement like a cheerleader that he found surprisingly adorable. "Your turn." She looked up at him. Her eyes were the color of dark chocolate.

He adjusted his sunglasses, which were still perched on top of his head. He was trying not to show that his heart was now pounding like a jackhammer in his chest, learning that Whitney was from Baltimore, too. His wavy brown hair blew in the wind as the boat glided along. His shoulders were broad from all the years of manual labor of construction, and his skin was kissed by the sun, giving him a dark midsummer tan. He sipped his drink trying to hide a wide grin.

"I also live in Baltimore. I work doing construction. My dad and I own the company. I kind of took it over when he had a heart attack back in 2018. And I did not go to college."

"I'm sorry to hear about your dad. Is he doing okay now?"

"He's actually doing really well. With me running most of the stuff, he has less stress, which is what the doctor wanted."

"Sounds like you guys are close."

"It's actually kind of cliche but my dad's my best friend. My entire family is pretty close. How about you and your family?"

"Yep. My mom and I are pretty close. It's just her and I now. My dad passed away from cancer just after I graduated high school. We spend a lot of time together. I hate to see her alone."

"I'm really sorry to hear that. But it's really nice that you've become closer because of it. I'm sure he watches over you two every second of the day."

"He shows up in the little everyday things. Like for example, 17 was my lacrosse number in school and 17 shows up on the clock or on a restaurant receipt. You know, things that that. On my college graduation day, I ended up getting switched to row 17 last minute. That's how I knew he was there watching. And a lot of times, it's when I need him the most."

They were standing side by side. Finn carefully took Whitney's hand. He held it up to his face and kissed the top of her knuckles.

Trying to keep the mood light, Finn asked, "Did your girlfriends mind that I stole you away for the night?"

"Oh no. Isla and I were college roommates. We're down with a group of girls from Georgetown. They won't even miss me." She regretted saying that and rephrased it. "What I mean is they will miss me... You know if I don't come home or I show up missing or something like that." She nudged him with her hip and eyed him jokingly.

"Well, there goes my plan then. What am I supposed to do with you now?" Just as he said that, they came to the end of the jetty. He opened the motor and the wind blew through their hair. The boat cruised over the calm ocean waves like a knife through soft butter. The sun was already below the horizon and the moon was high above them. Lights from the boardwalk streamed down the vast beach in the hot and humid evening air. Whitney could feel her skirt sticking to her legs.

For the rest of the ride out, Finn and Whitney just enjoyed each other's company. Several other boats were scattered along the ocean ready to watch the fireworks, too. Finn could see throngs of people on the beach fighting for blanket space. He was happy with his decision to invite Whitney out. He went through the motions of idling away from everyone and getting the anchor down.

"Can I help you do anything?"

"Yes actually. There's a blanket under the console on the side if you'd like to get that out for us. Even though it was near 90 degrees still, laying a blanket out would be cozy. Whitney opened the hatch and found a navy blue fleece blanket.

Finn walked to the stern and opened a white Igloo cooler.

"I wasn't sure what you liked to drink so I got a few options to be safe." He looked over his shoulder flashing a boyish smile. Whitney never had someone go through so much trouble just for her. It felt...lovely.

"That's so sweet of you." She walked toward Finn and placed her hand on his back. They were both peering into the cooler which was full of a mish-mosh of drinks—Natty Boh, White Claws, and Mike's Hard Lemonade. There was also a full bottle of Moscato. "I'll take Natty Boh, please."

Finn grabbed two ice-cold cans and closed the cooler. He popped the tops off both beers and handed one to Whitney.

"Cheers," he said.

"Cheers! To 4th of July, margaritas, and..." She couldn't think of anything.

Finn jumped in. "To 4th of July, margaritas, and taking chances." He smiled down at her sitting on the side of the boat.

"And taking chances." As they clunked beers, one single firework boomed. It was a perfect golden circle in the air, which melted like a golden weeping willow tree. Finn watched Whitney's eyes lock on the golden sky. She smiled like a kid on Christmas. And that's the moment that he knew. This was the girl he was going to marry.

He took a chance and leaned down and kissed her. It was soft and exhilarating at the same time. The time on the clock read 9:17.

TJ AND MARLIN

TJ and the men on *Big Distraction* arrived three and a half hours south of Ocean City Buoy to begin Day 1 of fishing. Kyle was busy getting everything set- outriggers, spread bar, and down riggers. Rods were all baited with heavy ballyhoo. On the way out, the guys were spread all over the boat. Some sat on the deck while others stayed tight inside. Two guys decided to hang out up top, on the bridge with TJ. Once Kyle got everything set, he dropped the lines in promptly at 8:30 am. No- sooner, no later. Looking at the depth finder, TJ could see that they were currently trolling in about 250 fathoms of water.

Down below on the deck, TJ could hear the cracking of beers opening.

"Let's catch some fish!" someone yelled out. He felt the vibrations of someone climbing the ladder. He looked back and saw Brendon, beer in hand, hat turned backward.

"Hey, Cap!" he said, patting TJ on the back. They must've been closer in age than he and Monty but he could already see that they had less in common. Brendon's party get-lit vibe was not TJ's style. Marlin lay at the bottom of the ladder. It was amazing how he had better sea legs than some people did. Maybe having four legs helped.

"Want a beer?" Brendon asked.

"No man, I'm good, but thanks. What are you having?"

"It's a smooth IPA called Harpoon." He turned the can so that TJ could see the label.

"Nice. I'm not a big drinker but save one for me later. I like to try new things."

"You bet, Cap." He took a look around. "So this is it, huh? We toss in the lines and just troll around?"

"It's a little more to it on my end, but yeah. I'll stay up here and watch the depth finder for ledges and drops. Fish love the edges. So we'll try to stay on the edge here." TJ pointed to the depth finder on the dash.

"That's cool." He took a seat next to TJ. Two-foot waves and little wind made for a hot and humid morning. TJ had already downed about four bottles of water. His mind was drifting to Jules.

Zzziiiii!!

"Fish on! Fish on!" Kyle yelled. "Who's on it guys? Get in the chair!"

Monty was on the back of the boat when the billfish took the line. "She's all mine. Let me at her!"

Kyle handed the rod off to Monty, put the rod in the holder between his legs, and began frantically yet methodically reeling in the other lines. Monty pumped his arms rhythmically as the fish struggled to get away. ***Pump. Pump. Pump.*** He made it look almost easy.

"Feels like a good size!" he yelled as he continued to reel. TJ followed the line, putting the boat in reverse to try and help the angler. Kyle was keeping Monty in check giving directions on what to do. Brendon had gotten his phone out to record the catch. Just then TJ saw the large fish thrash its large body out of the water. *Great looking fish! Yes!* he thought. *Get it in! Get it in!*

"Whoa! Did you guys see that?" Brendon called down. "Keep reeling, Monty! She's a beaut!"

TJ steered *Big Distraction* with excellence. Making sure the line didn't go under the boat was his main concern.

After twenty-five minutes of zig-zagging through the ocean, Kyle was able to grab the liter. With a lot of muscle and maneuvering, the first white marlin was on board *Big Distraction*. TJ was now on the leaderboard with a 77-pound white marlin. The large fish was shoved into the bag and then stuffed with ice. It was hoisted to the bridge making room on the deck to fish.

"God, that felt good!" Monty celebrated with high fives all around. Brendon had disappeared and then finally reappeared holding a bottle of Jack Daniels in one hand and plastic shot glasses in the other. He passed the cups around. Everyone obliged. Shots were poured for everyone—TJ included.

"To Day 1," Monty proclaimed.

"To Day 1," they all echoed.

But before anyone was able to get the shot down...

ZZZiiiii!

"Fish on! Fish on!" Kyle yelled. He grabbed the rod and shoved the handle at Brendon, who just happened to be the closest to him. The bottle of whiskey had quickly been forgotten as he pumped hard with a lot of force. Monty had made it look too easy. This one was a fighter. He pumped the reel hard, while the muscle in his right arm was quickly tiring. He needed to take a break.

"No man! Keep going or we'll lose him!" The fish thrashed its head while it swam in confusing patterns trying to break free. Back and forth, the rod went up and down with the waves. TJ could see the line but still hadn't seen the fish. The boat followed the sneaky patterns of the fighting fish until she finally came to the surface.

"There she is! There she is!" TJ called loudly, looking out the back of the boat toward the line. "Yee-ha!" It was a monster from what he had spotted from the bridge.

"Tight lines!"

Brendon was starting to get into the groove. Fifteen minutes... thirty minutes...and finally at minute forty-two, Kyle was able to get a hold of the liter while the monster fish thrashed and moved with vengeance. Dragging it in was a job but a job well done and worthwhile. An 84-pound white marlin was on board and would hopefully give *Big Distraction* a great lead on Day 1.

TJ looked at his watch. It was only 10:45.

The rest of the day was just as eventful. It never really stopped. Just as they brought in that white marlin, they ended up snagging back-to-back tunas that TJ was excited to put on the grill this week. After the tuna came another white marlin, smaller than the first but still made the minimum requirement. And you never know! Even a small one could keep you on the top of that leaderboard.

JULES

"So this guy you're going out with... You mean to tell me you fined him for having his dog off the leash... after he asked you out? And he *still* wants to take you out? I'm just sayin' don't get your hopes up. He's probably not even going to show up," said Jules' younger sister, Kit. She was over at Jules' house using her washing machine and eating leftovers.

Kit went to Salisbury University like many millennials around there. She was living near campus and taking summer classes. She often came to Jules' place on the weekends to visit to hang out at the beach—and of course, wash clothes.

"Well for one, 'this guy' has a name. It's TJ. And he has the most adorable yellow lab named Marlin. Second of all, it's my job to make sure that everyone follows the rules on the beach for safety. He really had it coming to him. I actually gave him a break. If another ranger would have caught him, the fine would have been doubled. How do I look?"

She came out of the bathroom wearing a flowy, baby blue sun dress that fell off the shoulder on one side, and tan strappy sandals that tie around the ankle. Kit was always jealous of Jules' hair because it had natural beach waves and hung halfway down her back while Kit's hair looked like she stuck her finger in a light socket if she let it air dry.

"Wow," Kit said. "Maybe you should save some of that for the second date. That is if he even shows up after that ticket."

Jules did feel a little bad; especially when she remembered how cute and attractive TJ really was. He stood about average height and wore a worn baseball hat that was torn on the bill. It definitely had seen better days. His shorts had been wet on the bottom from Marlin bringing the ball back and forth. His long-sleeved Quiet Storm T-shirt had a hole in it that was probably a snag from a fishing hook. He mentioned that he was a boat captain but the conversation that first meeting was pretty quick and of course mostly about Marlin's misdemeanor.

Kit was busy heating up cold pizza when a knock came from the door. *Points for coming to the door. Guys nowadays would just send you a text that says "I'm outside." One point for TJ*, she thought.

"I'll get it!" she yelled as she scurried to the door before Jules could get there. She opened the door to find a handsome guy wearing a ball hat, T-shirt, khaki shorts, and flip-flops. Standing to his left was the most adorable and friendly-looking yellow lab.

"Hi there," TJ said, unsure if he had gotten the wrong address. "I'm here to pick up Jules. I'm TJ," he said, reaching out to shake Kit's hand. Marlin stood by TJ's side watching—his obvious wingman.

"You're at the right house. I'm Kit. So you're the ticket guy, huh?" She led TJ down the hall into the kitchen.

"Oh yeah, that's me," TJ said with a laugh. "She told you about that, huh?"

"Yeah—there's not a lot we don't tell each other. Keep that in mind," she said pointing a finger toward him. "Jules will be out in a minute.

"Can your dog have pizza?" Kit returned to the microwave to retrieve the bubbling hot pizza.

"I'm sure he wouldn't mind a small piece of crust. Sometimes I think he eats better than I do." TJ slid his hands into his pockets.

Just as Kit was rewarding Marlin for being *such a good puppy,*" with torn-up slices of crust, Jules came into the kitchen. TJ smiled as she walked toward him.

"Wow, you look great! I was just talking to your sister about my outstanding violations that she somehow knows about." Her long tanned legs looked out of this world.

She couldn't believe the butterflies that she had in her stomach. He was so darn cute. His dark hair was peeking out from under his ball hat—the same one that she had seen him in at the beach. Jules laughed. "Yeah, there's not much we don't tell each other." Kit, who was now sitting on the floor with Marlin, burst into laughter. "Told ya."

"I'm ready when you are," she said to TJ. She walked toward him and lead him toward the front door.

"Don't wait up, and lock the door behind me, please. If you go anywhere, text me and let me know. Love you," Jules called to Kit from the hall.

"Love you, too! Remember TJ—we talk about everything!" she yelled back.

TJ and Jules walked out toward the navy blue Jeep. The tan top was down and it looked like it had recently been washed. TJ walked over to the passenger side and opened the car door for Jules. Marlin was right behind at his ankles waiting his turn.

"Go ahead! Hop up!" he said. Marlin effortlessly jumped in the backseat, showing off that he wasn't a first-timer. TJ gently closed the door, careful not to catch Jules' fingers or toes. He walked around, got in, and closed his door. He looked over. She looked incredible. He could feel his heart begin to beat just a tiny bit faster as he looked into those bright blue eyes.

"You look beautiful tonight."

Jules had her hands in her lap, feeling a little shy for the first time in a long time. She looked over at TJ, smiling.

"Thank you. And you did a nice job cleaning yourself up after your beach trip. You were both soaked the last time that I saw you."

"Yeah—us boys clean up nice sometimes, don't we boy?" he said looking back at his co-pilot. "I hope you don't mind that he tagged along. He insisted on coming."

Jules turned around to pet Marlin behind the ears. "Of course not. He's welcome anytime. So...where are we off to?"

"Well, I thought it would be fun for us to be tourists for the night. Head off to the inlet, wait in line for Thrashers French fries, and then head into the Haunted House. What do you think?" He pretty much held his breath waiting for approval. *Oh God, was it a bad idea? Did she think he was a complete moron now?*

"You had me at Thrashers," she said with a huge smile on her face.

The ride to the inlet was congested as it always was on a summer evening, but Jules' place wasn't that far into Ocean City. She stayed in a condo between the 7th and 8th on the bay side. It was a cute place off the main highway away from most of the noise and commotion that summer can bring. She had been living there for a few years now. Her landlords were excellent and loved having a steady reliable tenant. They kept the rent reasonable and let Jules decorate any way she wanted. She knew that they could get more money if they rented out to families over the busy season, but they were an older couple and just didn't want the hassle.

The radio in the jeep was playing The Beach Boys, *Little Surfer Girl*, one of Jules' favorite songs. It was the perfect background music for the night. Was this a sign? As they pulled up toward the inlet, they could hear the screaming from the Tidal Wave, the inlet's one and only roller coaster. The arcade was flashing multi-colors and the music from the Matterhorn played Lizzo.

As they pulled into the inlet, Jules could see the swaying waves of the ocean on the right, along with vacation anglers spaced out on the edge testing their luck. Because she's lived here so long, even though she couldn't see it, she knew that the long slender beach of Assateague Island was just beyond the inlet in the distance.

TJ parked the Jeep down by the Life Saving Station Museum. He opened the parking app on his phone and quickly paid. He walked around to open the door for Jules to hop out.

"We'll be back, Mar. You stay and make sure everything is safe here. Okay?" Marlin wagged his tail and sat down on the seat. He had a great view of the inlet waters from where he sat, looking a little disappointed that he wasn't invited. Jules felt a little bad, but dogs were only permitted on the boardwalk between Labor Day and Memorial Day—Ocean City's "off-season."

They could smell the vinegar from the parking lot. As they got to the boardwalk, the line and Thrashers were just as long as they both imagined. It was at least 15-20 people long with parents holding stuffed animals that were larger than their kids- obviously winners of the claw machine and kids that donned ice cream mustaches. But they were in no hurry and it gave them some time to talk.

"So do you and Marlin go to the beach every day after work,?" Jules asked.

"Actually, we try to. We spend a lot of time at the marina during the day, so I feel like he deserves a reward for that. Not much space to run around on the boat either. He loves the water."

The line inched forward as more and more people walked past them with heaps of salted fries in their overflowing buckets.

One of the guys behind the counter, who was pouring sweat from the heat of the fryer and the heat of the night, pointed to TJ. "Large," he hollered over the stainless steel counter as he reached for his wallet. He knew how much he loved Thrashers and could eat a whole bucket himself. He wasn't about to skimp knowing he had to share with another person. The huge bucket of deliciously cooked French fries was slid over as TJ paid.

"This may make or break the night right here and now," Jules said with the utmost serious look on her face. She picked up the heaping bucket of French fries from the counter and walked to the side table set up with napkins, salt, and vinegar. "Vinegar or no vinegar? Tread lightly, sir. This. Is. Serious." She tried to keep a straight face but her smirk was slipping from the corners of her glossy lips.

Jules popped a fry in her mouth as she giggled to herself. She had thought about how unless you're from Maryland, the whole vinegar thing might seem a little silly. However, Marylanders take their Thrashers french fries as seriously as New Englanders take their lobster—or better yet, people in Chicago take their pizza. In her lifeline thus far, when she had polled people, she would say about 80% of people make the right choice and douse their fries with vinegar—and the other 20% have no business being near a fry.

"Allow me," he said as he took the gigantic bucket of fries from Jules' hand. He reached for one of the many bottles of vinegar on the table that was also staggered with large industrial containers of salt. "Vinegar first—and lots of it! Followed by the salt, which sticks to the vinegar. I'm not a 'newb,'" he said, raising his eyebrows, head slightly cocked to the side.

Jules laughed as she took back the bucket of fries. "Good answer," pointing her finger in the air. "Never trust a person that doesn't use vinegar." She offered TJ the bucket but pulled it away at the last minute, teasing him as they walked toward the end of the boardwalk where benches overlooked the inlet and Assateague Island beyond that. As they walked the short distance past The Haunted House on the right and the tram station to the left, they both snacked on the salty vinegary

French fries. Children were spinning on rides and parents were purchasing their family's beach pet, the infamous hermit crab. They found a bench and sat, Jules still holding the bucket.

"I'm really glad that we bumped into you at the beach the other day. I guess it was a happy accident."

"I was actually on my last rounds when Marlin literally ran into me. I had been out all day. I helped a family launch their kayaks that morning, helped one of the ponies out of the road so people could actually drive into the park, then finished up some last-minute clean-up projects. I like going to the beach right at the end of my shift. It's a nice way to end my day."

"It was definitely the highlight of my day," TJ said smiling. "So tell me about yourself. Are you from Maryland? Do you live down here full time?" he asked, hoping that her answer was yes to the latter.

"I grew up in Harford County. My parents still live there actually. They have this huge backyard with a barn and two horses. Kit and I, my sister that you just met, we grew up taking care of them. They're the sweetest animals. We each have our own. My horse's name is Caramel. She's caramel-colored, with a silver and white mane. She has the best temperament. She's calm and gentle—would never hurt a fly. Anyone could ride her. Kit's horse on the other hand is more... Let's just say she's more. She's a red-headed handful. I said to call her Lucy. You know Lucielle Ball from the show *I Love Lucy*? That's what she reminds me of. But Kit ended up naming her Gingersnap because of her red hair. But I still call her Lucy. Have you ever ridden a horse?"

"Oh, no. Not me. I've never been near a horse really. I grew up on the water. Not many horses there. But I've got my Marlin," he said. Jules got a glimpse of a small dimple on the right side of TJ's cheek. Her heart fluttered for a split second and it caught her by surprise. She looked closely again at TJ as he was talking about Marlin. The butterflies that she had earlier in the evening were fluttering even more now.

"Marlin is almost four years old. He's the poster pup for 'Man's Best Friend'. He and I are best buddies. We go everywhere together. He even goes fishing with me during the tournaments. That's actually how I got his name. One of the first years I entered to fish, one of the other captains had a dog that had just had puppies. I was talking to him at the pier one night, ended up going to look at the little guys, and that was all she wrote. I knelt down in front of the litter and he was the only one that came up and laid by my side. It's like he picked me to be his best friend right then and there. I took him home that night. He slept on the passenger side of the Jeep, top down, wind in his ears."

"How sweet. How did you end up picking Marlin for his name?" she asked, reaching for a French fry.

"Well, that's a funny story. The next morning after I took Marlin home, I was scheduled to fish in the Marlin Tournament. We woke up around 4:00 to get a head start to the pier and get going. I told him on the ride to the boat that whatever fish we caught first that day was going to be his name. It could've been anything during that time of year- Tuna, Mahi, Marlin. And that day we got lucky. Not only did we boat a Marlin first that day, that Marlin actually sky-rocketed us into 2nd place for the tournament."

TJ and Jules had almost finished an entire bucket of fries and were now casually leaning their elbows on the back of the wooden bench. It was dark outside now and you couldn't see much further than the jetty.

"What a cool story. I'm glad you didn't get a tuna first," she said laughing. "It fits him. So you ended up winning 2nd that year?"

"Actually, no. The last day leading into weigh-ins, someone came in with a Marlin a little bigger than ours, so it knocked us out of contention. But who's the real winner in the story?" he asked with his eyebrows raised. "Still me. Because without that tournament, we wouldn't have found each other, Marlin and I."

"Aww. You guys do make a cute couple," Jules said giggling. She leaned over and playfully nudged him with her shoulder.

TJ looked at his watch. "I think it's time we get going on the rides. Don't you think?" He wiggled his eyebrows up and down, smiling slyly.

Wiping the salt off of her hands with a flourish, Jules stood up quickly. "I'll beat you to the Haunted House." She grabbed the nearly-empty bucket of fries and tossed them into the nearest rubbish can. She and TJ walked hand and hand down the ramp past the Life Saving Station Museum and Souvenir City.

They approached the lop-sided ticket booth with the mangled gate. The shutter was falling off at the corner to give the illusion of a crumbling house.

"We need to see if you fit the height requirements," he said. "Come stand here, please." He reached in his back pocket for his wallet. Jules laughed and stood next to the meter stick that came about to her waist. "That was a close one," she said looking down and wiping her head sarcastically.

TJ paid the $15, slid his wallet back in his pocket, and led Jules through the creepy gate and there they waited for their coffin to arrive. A man in an orange t-shirt advertising the words *Trimper's Rides and Amusements* slowly walked toward an open coffin. He held the ride while TJ and Jules climbed in. It was a snug fit. The coffin could only be three feet wide, leaving no room for spreading out. Their legs touched as their hips were squished against the outside of the coffin seat. The lid of the coffin was slowly closed and a loud screeching noise jolted the stuttering ride forward. They slammed through two dark and beat-up swinging doors as the lights inside the house showed only inches in front of their faces. To their right, a bald man eagerly devoured the intestines of a woman who was strapped to a splintered wooden table. Her arms pinned to her sides were no help as the man's face was dripping in fake blood. Jules turned away, leaning her face toward TJ's shoulder.

"I know it's fake, but that was disgusting."

"Well then, you aren't going to like what's up here on the left." The coffin cart crawled along the winding tracks toward a group of large rats carrying body parts and limbs as a torso lay eaten alive with only rags of clothing covering the remains.

"That's not so bad. Still gross, but I can stomach that."

"I don't know if that should worry me or relax me," he said laughing. TJ put his hand on Jules' leg. There really was no other place to put it. She looked over at him and smiled. She placed her hand on top of his and wiggled her fingers in between his.

They passed a man on the brink of climbing out of an insane asylum, another man screaming behind bars foaming at the mouth, and another human form chained up against the wall screaming while another came within inches of them with a chainsaw. A spinning tunnel lit up by black lights painted in yellows, oranges, and pinks gave a dizzy break to the scary scenes.

"My sister and I used to love coming in here when we were kids. It was a family tradition. Normally, she hid her eyes behind her hands while I tried to coax her to look at everything."

The spinning walls made TJ a little dizzy and he was actually glad when they exited the tunnel that led into yet another frightening room.

Jules pointed over to the other side of the room. A large circular saw hung from the ceiling, swinging back and forth giving the image that it was cutting a person in half. A gross-looking mannequin stood swaying back and forth enjoying the gruesome view. The tiny coffin then banged through another set of swinging doors where TJ and Jules' eyes were treated to some natural night sky. They were on the second floor of the haunted house now sputtering above the boardwalk. Vacationers down below waved to them as their children looked frightened to be near the ride. TJ and Jules waved back.

"Back inside! Here we go! Ahhh!" TJ gave a small scream for the kids watching below. Jules laughed again. And back into the darkness the coffin went. They knew they were toward the end of the ride when the track sped up to a brisk walking pace and almost slammed headfirst into an oncoming train but somehow twisted toward the right last second. Seeing the light at the end of the tunnel, Jules squeezed TJ's hand a little harder. She knew what was up at the end.

The black lights flashed as an inmate strapped by the wrists and ankles to an electric chair jolted in painful-looking spasms. That was always the worst part she thought. She could look from afar but always had to turn her head as the ride approached. It was just a little too real for her liking. As Jules was able to look back toward TJ, something began to drip from the ceiling onto their cart and dripped right onto TJ's forehead.

"Oh God," he said as he squirmed. "So nasty." They slammed one final time through the swinging doors that led them outside where they were greeted by a headless man who happened to be holding what everyone assumed was his own head, which warned the audience about the terrors that lay just beyond those walls. TJ lifted the lid to the ride and held Jules' hand as she stepped out glad to be alive.

"That was fun! It makes me feel like a kid again."

"Me, too," TJ replied. "One more ride? Your pick."

"Yes! But I won't tell you until we get there."

"Lead the way." TJ held onto Jules' hand as she walked them both toward the back of *Trimper's Rides*. They walked in the opposite direction of the Zipper, which relieved TJ. He had a bad experience with that one when he was little. He was kind of hoping for the Matterhorn. He loved the part when you were smashed up against the person on the outside from how fast it spins. However, Jules didn't go in that direction either. She looked at him and smiled as she stopped them both in front of The Tidal Wave, Ocean City's one and only roller coaster.

"Surprise! Do you like roller coasters?" Her face showed a gleam and he just couldn't resist.

"I've actually never ridden this one. But I am always willing to try something at least once. Do we need tickets?"

She clapped and showed her excitement. "Oh yeah. I forgot about the tickets!"

"It's okay. You stay here and I'll run over and grab them." TJ walked a few feet and returned with enough tickets for two riders. They walked up the ramp without checking their heights this time.

"Front seat?"

"Sure. Whatever you want." TJ only wanted to make her happy. He liked her a lot.

Jules hurried toward the front so that no one else would snag it. She climbed inside the ride and pulled the shoulder bars down toward her lap. TJ did the same.

"You've really never been on here before? This is Kit's favorite."

"Nope. Never. My family never went to theme parks. We were more fishing and beach people." The large machine lurched backward. Jules reached over and squeezed TJ's thigh. He placed his hand on top of hers. The roller coaster began its ascent up the tall and slanted track. TJ and Jules were now facing directly toward the ground below. The spectators looked like small bugs.

"My heart is racing. Oh my gosh. It's so much higher than I remember. Are you okay?"

TJ's grip on her leg tightened. "Yeah! It's so great up here! You can see so far!"

"Here we go!" The coaster's grip released and down they

flew! Jules threw her hands up in the air. TJ saw and followed. Both of them screamed like they were kids on vacation. Up and around, looping and swerving, upside down and back again. They were flying through the salty air enjoying each other's company like they had known each other for longer than just one night. The rollercoaster sailed up toward the top of the track, clicking in place leaving the two backward and ready to sail down again for round two.

"I am so happy! This is amazing." Jules was having a blast.

TJ looked over at her and gave a huge smile. "Me, too! Hands up!" The coaster released again and they flew downwards except this time backward. TJ and Jules screamed and laughed simultaneously. TJ grabbed her hand that was still flying high just as they were making the last upside-down loop and yelled, "Wooooo!"

When the roller coaster was done its epic acrobatics, it pulled back into the covered coaster terminal. The shoulder belts let them out of their tight grip and they climbed from the sunken seats. They walked down the exit ramp. Jules turned to TJ, her eyes lit up. Her hair was tousled from the wind. TJ brushed her hair from her face.

He couldn't take it any longer. He'd been admiring her all evening. Her long blonde hair danced around her shoulders. Her tan skin was freckled by the sun. She wore hardly any makeup, but she didn't need it. She was already beautiful. He wanted to kiss her. But he didn't want to ruin it. He liked her. Not just liked her but enjoyed her company. He could feel his heart beating in his chest. He slowly reached over and took her hand in his. She allowed him to. He stood there, holding her hand. She looked back at him—really looked back. Her eyes were dark brown with specks of gold.

He lightly touched her cheek with the back of his hand. Her skin was soft and warm. TJ slowly leaned in and kissed Jules lightly on the lips. A feeling of warmth and calm came over him at the very second. She was it.

It was approaching 10:00 when TJ and Jules decided to start walking back toward the Jeep. Hand in hand, Jules walked close enough that her hair was brushing up against his shoulder. He couldn't take his eyes off of her. It was a feeling that he'd never had and he didn't want it to end. Marlin had been patiently hanging out in the back seat of the Jeep awaiting their arrival. He stood up as he saw them approaching, wagging his tail. He received lots of kisses from TJ and rubs from Jules. Marlin returned some wet kisses to TJ.

"Oh! We missed you, too," she said, rubbing the back of Marlin's ears.

TJ opened the Jeep door for her and held her hand as she got in. In all of his life, he's never held the door for anyone- not even his own mother. But she deserved it. He'd dated other girls before, off and on, nothing serious—but not once did he even think about opening up a car door for them. It never even crossed his mind.

He got in and started the engine. He had set up the parking app on his phone already so paying for parking was already taken care of. They drove out of the inlet and passed the Life Saving Station Museum. Around the quick curve, they looked up and saw the iconic Harrison's Harbor Watch Restaurant that sat overlooking the inlet.

As they drove down Coastal Highway, the wind blew Marlin's ears back. TJ held Jules' hand as they drove all the way to her house. The Beach Boys now crooned *Wouldn't It Be Nice*. He pulled the Jeep into the driveway fifteen minutes later and turned off the engine.

TJ leaned his head back on the headrest of the seat. He tilted his head toward Jules. "I don't know if this is too forward, but when can I see you again? I want it to be sooner than later."

JULES

Jules was having a lot of new feelings inside. Feelings that she's read about in books or has seen in movies. The Notebook comes to mind. She brushed her hair behind her ears- a nervous habit that Kit has called her out on numerous times. She had an amazing time with TJ tonight. He was everything that a girl would want. He's completely adorable, with that torn-up bill on his hat. She had caught a glimpse of a dimple on his cheek as they talked over French fries. Her heart had fluttered then and the butterflies had come back for an encore performance.

"I had a really great time, too. I haven't sat and talked to someone like that in a long time. And the rides- I felt like a kid again. And I haven't eaten that many French fries in a long time, either." She paused for a second thinking. "I have off on Wednesday. And as of now, I don't have any plans..."

"I'd love to take you out for the day if that's okay."

"I'd like that but on one condition," she countered. "We have to be doing something outside. I can't stand spending a gorgeous day indoors." She smiled and brushed her hair behind her ear.

"Done and done."

Tuesday

Category: White Marlin
1st Place: No Limits
2nd Place: Big Distraction
3rd Place: The Other Woman

Category: Blue Marlin
1st Place: TBD
2nd Place: TBD
3rd Place: TBD

Category: Tuna
1st Place: Big Distraction
2nd Place: TBD
3rd Place: TBD

FINN

Finn and his team left the dock around 5 a.m. with the intent to run southeast about three hours out. He was lucky to have three of his good friends on board ready to just relax and have a good time. Their main goal was to have fun and maybe win some money while they do it.

When lines went in at 8:30, Finn kept an eye on the depth finder. Running along the edges and drops were where everyone had been having their luck, so he thought he'd start there.

Alex, Finn's best friend, was the working mate on board and was managing the lines. The weather was beautiful but hot. Nothing really out of the ordinary for the first week of August. All the guys were hanging out by the back of the boat enjoying a few cold ones. They had all known each other since middle school. Alex and Finn had been best friends since they were in elementary school. They had grown up down the street from each other. The two of them had been in the same class starting in fourth grade. The boys played on the same rec baseball team, rode bikes around their neighborhood, and fished just about every evening they had the chance to.

The "fast four"—they had called themselves growing up—looked more like a boyband. Finn, the heartthrob, Alex, the rebel, Trevor, the gym rat, and Luke, the one you take home to Mom. Just don't ask them to dance in sync. They even got their first tattoos together. The wave/ shark fin design wrapped around all of their left calves and will always be a memory from their very first fishing charter many years ago here in Ocean City. Not one of them had any idea what they were doing- except Finn obviously. Like any good boyband members, they just had to follow their favorite heartthrob's lead.

97.1, The Wave, was on the radio playing *Feels Like the First Time* by Foreigner. Lines had been dropped over an hour and a half ago but no luck quite yet. Finn was trolling slowly around Baltimore Canyon, which was known to be a hotspot for marlin, wahoo, and mahi. He usually didn't have to wait more than an hour for at least a hit on the spread bar out here.

"Do you guys remember the very first offshore trip we took when we were 21?" Alex asked. "Man, that was fun."

"How could we forget? It was Trevor's turn to bring in a fish and he was too busy puking off the side of the boat to even sit up straight." Luke pushed Trevor on the arm. "Good thing he finally got his sea legs. It took how many years before you could come out here without getting sick?"

"Guys. Being seasick is not a joke." His face was serious. I don't wish that on anyone. And I just take a ton of Dramamine beforehand now. I didn't know I was going to feel every wave the boat rolled over."

"I remember Finn was the only one that actually had an idea of what was going on."

"Yeah. You guys were so embarrassing!" Finn drove the boat southeast as the sun was directly over top of them now.

"And look at us now," Alex replied, lifting his beer, his bicep full of tattoos. "Cheers fellas!"

"Yeah. Would you ever think that the "fast four" would ever settle down and get married? And even have kids! Some of us three kids and one on the way." Trevor was referring to Luke. He and his wife Amanda have three beautiful daughters all under 5 and another girl on the way.

"Four girls! That's some type of pay back from the universe right there," Finn laughed out loud.

"And you, Finn! Engaged to Whit."

"How is Whitney doing with everything that's happened? I mean does she still want to have kids even with...you know?" The guys all knew how touchy of a subject family and kids were.

Sigh. "I mean yeah. The doctor says there's nothing that would prevent her from having a normal pregnancy. But you guys know how hard it was for us both. We were blindsided. And then with her miscarriage..." He paused. "I want a family with her. It's one of the things that I feel as a man, I should be able to provide. But—"

"But it's no one's fault—any of it."

"Yeah, man. Don't beat yourself up over it. It'll happen when it's supposed to." Luke got up and passed around another round of beers.

"Everyone can say things like that. But if you've never experienced it, then you have no clue about the turmoil that it sends you through. We felt...defeated...from all ends. But luckily for Whit and me, we had a huge support system that we could go to. And I can't thank you guys enough for it."

"Cheers to that, buddy. Cheers...to...that."

Alex looked at his watch. "How long have we been out here without a bite? You know what happens after the two-hour mark."

"No way," Luke protested. "No. I'm too old for that now."

Trevor chimed in. "Nope. You're doing it. We all have to. Even the captain."

"Rules are rules," Finn looked over at Luke. He put both hands up in the air in a surrendering motion.

I've got two tickets to paradise! Won't you pack your bags, we'll leave tonight!

Alex belted out the lyrics as he got a bucket and filled it with salty ocean water. Trevor rounded up another bucket and loaded it with ice, filling it to the very top. And Luke begrudgingly got three mini shots of whiskey from the cooler. Finn was captaining and wouldn't do the shot, but the other part—he was allowed. This was another "rule" that Alex made up.

Alex poured the water into the bucket of ice creating an ice bath.

"It's time, boys!"

One year on an offshore fishing trip, they hadn't had a bite in over three hours. They were getting bored and pretty drunk by then. So to liven things up, the band created what they have properly named 'the dunkaroo'.

The three of them crowded around the ice bucket, Finn stayed up top driving the boat. Raising their shots, all four loudly recited, "*I love it when she bends over! Let me see that bend, baby,*" referring to the fishing rod when it has a fish on. Shots were twisted, opened, chugged, and one by one each guy performed a headstand over the ice bath and dunked themselves all the way in headfirst to their shoulders!

Years ago when dunkaroos were invented, Trevor was able to fit in the bucket. Now with all his hours at the gym, he was lucky to get his head in.

Shaking off the sting and shock of the ice, he climbed the ladder to the bridge. It was Finn's turn. Just because he was the captain didn't mean he was exempt. The liquor boundary was for safety.

"Let's go, baby! Come on. Give me a boost!"

Just as Finn's head was under the ice blocks, he could hear through the bucket and water that magical sound they'd been waiting for.

Zzzzziiii

Darting out from inside his dunkaroo position, Finn jetted up top to the wheel, and Trevor pretty much jumped from the top down below. He whipped his hair like the heartthrob he was to get the wet hair away from his eyes.

"Bend baby! Look at that bend!" The rod was bent so far over from the strength of the fish, it looked like it would snap in half.

"Hell yeah! Dunkaroos for the win!" Luke was reeling in the other rods to avoid getting tangled with the prize money on the end of the other line.

Trevor was on the line grinding away like a machine. It looked like he was reeling in a minnow from the power he was emitting. Tightening the drag a bit, he reeled, feverishly stopping to wipe the sweat and salt water from his dripping face.

"It's a big one. I can feel it. We got this one boys! Can anyone see it yet?"

From the bridge, Finn looked hoping to see a huge blue marlin sweep across the horizon trying to free itself. "Not yet! Keep going! Get it closer!"

Another one bites the dust! And another one bites, and another bites. Another one bites the dust.

"She's pulling hard man!" Luke stood nearby in case Trevor took a tumble and needed to be caught, yet far enough not to touch him resulting in a disqualification.

Reel downward. Pull up! Reel downward. Pull up!

Finally, a monumental tail splashed around the back of the boat after thirty minutes of fighting. Alex reached the liter and wrestled the fish until he was able to grab the bill. The struggle was real and with some serious manpower, an enormous blue marlin was finally on board *Weekend Vibes*.

Hollars and yells were uncontrollable as 'the band' rocketed themselves onto the leaderboard.

"There's no way anyone has a monster like this on their boat today!" Trevor was still on a high from the reeling.

"Oh yes there is! Weekend Vibes, baby!" High fives and hoots were given all around.

And it only picked up from there. By 3:30 *Weekend Vibes* had boated four tuna, released a white marlin, boated another white marlin at 72 inches, and 6 mahi. As they made their way in, they cranked up some Bon Jovi. *Ohh! Halfway there! Ohh! Living on a Prayer!*

WHITNEY

"Distance...5 miles. Pace...10 minutes, 13 seconds. Split pace...10 minutes, 45 seconds." Whitney came to a slow stop as her running app alerted her that she was finally done with her morning run. And the best part was, it was only 7 a.m.

She took out her earbuds and placed them in her pocket. She'd probably leave them in there and wash them by mistake. She's been through at least 3 pairs in the past few months out of plain carelessness. She stretched and walked across Coastal Highway toward the beach. This early in the morning, people were still sleeping. It's their vacation—why would anyone wake up this early? She made her way up through one of the dunes that were surrounded by seagrass.

It was a gorgeous morning. The sun had come up over the horizon and she could already feel that it was going to be another scorcher. Yesterday had been near 100 degrees and the weatherman from the news had predicted another day near, if not over the hundred-degree mark.

She has no concrete plans today until around 6 when her fiancé came in from fishing. Finn was the captain of *Weekend Vibes* and was fishing the annual Marlin Tournament. He had gotten up around 3:30 a.m. to get to the boat by 4:00. Their plan was to leave by 5:00 to get a head start on the competition. Since today was Finn's first day, he hadn't placed yet but was extremely optimistic. In 3rd place were *The Other Woman*, Rob Hennesy's boat, and *Big Distraction*, TJ Moxley's boat was always one to watch according to the White Marlin Open website and social media was in 2nd. TJ's yellow lab, Marlin, was his unofficial first mate and made every fishing trip that TJ ever took. Marlin was famous at the dock.

Since it was so early and Whitney had the whole day in front of her, she took a short walk, not that she needed any more exercise, to her favorite breakfast spot, Layton's. She walked in and sat at the counter, ordering a cup of hot black coffee and two French crullers. She was starving and heck—she deserved it!

People were envious of Whitney. She had an athletic build because she ran at least 5 miles a day, ate extremely healthy (aside from her French crullers), and hit the gym multiple times a week. Her dark brown hair was cut in a shoulder-length blunt bob. When she exercised, several chunks of hair fell in the back, sticking to her neck.

Whitney was down the ocean for a few days while Finn was captaining *Weekend Vibes*. He was down here for a majority of the summer and she came back and forth from Baltimore as often as she could. Whitney worked as a nurse in labor and delivery at Johns Hopkins Hospital in Baltimore City. She'd been working there for about 4 years now and loved her job. With her schedule, 3 twelve hour shifts a week, she's able to get away for 3-4 days at a time, which works out perfectly during Marlin Week.

"Here you go. Hot coffee and two French crullers," she heard a man say.

As she looked up, it was Mr. Layton himself. Layton's was a staple in the town of Ocean City. Whitney loves the 16th street location, but their second location on 92nd was also extremely popular.

"Good morning. I haven't seen you in a while," she said.

"I know. It's been busy around here. How long are you in town for?"

"I have off the rest of the week. Finn's in the Marlin tournament, so I get to relax by the pool until at least 4:00. I'm hoping for a lucky day. It's his first day out."

"Well, that sounds very promising! I wish him all the luck in the world," he said as he carried around his tray of free samples of their delicious donuts.

Whitney sat at the counter enjoying her crullers and coffee while scrolling her social media accounts. She has to admit, she's kind of an addict. She's not someone who posts a lot but does enjoy seeing other people's pictures. Pictures of vacations, new cars, people buying a new home. But there was one thing that tugged on her heartstrings harder than others and that was pictures of moms holding their newborn babies. Whitney had always wanted to be a mom. But one year ago, that all changed with a simple annual check-up at the gynecologist.

Whitney had made an appointment with Dr. Maggio, her OBGYN she had been seeing since she was in high school. She went in for her annual appointment on a Thursday morning at 9:10. She liked early appointments so she could get them out of the way. She remembered it like it was yesterday.

Whitney sat in the waiting room. Whenever she went to the gynecologist she remembered an article she had read and it always made her laugh. This girl was on her way to the gynecologist and was running late. She didn't have time to "freshen up" as the article stated so she sprayed some deodorant down there to give it a light rosy smell. The girl gets to the doctor's office and right as the doctor starts to examine her, he gives off a little giggle. The girl gets put off and asks why the doctor is laughing. He says, "Well, I've never had a patient get so fancy and sparkly just for me." Turns out that she hadn't used spray deodorant but spray glitter and her vagina looked like a disco ball under the examination light. Mortified would be the word Whitney would have used.

Her name was called and she went back, got her weight—121 lbs.—and was directed into room number two. The nurse took her vitals—temperature and blood pressure— and told Whitney she could change into the hospital gown and reminded her to leave it open in the front. The nurse left the room and a few minutes later Dr. Maggio knocked and entered the room.

"Hi there, Whitney. It's so good to see you. How have you been? Still running?" Dr. Maggio had long, thick black hair that hung halfway down her back. She looked to have been of Asian Pacific descent. She was shorter than Whitney and wore thick, black-framed glasses and little makeup. She also happened to be a runner. She knew this because she had literally run into Dr. Maggio during a half marathon that Spring around mile marker 6.

"It's good to see you, too. Yes, you know me too well. Still running about 5 miles a day, longer ones on the weekends."

"That's good to hear. How are you feeling? Any aches, pains, or complaints?"

"Nope. I'm just here for my annual," she replied.

"Ok good. That's what I like to hear. Any spotting or cramping that I need to be aware of? Anything that sticks out in your head as uncharacteristic," Dr. Maggio asked.

"No. Everything feels fine. I still take my birth control daily. I'm a stickler for that."

"Perfect. Well, let's have you slide down on the table and let me take a look." Whitney placed her feet in the cold and unwelcoming stirrups. And right then and there, that's when Whitney's life began to spiral.

Everything that happened in Dr. Maggio's office after the words "*cervical cancer*" came out of her mouth was a blur. There was talk about stage one, operations, chemotherapy, medicines, IB2, 4 cm, hospitals, family support, insurance, and a lot of other things that Whitney hadn't heard. But one other thing that Whitney had heard loud and clear was: "Whitney, you're pregnant."

LEANNE

Leanne had a showing today in midtown Ocean City. It wasn't exactly what the client was looking for. In fact, it was nothing like the client was looking for. But it was her job to help clients open their minds a little more than they knew they wanted. It usually leads to a more successful closing, she has found out. This particular condo was bayside overlooking Assawoman Bay. It was a two-bedroom, two-bath, one-level condo with neighbors on one side only. The living room had two sliding glass doors, which opened all the way leaving the living room exposed to the gorgeous nightly sunsets. The paint throughout was a light blue with touches of beachy decor all around. An updated kitchen with a double oven and white marble countertops with specks of gold and silver.

Leanne had to be at the scales later in the afternoon, so she purposely made this meeting for late morning knowing that she would want to spend some extra time getting to know this client a little more intimately.

As always, she arrived early to open the doors and make sure everything was in its place. Normally this client she was meeting was early, however she didn't see his car in the parking lot. Leanne climbed the three flights of stairs in her four-inch tall black sandals that made her legs look even leaner than they already were. She had always gotten compliments on her beautiful tan legs in the summertime. She had chalked it up to the many years of walking the track while the boys were at baseball, lacrosse, and soccer practice. She missed those days. The boys were almost grown and in college. It felt like yesterday she was cleaning Cheerios and popcorn from the inside of her car and chauffeuring kids to the movie theater.

As she waited for the client, she walked out to the open-air deck. It was fully furnished with a 7-piece Rattan wicker sectional on the right side. The left side of the deck housed a large hanging umbrella with a lounge chair resting in its shade. She looked out over the bay. It was early and people were already out clamming on the sand bar. Low tide comes in the early afternoon, but the diggers were only in knee-deep water in most places. A black lab was running the sandbar gripping a tennis ball in its mouth. The dog's owners had their Whaler anchored up and were enjoying a few beers. Another boat was anchored up further out toward the deeper end of the sandbar. Leanne could see an old milk crate floating nearby with the help of an old pool noodle tied around its edges.

A knock came from the entry hallway.

A man's voice, deep but cheery, echoed through. "Hello? Anyone here?"

Leanne walked back through the opened glass doors, to the living room and met him halfway. He was over a foot taller than her. His eyes were the color of the ocean in the middle of a hurricane. Danger.

"Hi," was all she could get out.

The client approached her. He kissed her on the cheek as he slid his hand down her arm. Chills.

Leanne tried to compose herself.

"So I'm trying to figure out why you brought me here. This isn't as secluded as I wanted to be." He strolled around the living room and then out to the deck. It was sunny outside so he slid his Christian Dior sunglasses off of the top of his head. Propping himself onto the edge of the railing, his one elbow over the side, he turned around toward Leanne.

"Well, it's my job to show you options. I know this isn't exactly what you had in mind. But it has a lot of what you wanted. Open living space, two bedrooms, an extraordinary view of the sunsets every night."

"Privacy?" he countered.

Leanne sat on the beautifully upholstered outdoor sectional. As she crossed her legs, her dress smoothly slid up her thigh. She tried to cover herself with minimal luck.

He came and sat next to her. He put his arm up behind Leanne on the back of the sofa.

"Well, really any place can have as much privacy as you want. This condo only has neighbors on one side. And I did some inquiring and they live in Florida and only come up a few weeks out of the year."

She faced her body toward his.

"It does have a great view. The neighbors, I'm not a fan of. But I did see a nice private pool as I walked in. What do you say we go and take a dip and relax. I'm tired of business already today."

"Tired of business? We just got here. And you know that swimming isn't really an option." She tilted her head a little giving a sly smile.

"Well I guess then I'll have to go back to my rental and enjoy the picnic basket of martini glasses, gin, and vermouth that I brought with me all by myself. I was hoping to share it with someone, but..." His arm came down over Leanne's shoulder. His touch was...hot, electric, sultry. Dangerous. He brought her in closer. His lips touched hers and she responded back. His hands were on her rubbing down her thighs near the top of her dress which wasn't covering much at this point. He traced his finger down the middle of her chest down to her breasts with his pointer finger.

"Did you bring your suit? Like I asked?"

"It's in my bag," she said. "I'll go change." She went to stand up and he pulled her back down.

"Why don't you let me help you." He slowly moved her hair to the side. The zipper on her dress slid down seductively all the way down past her waist revealing a lacey, maroon bra and thong underneath.

The dress was now long forgotten and on the floor leaving Leanne in her panties, bra, and as she used to call them her "kitten heels."

She straddled her client on the newly-upholstered outdoor furniture as they made out like high school students in the back of a car, except the seven-piece sectional had ample room for movement. However, Leanne had zero intention of moving far from him. The attraction they both felt was magnetic and undeniable. They both wanted it.

Twenty minutes later, Leanne was coming out of the bathroom adjacent to the living room sporting her solid black bikini. He was in the kitchen, donning swim trunks and opening a large picnic basket on the marble countertop which had been empty when she arrived.

He looked her up and down as he opened the bottle of gin.

"Shaken, not stirred," she said.

"You are in luck. I just happen to make the best martinis. He poured the gin into the tumbler which was already full of ice. A splash of vermouth followed. He capped the tumbler and began to shake the luscious cocktail as the outline of his biceps showed. Just a few minutes beforehand, those tan arms had enveloped her body on the brilliant king-sized bed which overlooked the bay.

He opened the freezer and presented two frosted martini glasses. He slid one of the glasses slowly down her arm. "Let's take this party poolside, shall we?"

The martinis were salty and strong. The breeze was divine and the pool was empty. Even though this pool was smaller in size for a complex this grand, what it lacked in size it made up for with its view. The entire perimeter of the pool was lined in bright pink roses with lavender and cyan blue hydrangeas. The smell of the sweet flowery aroma mixed with the salty briny whiff of the ocean was enough to relax even Leanne. A smaller grassy area extended past the flowers leading to a dock lined with Bayliners, Whalers, and Sea Foxes. The white fiberglass boats bobbed calmly just waiting for their day to drift through the waves of Assawoman Bay.

Leanne sat on the side of the pool, legs dangling in the cold water, her martini close by. Dean swam back and forth a few times, which didn't take long considering its tiny size. Rob was out on the boat. Day 2 of the tournament. She felt a little guilty doing this, being poolside with a client, drinking martinis. But it was business, right?

He slowly swam underwater, coming up for air right at Leanne's perfectly pedicured feet. His hands glided up her ankles then calves and gently up her outer thighs. He pulled her off the ledge and lifted her down into the water. Instinctively her legs wrapped around his waist as he pressed her back up against the side of the pool.

They gently kissed, even feeling romantic at one point. He placed his hands on her rounded hips as he pushed against her. She could feel him again. But there was nothing they could do in this public setting. At least that's what she thought.

Reaching toward the front of her bathing suit, she could feel what he had planned. Looking around, she felt almost scandalous. In a public place? They were the only two people around. Privacy was important to him, yet here they were on public display.

He began to use his hands...and she didn't stop him.

● ● ●

After the escapades in the pool had come and gone, they both lay in the shade sipping their martinis, each with three olives. She couldn't think of a better way to spend a morning at work. As she looked at her watch, she read that it was nearly 10 a.m. People would be coming to the pool soon with their kids, noodles, swimmies, and suntan lotion. For the next hour, she wanted to enjoy the quiet. As her martini glass was running low, another pour was waiting—shaken, not stirred. He leaned over and kissed her collarbone, then her lips. It was sexy.

Out of the corner of her eye, Leanne saw a younger girl appear at the pool gate. She apparently punched in the same code as they had, given the gate swung right open. She was taller, lean, and athletic looking. She took a spot furthest away from them in the shade. Leanne had purposely worn large dark sunglasses and kept them on while at the pool. She couldn't risk being seen here.

"Ready for another dip?" His eyebrows jumped twice.

"Just a dip. It's getting hot already."

"Let me help you up."

Leanne took his hand while balancing her drink in the other. She took charge this time and leaned in for a kiss. Her hand was on his tan shoulder as his hands cupped her from behind.

His mouth got close to her ear. She could hear his breath. "The more I touch you, the more I want you."

She slid her hand down his back and kissed his chest then lips. Their passionate, playful kissing was finally stopped when they were able to pry themselves apart. They walked down the steps into the shallow end of the pool and let the crisp water wash over them...and try to cool them down.

WHITNEY

After her much-deserved breakfast, Whitney walked a
few blocks back to the condo. It was midweek and the
hope was that the pool would be empty. She rinsed
off her run and then went to change into her bathing suit. She
caught a sideways glimpse of her body as she walked by the
mirror. Something had caught her eye but she was unsure of
what it was. She tenderly rubbed her stomach. It was always
in the back of her mind. Having a baby wasn't just something
that she and Finn had thought about—it was a dream of theirs.
To have something that the two of them had created together
and were going to care for and love together. They wanted a
family. But it was her fault that she had miscarried multiple
times. Her body had failed her—had failed them.

Whitney's phone pinged, alerting her of a text message.
It was from Finn...

> *Hey Honey!*
> *Just wanted to say I love you*
> *Hope you had a good run!*
> *I'll let you know when I'm on my way back in*
> *Love you!*

He knew her so well. They hadn't spoken since last evening
before bed. Both she and Finn were exhausted. She had each
just gotten in from Baltimore on Monday. Finn had driven
right to Sunset Marina and prepped the boat with the band.
She hadn't gotten in until late evening after a day of errands
and bills. They ordered sushi from OC Wasabi and ate in front

of the television in their pajamas. They fell asleep on the sofa, smushed under one blanket because neither of them wanted to get up for another. They watched old reruns of *The Jersey Shore*. When Whitney awakened the next morning, Finn was long gone, but the sushi take-out boxes were still scattered on the coffee table. Nights like that were her favorite.

Whitney tried to set aside the sad feelings about the miscarriages and tried to focus on a day of relaxation by the pool. She packed a pool bag with her essentials- water, sunscreen, snack, an Elin Hilderbrand book, her phone, towel, and sunglasses. She grabbed her keys and headed out toward the waterfront pool.

It was turning out to be just as hot as it was yesterday. Maybe she would be able to snag a chair with an umbrella for shade. As she opened the gate, which revealed a very quaint, very quiet lounge area, she realized that the pool was empty. Except for a couple in the corner farthest away from her, she was the only one there. She found the perfect spot, half-shade, half-sun, and set up her own little piece of paradise.

The pool was calling her name so she slipped off her sundress and walked toward the steps that descended into the glass-like water. It felt as good as it looked. The sun was already so hot that it had heated the pool water up enough to where there wasn't even that shock of cold. It was like cool bath water as she slid in. She held her breath and swam underwater from one end of the pool to the other. A calm wave of relaxation came over her and she walked up the stairs and back to her shady, sunny spot. As she settled down with her book, she could feel her early morning run catching up to her. She lay her head back and closed her eyes. *Oh yeah. This is it. That breeze. The smell of the ocean air.* And off she went...

Two glorious hours later, Whitney slowly woke up from the most incredible nap in the history of all naps. She hadn't even stirred once during her light slumber. She slowly glanced around and noticed that she was the only one there now. The couple she had seen earlier was now gone. She wasn't one hundred percent sure, but the woman had looked familiar—but she couldn't put her finger on it. The only evidence that the couple left was a couple of martini glasses strewn here and there. She shrugged her shoulders, closed her eyes, and dozed off again.

Katherine Ruskey

FINN

When Finn wasn't captaining a boat in the summer months, he worked construction back in Baltimore. He worked for a small company that worked mainly in residential construction. They bought and flipped shabby old houses and transformed them into shabby chic homes. From September through April he hung drywall, installed kitchen cabinets, tiled bathroom showers, and even dabbled in some outdoor landscaping. He was the Chip Gaines of Baltimore. The house that he and Whitney currently lived in was actually bought as a flip but he ended up falling in love with the old school charm mixed with the new modern feel.

The band relaxed on the deck of the boat while Finn lead them back in.

Alex inhaled the ocean air.

"Do you smell that, boys?"

"Yep. Fish." Luke was always good with dad jokes.

"No, bonehead. Smells like victory." Both arms spread wide open as he inhaled again.

Finn joined the boat parade that led into the inlet. Of the 500 some-odd boats that fished this week, he estimated that three to four hundred of them were heading back home through this channel. People lined up on land waving and cheering.

The band wasn't quite sure what place the blue marlin they had on board would put them, but they were eager to get into the scales and find out.

When he finally got cell service, he had sent Whitney a quick text saying that he'd be at Harbour Island Marina on 14th street around 5 p.m.

Weekend Vibes was one of the first boats to arrive at the scales today. They drifted in between the tight piers of Harbour Island. Tank and his crew of guys waited to weigh in the million-dollar fish that were being brought in from the canyons and beyond. Crowds were already gathered, several people deep, all anticipating the excitement that was the White Marlin Open.

Over the intercom, Finn heard, "*And here comes Weekend Vibes captained by Finn Donahough. Let's see what they brought us.*" The crowd clapped and whistled.

The band stood port side as the boat pivoted, gliding right into the dock. The dock crew tied them off as they began to unload their haul.

"We got quite a bit for you today! Wait until you see this beauty." Trevor began to drag the blue marlin by its tail across the deck.

The announcer came back over the loudspeaker.

"*Looks like we have ourselves a nice big qualifying blue marlin on board!*" The crowd yelled their approval. Mack looped the large billfish by the tail and let the scale begin the difficult job of hoisting her up. The crowd's "whoas" was echoed all over the cul-de-sac. Digits on the screen began to slowly climb as the rope tugged the fish upwards.

The guys all stood around. Their hearts were racing and they couldn't peel their eyes away from the screen.

The numbers locked in. One thousand one pounds!

The crowd erupted and Finn yelled out! "Whoa, baby!! Yeah!" The band all hugged and high-fived! They were now in first place in the blue marlin category winning approximately $1.4 million.

"Let's go, baby!" Alex jumped around, running down the line of spectators high-fiving them all. The band was on a high and they wanted to keep it running. They unloaded the rest of the fish including a 72" white marlin that put them in third in the category winning around $100,000. The boys were back in town, and everyone at the scales knew it.

The blue marlin sent them to the top. However, it was still too early to know whether or not he held his spot on the podium. Several boats were still on their way in. As he looked around the marina, he noticed his number one competitor, *Big Distraction*, wasn't there. It looked like TJ Moxley may have taken the day off.

Back at the boat at Sunset Marina, Finn was heading up the ladder to finish up some minor details. He saw Whitney in between the crowds of people. She was walking toward him smiling ear to ear. *God, she was stunning*. He thought that every time he saw her. *What did a girl like her see in a guy like me?* he often thought to himself. She finally made her way through the crowd and embraced him in a tight hug. He kissed her long and hard, grabbing her butt while he did so. She playfully shooed him off her and laughed.

"How did you do today?" she asked.

"Brought in a 1,001-pound blue, a few tuna, a white marlin, and some nice mahi. We're in first place! The boys are at the fileting station waiting for the bags of fish."

"Oh my God! That's incredible!" She threw her hands up in the air. "Now what? Are you all done for the day or do you need to tidy up the boat?"

"I need to tie up a few loose ends real quick with the guys. Then I'll be ready to go. Meet you at the bar in a few minutes?"

"You know where I'll be," she said, smiling. She gave a quick peck on his cheek and squeezed his bicep. His arms were so big and strong from all of the construction. Not only was he strong—he was sexy.

The bar was pretty crowded because it was midweek of the tournament. It would be tricky to find a seat. She made her way through the throngs of people and ten minutes later, she just happened to snag a chair right in front of one of the bartenders. They were running around like mad making Ocean City's famous orange crushes and pouring Flying

Dog beer on tap. She quickly ordered a Natty Boh on tap—a straight Baltimore-style beer.

Whitney sat people-watching and sipping her drink. She saw a few people that looked familiar only because she had been down the marina on other weigh-in days. There were lots of families eating dinner around the restaurant. A twinge of pain hit her heart each time she saw a young couple like her and Finn having dinner with their children. It made her sad at the fact that she had failed them as a couple. It was her fault that she and Finn didn't have a baby yet.

Just then, a brunette woman squished her way to the bar. The gentleman that was sitting on the stool next to Whitney offered the woman his seat. Whitney loved old-school manners and charm. The woman sat down next to her and ordered a dirty martini with extra olives. Whitney loved to talk and mingle with people. She was what Finn called a "people person." If they were in line at the grocery, Whitney would talk to them. If they were at a party, Whitney knew everyone's name halfway through the evening. Bars—forget it. She talked to anyone and everyone who sat next to her. She had a magnetic energy that people were drawn to.

"I've never liked martinis. I could never handle them," Whitney commented. "They always look so delicious. But I just can't do it."

The other woman laughed. "They are an acquired taste. I like mine with gin, not vodka. Try it that way. Maybe it'll change your mind."

Whitney pointed to her beer. "This is more my speed, I guess. I'm not a huge drinker. But martinis just look so sophisticated."

"They're a good decoy then, I guess," she said and laughed, winking at Whitney.

"So are you down here for vacation?" Whitney asked the woman.

"Not particularly. My husband, Rob, is fishing in the

tournament. He lured me down here to the pier. He's in 3rd place I think."

"Oh, that's great! My fiancé is fishing, too. He's on Weekend Vibes. What a coincidence. Does that mean we should be rivals?" Whitney laughed. Her new friend laughed too, but more of a nervous one. "Cheers!" The ladies clinked glasses and sipped their summer drinks.

Whitney's phone pinged a text. It was from Finn.

I'm done, honey. Wanna go grab dinner?
Sure, Whitney replied.
I'll pay for my drink and I'll meet you at the boat. Muah!
OK

Whitney turned to say goodbye to the woman who was next to her. But when she looked over, the woman was already gone. The only thing there was half of a sophisticated-looking martini.

LEANNE

S he sat at the bar of Sunset Marina sipping her martini. There was a friendly girl next to her sipping on what looked like a crappy beer. As she made small talk with the friendly girl, her heart jumped into her throat. *What the hell was he doing here?* Across the bar, her client was leaning along the bar, sunglasses perched on her gorgeously tanned face. Lifting his hand up, he slid his glasses down. He winked at her right before he ordered a drink. She needed to leave and quickly. She couldn't believe what she was seeing. Luckily, at that very second, her friendly companion's phone pinged what was hopefully something to keep her distracted. She quietly set her drink on the bar and quickly walked toward her car. A kind gentleman who had been standing behind Leanne patiently waiting reclaimed his seat and ordered another drink.

JULES

It was mid-summer, and family vacations were in full swing on Assateague. Every camping site was booked from now until Labor Day Weekend. Families came in with coolers, canopies, tents, bicycles, kayaks, fishing rods, and anything else you would need for an exciting week of camping.

It was Tuesday morning. Jules' job was to drive the golf cart, visiting sites to make sure campers were emptied out by 11 so that the next family could come in and set up shop. It was normally an easy gig. Families obeyed the times for the most part. Every now and then she found a couple that had overslept and had to wake them. Or a family that just lost track of time at the beach. Other than that, her job was pretty great. What was there not to like? People were happy on vacation. By day, they were splashing in the waves, eating chicken salad sandwiches, and marveling at the wild ponies. And by night, they were cleaning off the day's sand in the outdoor showers, playing a game of flag football with their families, and cooking s'mores over a campfire.

Jules was a year-round local. She lived in Ocean City in a small sublet on the bayside near 9th street. She'd been there a few years now. Her younger sister goes to Salisbury University and comes to visit Jules weekly, meaning doing her laundry and eating Jules' leftovers. She never minded Kit's visits. She welcomed every moment the two had together. There was a pretty large age gap between the two—10 years to be exact. Kit had been what their parents called their 'rainbow baby' growing up. She never understood that until she got older.

It was around 8 a.m. and it was already hot. Her long blonde hair was pulled up in a flowy bun to keep it from sticking to her neck. Riding from the bayside to the ocean side in the golf cart, the air was humid and stagnant. She spotted two ponies on the road just hanging out. People were stopping their cars to get out and snap photos. Jules hung around for a few minutes to make sure no one was getting too close. Once the crowd thinned, Jules made her way to the oceanside lots with her clipboard. On it was a list of reservations. She needed to make sure the lots were cleared out and maintained.

Walking from lot to lot, Jules climbed the dunes around Lot 88 and took in the view. The ocean lay out in front of her, calm and mellow due to the lack of wind. No surfers wading on their boards, and very few people had set up their beach equipment. However, the smell of bacon, sausage, coffee, and pancakes danced in the air around her. She took a deep breath in. She loved her job.

TJ AND MARLIN

TJ was never one to sleep in. He felt that if he slept later than 7 a.m., then his entire day was shot. And today was no exception. He woke up to a cold nose on his neck and he knew he only had two minutes before Marlin started to climb on top of him to go outside.

"Good morning, boy. Did you sleep? Good?" He rubbed the back of Marlin's ears while Marlin's tail swooped from side to side. He buried his face in the crook of TJ's arm and sneezed.

"Oh, God bless you. Is it time for coffee?" TJ climbed out of bed and threw on a Boston Red Sox hoodie. A few years ago, a group of college guys came on board to fish and one of the guys left it behind. He didn't want it to go to waste. It was warm and he didn't mind the Red Sox. He was actually a fan of the city itself. Well, the ballpark at least.

He opened the door for Marlin and brewed his morning coffee. The clock read 7:15 a.m. He had a list of things that he wanted to do today: get a haircut, wash the Jeep, Marlin needed a bath, and a few other odds and ends at the house. He looked at the surf report and saw that this afternoon looked promising as far as wind. He needed a good wave session and with the heat so unrelenting in August, a long dip would feel great.

Marlin came in and had his breakfast. TJ took his coffee to the deck that overlooked his backyard. He settled in his rocking chair and propped his feet up.

He couldn't stop thinking about last night.

He had had an incredible time with Jules. It was relaxing and fun. It was easy. He didn't feel the need to try to impress her.

He could really be himself. She wasn't like other girls. He loved that she was close to her sister and thought it was kind of cute that Kit had given him a hard time. And Marlin seemed to like them both. That could've been the pizza Kit was feeding him, too.

Marlin brought TJ one of his many tennis balls that TJ stored in a bucket on the back patio.

"What do you think about Jules, huh? Did you like her?" Marlin plopped the ball at TJ's feet.

"Me, too. We're going to see her again tomorrow, okay? But you need to behave. Don't spoil it for me."

TJ leaned down. Marlin was fixated on the tennis ball that was about to be tossed into the yard and could care less about what TJ was saying. He flung the ball in the far corner of the yard. Marlin sailed off of the top step and landed lightly on his feet as he scooped the ball up in his mouth. They did this about fifty more times before TJ had to break the news that playtime was over.

After doing some dishes and starting a load of laundry, TJ headed out for his errands. *The early bird catches the worm.* He enjoyed waking up early. He had the world to himself most days. Occasionally he would pass trucks that were heading to the docks or the beach for some morning fishing.

He made a left at Assateague Island Surf Shop. Assateague Island farm stood on the left already burning wood that attracted several campers daily. In addition to firewood, their produce was to die for. Bright red tomatoes and summer squash were some of his favorites. They always had fresh-cut flowers. *I'll stop and get some for Jules before our date,* he thought. He'll look on their Instagram page to see what's available. Marlin never passes up an opportunity to visit Jasmine and Cosmo, the farm goats.

A little further down he passed a large field of what will be sunflowers come Fall. The road gets crowded with families taking annual photos and young kids apparently called influencers taking selfies with unnecessary filters.

His haircut was scheduled for eight. He'd been coming here for years. The owner was right out of Italy with his thick accent and all. Before Marlin even jumped out of the Jeep, Guillermohad already opened the food with a hot cup of freshly brewed Italian coffee and a dog bone.

"Mornin," TJ greeted as he climbed from the Jeep. Guillermo passed the hot Italian brew over and knelt down to say 'Buongiorno' to his favorite furry customer. He sipped his coffee, which smelled like he was sitting in an Italian cafe overlooking the cobblestone walkways.

"How are you? Sorry it's been so long. How is Celia?" Guillermo patted TJ on the back. His stature was small, shorter than average. His hair was silvery grey and white.

"Bueno! Bueno! She's inside waiting for her favorite guy to arrive."

"Oh, I'm flattered."

"Don't be. It's not you. It's that guy," he said, pointing to Marlin. The door swung open and Marlin led them both into the shop. High-pitch squealing came followed by a bunch of Italian that TJ had always thought sounded romantic. Before he died, he wanted to learn.

Celia, Guillermo's wife, worked alongside him cutting hair for over 40 years now. He loved watching them together, bantering in Italian and English.

"Celia, how are you?" TJ slid in for a one-armed hug not wanting to lose the delicious potion in his mug. Celia was just as short as her husband. TJ had always thought that they matched. They were the perfect couple. Her dark hair was always fixed and her make-up was always done.

"We have missed you. It's been such a long time." By this time, Celia had already taken Marlin over to the hair-washing station where everyone else would be ignored until Marlin left. Celia loved Marlin.

"Well, you know she's occupied for another thirty minutes.

Get her off my back for a little about seeing a doctor." He swooped the black hair cape around TJ and buttoned it up on the back.

"Doctor? For what? You feeling okay?" TJ asked, concerned.

"Just growing pains, you know? I'm no spring chicken...but hell—neither is she." He made sure to whisper that last part. "Head down," he directed. TJ followed. As he talked about his "growing pains", he went about buzzing, snipping, and trimming TJ's hair in a swift dance that he had mastered years ago. He would be able to cut TJ's hair blindfolded if he needed to. "Hey, how's your granddaughter? She's graduated from Salisbury, right? Or almost graduating?"

"Cici! Yes! She is in her junior year and will be graduating next year. We are so proud of her. She comes and visits when she has time off."

"I'm so glad to hear that. I remember when she used to run around the shop here. She still hasn't met Marlin. It's been that long since I've seen her."

"She is always studying. At least that's what she says she's doing."

The cape was taken off with just as much flourish as it had taken to put on. TJ paid Guillermo and Celia and tipped extremely well.

"Okay, you two, it's time to break this up. We have errands to run before tomorrow."

"What's tomorrow?" Celia asked, looking up while rubbing Marlin's ears.

"Nothing special. Well, it is kind of special." TJ adjusted his hat with both hands, one on the bill and one on the back. "I met this girl the other day and I'm taking her on a date. And...I really like her."

"Oh, that's so good to hear! Especially after that other girl that you had dated. I knew that wasn't going to last," Celia stated. She stood up and placed both hands on TJ's face. "You deserve the best, and I want nothing other than that for you. I hope she sees how good she has it."

TJ's face was beginning to turn bright red. They treated him as if they were his parents. He gave a huge hug to Celia, gathered Marlin, and out the door they went.

It was still early and TJ had a list of things that needed to be done. Haircut, check. Laundry started, check. Clean Jeep. Okay.

"Let's get home and clean her out. And while we're at it, someone needs a bath." Marlin's ears perked up at the mention of that word. While most dogs he's seen on tv and in movies hated the idea of even touching water, Marlin was the anomaly. He loved a good bath. And once that word had come across his ears, he wouldn't let you forget until he got one.

...

Jeep. Check. Bath. Check. TJ looked at his watch. It was approaching almost 11:30 and TJ's stomach was beginning to rumble. Maybe he'd take a drive to Harborside and grab a bite at the bar. He hadn't been to the grocery store and knew it was a mistake to go when he was hungry.

He and Marlin jumped in the Jeep. The top was up and the windows out. It was scorching again and the shade was nice. The traffic was backed up on the way to Assateague with other Jeeps that were rolling along with surfboards hanging out the back. He would make sure to get some waves in this evening.

Pulling up to the bar, TJ tried to find a spot in the shade to keep the Jeep cool. No such luck. The lunch crowd had already arrived and he took one of the last available spots. He and Marlin walked through the outside door and walked down the pier. He found a spot facing the water near a fan while Marlin found his place at TJ's feet.

The open-air bar faced out onto the open dock. Boats lined up in their slips. Couples sat with their legs propped up, sipping their favorite beer. Dogs perched on the bows of their boats exercising their authority.

"What's up man!" a larger man wearing a bar rag across his shoulder greeted TJ. He used the water gun to fill up a bowl for Marlin. His shirt was soaked through and TJ could see the sweat running down his temples.

"How's the fishing this year," he asked, sliding Marlin's water over the bar top.

"It's really good! Looking promising. I have a feeling this is going to be the year."

"Well, you know where I am when you have some leftover tuna!" Roman had been working as a bartender here for years. He was notorious for the night that a bar fight broke out. Two guys started going back and forth after several shots of Proper 12. Next thing you know, they're swinging punches like Connor MacGregor. One of them connected hard, breaking the other guy's nose. Roman, at 290 pounds of beer belly and muscle, hurtled over the bar like an Olympian to break them up. Blood covered the guy's broken nose and shirt. The other guy had then come after Roman for meddling. He charged Roman and swung toward him. He'd swung so hard he had lost his balance and stumbled backward falling right overboard! Roman reached into the bay, grabbed the man by his shirt collar, and left him on the pier like a wet towel from a boat.

"I'll make sure you get some good fish this year."

"Thanks, bro. Whata ya eatin?"

"Coconut shrimp and a flounder sandwich. I'm starving."

"You got it." He turned around and punched TJ's order into the computer.

TJ looked around the restaurant. There were tables surrounding the bar and out on the waterfront. Beach-goers and boaters were enjoying mahi sandwiches and shrimp salad wraps. Later tonight vacationers would taste the plump stuffed shrimp and the local scallops seared in white wine.

He watched the highlights from last night's Orioles game on

the television. They won against Tampa Bay and were gearing up for another game tonight.

Marlin relaxed in the shade, and people watched like an older gentleman rocking on his front porch. A younger kid in a Harborside t-shirt came out and delivered TJ's lunch. The golden coconut shrimp glistened with flakes of crispy white coconut. He could eat these every day; they were divine. Even though the temperature is approaching Hell outside, they hit the spot. Marlin sat patiently waiting- never begging. TJ slipped him a piece of the coconut shrimp.

As he enjoyed his first bite of the salty founder sandwich with lettuce, tomato, and mayo, he looked across the bar. Mallory was sitting sipping a seltzer, probably black cherry. She was your typical basic girl— pumpkin spice, sweater weather, and selfie-posting. But there was no spark. They had dated on and off for about a year. Last year, he broke it off as gently as he could. He remembered going to Frog Bar that night after he drove to her apartment. He thought she had taken it very well. There were no tears. No screaming. Until the next morning when he got a phone call from someone at the marina. Someone had vandalized *Big Distraction* with some spray paint and a few colorful words. It cost him a few thousand dollars to have it fixed and cleaned up. There was no proof that she had anything to do with it, nor did any of the cameras catch anyone. The coincidence was just too close. And obviously when he asked her about it, she had no idea what she was talking about and was "truly offended."

Roman walked over holding two shot glasses of what looked like tequila.

"From the pretty girl drinking the black cherry White Claw." He nudged his head toward his right.

Now he knew it wasn't tequila. She was never able to stomach it. *Lemon drop?*

"Lemon drop."

Predictable.

"I really don't want it."

"That would be rude to say no."

"We used to date. She vandalized my boat. No—I *think* she vandalized my boat, last year. When I broke up with her."

"Oh man," Roman said. "Bro."

"Yeah." He reached down and rewarded Marlin with a French fry. He had lost his appetite.

"Well, we have two shots here. One for each of us. Let's just say they're from me.

Fine.

They threw the tart liquid of the lemon drop back. TJ waved politely as a thank you. But not an invitation. He could see her move from her barstool and begin to walk around the bar that was now full of lunch patrons. She had her long blonde hair pulled up into a messy bun and a red bikini under a see-through cover-up. He never understood the point.

Setting her drink on the bar and sliding the stool out, she said, "So you missed me I see."

"Excuse me?"

"You took the shot I sent over to you. You know lemon drops are our thing." She was leaning up against the bar, batting her eyelashes.

"No. Lemon drops are *your* thing," he said, annoyed.

"That's not how I remember it. Remember that night at Fishtales with that group of people we met from Florida? I hardly remember the bar scene, but I remember the night back at my place vividly. We rattled that place so hard, I had a noise notice taped to my door the next morning."

"That wasn't me," he countered flatly. He finished his drink and placed it back on the bar then signaled for Ramon for his check.

"Oh! Well, that's embarrassing." She paused. "That was still a good night," she said, clearly not bothered by the mix-up.

Mallory flipped her ponytail from one side to the other. "Buy me a drink?" He chuckled. If it will make her go away, then fine. This isn't how he wanted to spend his lunch.

"Hey, Ramon. Add whatever she's drinking on there before you cash me out?"

Romon's eyes said what TJ was thinking. He walked over, leaned in the chest cooler, and plopped another can of seltzer on the bar in front of Mallory.

"Thank you," she said and pecked TJ on the cheek. Her hands were now on his upper thigh. This was the reason he had ended it with her. *Flirt. Loose.* He handed his card over to Ramon who was shaking his head.

Romane felt for TJ. *Bitches be crazy.*

TJ made it out of the bar unscathed. Mallory got her free drink and walked back to the other side of the bar and sat down next to another guy who was sitting alone.

"I wish I could have warned him," he said to Marlin as they walked out.

• • •

TJ and Marlin spent the rest of the afternoon mowing the lawn, weed whacking, and finishing laundry. Around 5 o'clock, he changed into his trunks and grabbed his surfboard. The wind was just right for some nice waves and he hadn't been in a few days. Marlin tags along of course; however, he knows because of the surfboard he'll need to stay on his blanket.

All of the families were headed off the beach for showers, Dough Roller Pizza, and Dumsers Ice Cream for dessert. A line of cars crawled over the Assateague bridge because some of the wild ponies that live here were blocking the road. A younger ranger stood cautiously nearby making sure that cars and cyclists stopped for photos and only that. It's illegal to feed them or even pet them.

They're wild and enchanting. Their history of how they came to be on the island is remarkable. But they're still wild animals and have a mind of their own. He's seen them go into people's open coolers on the beach and help themselves to a snack of apples and peanut butter and jelly. And he will never forget when one foal went into a woman's beach bag, grabbed her shoe, and walked away with it!

After paying for his parking, he and Marlin walked up to the beach. He made Marlin a little area on his blanket. Marlin sat and watched as TJ strolled toward the breaking waves. He spotted two kids out there. It looked like Josh and Nathan, Rob Hennesey's twins. They were always together.

His time out on the water was relaxing and therapeutic. The waves today were crisp and sharp. The barrels were on point and his board glided along the waves like a knife through butter. He checked on Marlin a few times and gave him a little pat on the ear. Laying paddling out, he began to wonder if Jules was around. *Would she be making her way down to the beach for her end-of-shift peek at the beach? If so, would she see me?* Marlin would probably run up to her again and get him another ticket. He didn't mind the first one because he would've never met Jules. But he didn't want to go broke on beach violations.

He sat in the lineup, really just the twins and him, each waiting patiently for their next ride. He saw his coming in. He turned and began to paddle ferociously. He felt the back of his board become in sync with the wave. His legs popped up. He swayed first right to keep riding down the line, then pushing with his left foot in front he sped up. The salty water splashed on his legs, and foam enveloped the sides of the board. His ride fizzled out a few yards down the beach as the strength of the wave dissipated. The leash pulled at his right ankle and he yanked it back leading his board back to him. Glancing up, he checked on Marlin. To his surprise, he saw a blonde sitting on the blanket with Marlin. His heart surged at first then took a spill as he began to walk over. *Seriously. This cannot be happening*. She stood up and brushed off her see-through cover-up.

"I knew I would find you here. You were always drawn to the

sunset waves." She covered him up with a striped beach towel. "Look, Mallory. I'm not sure what this is or what you're trying to do, but—"

"Shh." She set her finger on his chin. "When I saw you today at the bar, I couldn't believe how cute and adorable you looked with that old hat you wear. I started to miss you all over." She ran her hands along his newly-cut hairline.

He leaned away.

"There's nothing between us." He had passed the point of sparing feelings. "I tried to explain this last year. We both agreed."

"No, *you* came up with that silly idea. I still have feelings for you."

"I'm sorry. It's not going to happen. Please understand." TJ removed the towel and handed it back. He leaned down and petted Marlin. "Come on, guy. Let's get home." He gathered Marlin and his blanket. With one hand carrying his board, he flung the blanket over his shoulder with his other hand. He was trying not to let Mallory ruin his good mood. His date with Jules was tomorrow, and he was so stoked!

He looked back behind him. Mallory was sitting on the striped towel that she had just covered TJ with. She was on her phone. Taking selfies, of course.

Trying to stay unphased by whatever this was, he found his favorite spot in the park for the sunset. He pulled over and turned off the engine. From the backseat, Marlin rested his head on TJ's shoulder. The coral sky brushed with wisps of purple and blues never disappoints here. The hot orange ball of sun began to dip below the line that connected the bay with the fire-covered sky. Lower and lower it drifted off to sleep, yet still beaming the colors of flowers from Assateague Farm from below the horizon.

The streams of painted sky began to darken. TJ started the engine. He and Marlin enjoyed a cool breeze coming from the bay as they headed out of the park. A few silhouettes from the ponies were standing by the water's edge. Tomorrow was just around the corner and TJ couldn't wait.

ROB

It was the second day of fishing in the tournament and the Wallace family had a great time! Everyone had a turn at reeling in their own fish. They charged to shore with two marlins on board. One weighed in at 83 pounds and the other at 54 pounds. They were also lucky enough to board one large tuna and three mahi. They were one of the most decorated boats at the scales for the day. They started out on the leaderboard at number 3, just behind no other than TJ Moxley and Marlin. And taking the top of the board at number 1 was *No Limits* out of Ocean City.

We did good, but not good enough, he thought. Today was another day out on the open sea and he intended for it to be a worthwhile trip.

Everyone boarded *The Other Woman* at 5 o'clock and off they went.

"Everyone seems a lot less awake today than yesterday," Rob said to Bill.

"Yeah. The excitement of the first day has its charm." The two sat on top of the bridge and chatted as they left the marina. Everyone else was down in the cabin relaxing and having their morning coffee.

"We were all beat after yesterday's excitement. We went back to the condo, showered, and ordered pizza for dinner."

"Mione's pizza?"

"No. Grottos. Family tradition. We took the boys there growing up. And now we get to take our whole family- the boys and their wives. And then eventually our grandchildren. God willing."

"I look at your family and am in awe at how close you are. It makes me hope that Leanne, the boys, and I will someday be like that. You've got it all, my friend."

"Well, don't get me wrong—it wasn't always like this. Sharon did a lot of the work when they were younger. You know the parent-teacher conferences, sports practices, and all. I was always working so we could do all of this stuff. Trying to set a good example and instill a good work ethic into them. It wasn't easy. I missed a lot. A lot of home runs, a lot of opportunities to practice playing goalie in the backyard. I'm trying to make it up to them now and show them it was all for them."

"I'm sure they know." Rob remembered recently coming home one day and Nathan had scored the winning goal in his lacrosse game to take them into the playoffs his senior year. He had missed it because he was at the marina. With Summer. He will always have the worst guilt over that. And to make it even worse, they had won the states that year. He wasn't there for every step like he should have been. I bet Bill doesn't have guilt over an affair.

Snapping back to reality, Bill continued. "Even though it's fun when they're younger- it's even better when they're older. They have their own lives established. They have their own houses, jobs, and money. Even though Sharon loves when they come over to "grocery shop" our cabinets. They become your friends- best friends even. There's no one else I'd rather be around than my family."

The rest of the ride out to Poorman's Canyon was a quiet one. The water started around 100 fathoms but could reach well over 200. Kevin began the ritual of getting outriggers and down riggers in place. It was a dance he'd done so often, he could do it in his sleep. Eve, one of the wives, sat on the deck enjoying the view of the now navy blue waves, careful not to get in Kevin's way.

"This is the most peaceful place that I've ever been. There's no one around and it's like an aquatic paradise." Kevin listened as he worked.

"It's one of the reasons that I love being on the water. You can't get quiet like this at home."

"You're sure..."

Zzzzz! Zzzzz!

"Fish on! Fish on, boss! Get in that chair, girl! You're quiet just got much louder!" The line ran out so hard and fast that he almost lost the rod. Eve just happened to be in the right place at the right time. Everyone else was either still relaxing inside or in the head.

Kevin strapped her in the fighting chair and maneuvered the rod into the holder between her legs.

"I get the first one today!" she yelled, bragging to her husband, Adam. He was taking a picture of her in the chair on his phone.

"Let's see you reel her in then! Show me the trainer I pay for isn't a waste."

The fighting fish was still running with the line but you could tell was losing steam.

"Start cranking," Kevin yelled! "Go! Now!"

Eve began to reel quickly and steadily. She couldn't feel what was on the other side of the line but was eager to find out.

"Keep it up." Bill emerged from the head to see what they'd gotten on.

"Looks like a mighty marlin by the swim patterns! Reel girl! Reel!" Kevin was encouraging yet firm.

"My arms are getting a workout," she said, now huffing in between breaths. She considered herself healthy, but after just twenty minutes, her biceps and shoulders were screaming. *Just keep swimming. Just keep swimming.*

The rod line started sailing straight out of the back of the boat again.

"Let her go. She'll get tired," Kevin said loudly.

The whizzing of the large fish running off with the lure

was exhilarating! It felt like she was in the eye of a hurricane just waiting for all hell to break loose and have to reel again.

"Now go! Start reeling," ordered Kevin.

The line made a zig-zagging motion under the azul of the ocean.

"I see her! Bring her in closer!" It was a beautiful pattern that only a marlin knew. Rob maneuvered the boat this way and that, trying to keep up her pace.

Kevin leaned over trying to grab the liter. His gloves were the color of summer tangerines. His hat now backward showed off his three-day scruff of beard.

"Get the gaff! Get the gaff!" It was on the floor next to his feet and this old girl wasn't playing around. The line thrashed back and forth as someone handed the gaff over. And with one spear throw of the sharp tool, *The Other Woman* sprang to what he had hoped would be first place! That magnificent fish had to weigh over 100 pounds. It was exactly what they wanted!

"Way to go!" Rob yelled from the top of the bridge clapping his hands.

The rest of the day brought in two mahi and one small tuna weighing around 80 pounds. He was happy to be sending them home with a cooler full of fish. That was the goal, right? Lines came up around 3:30 p.m. and their happy journey back to Harbour Island began. Earlier that week, he had tried to coax Leanne down to the marina for a drink or two. He'll text her when they get a little closer to shore. He knew she had a large workload and he wanted to try to alleviate the stress a little. And a little one-on-one time would be nice. They needed it.

WHITNEY

It was later that evening and after a long day of fishing, the last thing that Whitney wanted was to drag Finn to a crowded restaurant. But since they were within walking distance to Fish Tales, he didn't mind. They parked the car and walked over through the entrance. The wait was about 35 minutes, not bad for an August dinner time.

Sitting at the bar waiting for their text that the table was ready, they chatted about the fishing excitement on the boat.

"How was 'the band' today?"

"We had a slow start, not going to lie." He sipped his beer. "But after two hours, things really picked up." *I mean, we just dunked our heads in ice-cold ocean water in hopes that the fish would start to feed*, Finn thought to himself. There was still time for boats to come in and weigh in. Movement on the leaderboard later in the evening was possible. They had to wait until 9:15 for the scales to close to see the final standings for day two.

"Well, I am excited to see the standings. I hope you rocket to the top."

"Cheers to staying on top," she said and winked at him.

When their table was ready, they followed the hostess through the maze of pink and green picnic tables and Blue Moon umbrellas. They shimmied their chairs down in the sand and got comfortable. Whitney didn't even have to look at the menu. Even though it wasn't the healthiest choice on the menu, she always orders the seafood baker. It was a large baked potato covered in crab meat, shrimp, scallops, cheese, and bacon. And it was worth every single calorie. Finn ordered the blacked mahi Reuben.

Fish Tales was a nice family restaurant. They had a large pirate ship playground where families could take their kids while they waited for their dinner to come out. On the side of the playground was a small arcade area where the older kids could go hang out. Often on the weekends, a friendly, local woman volunteered and painted faces, transforming kids into pirates, puppies, and unicorns. It was a popular amenity.

"I love that the sun doesn't set until later in the summer. We have more time to spend outside and enjoy this view." Whitney pointed to the setting sun over Assawoman Bay.

Finn reached over and gently held Whitney's hand. "I love that you love sunsets." He leaned over and kissed the top of her hand. He was so romantic.

A young surfer wearing an aqua blue Fish Tales t-shirt walked over and delivered their food.

"Hey, Josh! What's up, man! Good to see you working here." Finn had known Josh and Nathan from fishing with Rob. Every now and then the boys would join a charter that needed filling. They were cool kids.

"Hey! How did you guys do today? Get any big ones?"

"As a matter of fact, we did. I might even be beating your dad." Josh lifted his hand and fist-bumped Finn. The boys thought Finn was cool.

"Well, I gotta get back in there. Good to see you. Good luck!"

Whitney and Finn relaxed and ate their dinner by sunset. Sipping on ice-cold beer and then later splitting the key lime pie. They paid the check and headed home.

On their walk home, Whitney began to feel a little queasy.

"That dinner was so good, but I have a bit of a stomachache. I think I ate too fast."

"We did eat a lot."

"Yeah." She sighed. She had a long day. "All I know is I am looking forward to a hot shower, my jammies, and cuddling up on the couch with you."

Finn grabbed her hand and kissed it again. "Me, too."

Wednesday

Category: White Marlin
1st Place: The Other Woman
2nd Place: No Limits
3rd Place: Big Distraction

Category: Blue Marlin
1st Place: Weekend Vibes
2nd Place: TBD
3rd Place: TBD

Category: Tuna
1st Place: Weekend Vibes
2nd Place: Big Distraction
3rd Place: The Other Woman

LEANNE

Leanne woke up around 5 a.m. Wednesday morning. Rob was not fishing today, but his spot in bed was vacant.

That's strange. He never wakes up this early on an off day. Oh well.

Either way, she loved having the king-sized bed to herself in the morning to sprawl out. The crisp white summer linens felt good on her skin. She slept naked when Rob wasn't around; she knew it would lead to sex. And to be honest, ever since last summer, sex wasn't very appealing with Rob anymore.

She opened her text messages. 11 missed texts. None of which were from Rob. She scanned the list. All work. Clients and potential clients were all interested in getting their hands on their dream property in the Delmarva area. In the past few years, the real estate market at the beach has been booming. As soon as a place is listed, no more than 48 hours go by without an offer, followed by a sale, usually well over the asking price.

However, there had been a time when Leanne had trouble even getting a listing. There were several weeks, even months at a time where she sold nothing. Her job solely revolved around people buying and spending. If it wasn't a buyers' market, then she was slow. But something had happened in the past few years in the Delmarva region. People were flocking to the Eastern Shore of Ocean City: Dewey, Bethany, and Rehoboth. At first, she still had to fight hard to get a listing. She wasn't a big name in the real estate game back then. She mingled at parties and gave out her cards any time an opportunity was given. She spent many late nights at the office researching and making phone calls. More often than not, Rob would be home cooking dinner and getting the boys to practice. But she never missed a game. Up until about a year or two ago, she and Rob were the involved parents type when it came to the boys. Every game, every school event, they were there for them. On the outside, they were model working parents. On the inside, their relationship had begun to implode.

Last *Summer*. She even began to hate the sound of the season. Rob had been fishing the White Marlin Open like he does every year. He stays on the boat before a fishing day. Again, nothing out of the ordinary. Leanne had been working nonstop back then. To her, a 12-hour day was a gift. On this specific summer evening, a client had canceled a viewing of a house and decided to buy, site-unseen.

She had begun the paperwork to get ahead for the following day. It was around 8 p.m. when she headed out of the office for the evening. She had gotten a text that morning from Rob saying he was going out for the day, but still hadn't heard anything about him coming back in from his trip. She knew rods were in at 3:30 and that he usually arrives back around six or seven. She had felt a twinge of guilt working so much recently. Rob was the type of husband who loved to be loved. He loved when she did out-of-the-blue things that were spontaneous. She decided to go home and check on the boys to see what their plans were for the evening. Even though it was already 8, she knew their nights usually began around this hour; sometimes even later as the summer progressed.

After a slow 45-minute crawl down Coastal Highway, she finally arrived home. Both Nathan and Josh's trucks were home.

She opened the door and saw a half of a Mione's pizza and an empty take-out box full of chicken wing bones. *Sigh. Boys.*

"Hey boys!" she greeted as she hung her bag on the hallway hooks.

"Hey Mom," they replied in unison. It was true that twins had some type of special connection. Nathan and Josh often answered simultaneously or shared looks like they could read each other's minds. I guess being identical did that to you.

They were both vegging out on the couch, which was odd for an August night.

"I'm surprised to see you both home. Are you doing anything tonight?"

"Nah. We decided to stay home tonight. We went surfing earlier, but there's so much traffic, we just ordered food and brought it home." Nathan was her low-key mellow child.

"I have to work tomorrow night, too. So I just wanted to lay around." This is strange for Josh. He was her get up and go, always-in-the-mood-for-fun one.

Both boys had gotten seasonal jobs that fit their personalities to a T. Nathan got a job bussing tables at Ropewalk. It's family-oriented, more on the calm side. They have firepits and an outdoor playground for their families...whereas Josh applied to Fish Tales as a barback. It's more of a bar-marina-type atmosphere. Both boys loved their jobs. It was nice to see them thriving in the real world.

"It's nice to see you guys relaxing for a change."

Leanne walked upstairs to change into a summer dress. Even though she was tired, she decided to drive to Sunset Marina and surprise Rob. She checked her hair and makeup, added a little more eyeliner and mascara, and last minute, grabbed her sexy black lace lingerie. She could slip it into her bag and change on the boat, she thought. She walked out of their bedroom, which was adjacent to the living room, trying to hide her unmentionables.

"Okay, guys. I will see you in the morning. I'm going to the boat to see your Dad."

"Okay, Mom," Josh said, neither one taking their eyes from the television.

"I love you!" she called on the way out as she successfully concealed the lace in her bag.

"Love you," they said in unison.

Leanne closed the door behind her and began the drive toward Sunset Marina.

By the time Leanne pulled into the spot, it was just before 10 p.m. Many fishermen still hung out and drank on the docks. The bar was flooded, which was normal for a summer evening during tournament week. She knew which slip Rob's boat was tied in. She wiggled through a few groups of guys sporting Guy Harvey, Sperry's, and sunglass tan lines. Some looked so burnt, they resembled raccoons. But they didn't care. They'd all been drinking since 8 a.m.

The Other Woman, Rob's boat, was further away from the bar. The crooning of *Jesse's Girl* by Rick Springfield was fading as she walked. Fishing rods loomed over the dock like battle swords ready to slay. It was quite a sight. From afar, she could see that the boat's lights were off as she approached.

Good, she thought. *I can slip in and freshen up before I text him to come see what he's missing on board.* She slipped off her Michael Kor's sandals and picked them up with her fingers. She carefully stepped onto the boat, which she always thought was grand in size. She went to the door and slowly slid it open. She also didn't want to make a lot of noise in case Rob was already asleep.

A stream of light dimly lit the living area. She had no idea that just beyond that stream of light would be something that would rattle her world entirely.

Leanne couldn't believe what she saw—the back of a naked woman, kneeling in front of her husband. She flipped the light on mid-moan. Rob, her husband of over 20 years, was sitting on the couch, wearing only a light blue T-shirt with sunglasses perched on top of his head, bare ass on the faux leather. Shorts nowhere to be seen. And her. This woman couldn't have been more than 5'2", now calmly collecting her khaki skirt and t-shirt that showed STAFF written across the back.

"Shit—Leanne! I can explain," he said, covering himself up as he frantically searched for his shorts with no success.

Leanne stood there as the STAFF had already slipped out of the door and off the boat. Rob had disappeared to find a pair of bottoms and reappeared as she was turning to leave. He grabbed her arms. She remembered how rough his hands had felt on her skin.

"No, no, Leanne. Wait."

She turned around as tears were pouring down her face.

"Let me explain, please."

"Fuck you!" she screamed. She was so loud that she was sure that people could hear. But at this point, she didn't care. She could feel her adrenaline beginning to skyrocket. The room was beginning to spiral.

"Look, Leanne. I'm so sorry. This was a mistake. It was not something that was planned. We just kind of got to talking and one thing led to another..."

"Who is she?" Leanne could feel her heart racing, and now her heart pumping with rage.

"Who the hell is she!" Rob was looking at the floor. He sighed.

"Her name is Summer. She works at the bar. I've only seen her a few times."

"What?" Her body was actually on the verge of collapsing. Her chest felt tight and her heart actually felt shattered like crystal.

"No, no! Not *see* her, see her. Like in passing. She's a bartender. That's all."

"Oh, okay," Leanne said, her voice shaking with anger, still clinging to her hurt heart. "Because she's a bartender, I can forget the whole thing. Forget that your dick was in her mouth and God knows where else. Did you have sex with her, too?"

"God, Leanne. Does that really matter?"

"Did you...have sex with her?"

Rob fell back limp on the couch. He put his head between his hands, elbows on his knees. That's all Leanne needed to see. She walked off the boat, collected her sandals and the shattered pieces of her heart, and walked slowly toward her car.

At that very moment, she honestly didn't know where to go. She opened the door to her car and sat inside. The top was down and the warm weather of summer blew a nice breeze through her hair. She sat not knowing what to do. She couldn't go home. The boys were there and she couldn't face them right now. She felt anger and rage and heart-shattering chest pains. Just how she could be feeling all of this at one time?

She needed a drink. She put the keys in the ignition and started the engine. She drove back into Ocean City and veered right after the bridge, heading toward the inlet. She didn't want to be around people and knew of a small bar that sat overlooking the inlet. She made the small turns that led into the inlet and put her car in park near a small marina. As she took a deep breath of ocean air, a large restaurant loomed in front of her. *Harrison's* stood at the south end of the boardwalk. It was a special place for her and Rob. It's where she told Rob that she was pregnant with the boys nearly eighteen years ago. She wanted to cry but also take a baseball bat to their front door. She passed and walked through the teeny shopping village lined with chachki shops where the Frog Bar was hidden. At this hour, the bar was pretty dead—just how she wanted it. As she sat down at the bar, Leanne was hoping that her face was less swollen than it felt. The bartender, an older woman who looked as though she never used sunscreen in her life, greeted her.

"Hey honey," she said. "What can I get you tonight?" She looked rough on the outside like she has broken up a bar fight or two in her lifetime, towel slung over her shoulder.

Leanne's go-to was a gin martini with extra olives. But not tonight. She needed something to take the pain out of her chest and the image of Rob with the bartender out of her head.

"Tequila. Double. Chilled. Please," she stated with a blank stare, more firm than she intended.

"You betcha. Can I get you a menu? We're only serving fried stuff now since it's getting late and we're cleaning the kitchen up."

She felt sick to her stomach and knew she hadn't eaten anything since lunch. And why not eat her sorrows along with drinking them.

"Cheeseburger and fries. Medium?"

"I'm on it, darling."

"Thanks."

She watched the woman glug the Jose Cuervo into the silver cup, generously splashing in a scoop full of ice. The bartender strained the golden liquid into a short glass, chucked the ice into the sink, and slid the glass in Leanne's direction. She picked it up and took a big sip of the icy liquor. It burned as she swallowed. She wasn't a tequila drinker normally. It wasn't that she didn't like the taste, but she felt that it was better off mixed inside of a margarita. But not tonight. She would drink whatever it was to numb the crushing of her chest.

Leanne wasn't the only patron in the bar. At the far end, nearest to the modern-day jukebox was a guy maybe in his thirties. He was wearing a baseball hat with a torn-up bill. In front of him was an empty Landshark bottle. He was staring at the television where the Orioles were playing. The bartender set another bottle in front of him. He looked over and 'cheered' Leanne from his stool. She raised her tequila back at him and took another sip. It didn't taste as bad as it did at first. Her head felt a little lighter and her broken heart seemed to ache a bit less than it had ten minutes before. She took one more sip, this one bigger than the last. She could feel the liquid warming her insides, almost like it was trying to glue the pieces of her heart back together. Unsuccessful.

What in the world am I supposed to do? she thought. She looked out of the window that was wide open in front of her. She could see the tide moving in with the motion of the waves. She could feel her limbs loosening up as she adjusted herself on the stool.

The bartender was mixing up some type of shot behind the bar. She poured the cloudy mixture into four small plastic shot glasses. She placed one in front of the guy with the torn bill then walked down and set one in front of Leanne. Just then, what appeared to be the cook came out and placed a hot grilled cheeseburger and fries in front of Leanne.

"Oh, thank you."

The third and fourth shots were for the cook and the bartender. The cook looked at Leanne and the guy at the bar.

"Salut! Kitchen's closed."

The four of them silently raised their cups and shot their drinks back, which Leanne now knew was a red-headed slut. *Try a blonde-headed whore*, she thought as she slung it back. Looking down at the melting cheese on her burger, Leanne picked it up and took a bite. She was really beginning to feel the tequila and knew this would help. The grease ran down her fingers and onto the checkered paper inside the red basket. As she wiped her hands on a napkin, she called down the bar.

"Rough day? Or do you always drink alone?" Clearly, the tequila was helping her relax.

He looked at Leanne.

"Little bit of the first I guess you could say. I'm not a big drinker, to be honest. But it just kind of felt like the right thing to do."

"Girl trouble?"

"More like happy that it's over. Like a feeling of relief. I broke it off with a girl I'd been seeing."

"Was it serious?" Leanne looked at him and put her hand

out in front of her, almost apologetically. She immediately drew back, catching herself being nosey. "Oh my gosh. I am so sorry to be rude. I shouldn't be asking all of these questions. I'm sorry. You don't need to answer." She turned back toward the bar and took another sip of her tequila.

He smiled and shook his head. A little dimple came out on his cheek. "No, no. It's fine. It wasn't serious. We had only been dating a few months, off and on. But I still feel a bit bad. Even though we both knew it wasn't going anywhere, you know? She and I were pretty opposite. She liked going out all night and I'm more low-key. And she wore way too much makeup in my opinion."

"Well, at least you did it. You could have stayed and then made it even harder later on. It'll get better."

"And what about you? Troubles in paradise?"

Taking a huge mouthful of burger, she held a finger up as she chewed. *God this is good.* She nodded her head and wiped her mouth with a wad of paper-thin brown napkins.

"Well. While I have been busy trying to set up a successful business and do something great for myself, my husband has been sleeping with a bartender at his job. A bartender." She quickly looked over at the woman behind the bar. Luckily, she was far enough down the bar that she didn't hear her. She downed the rest of her Jose.

"And just before I came here, I went to surprise him at work and caught them on his boat. She was *ducking his sick.*" She closed one eye. "No, that's not right. But you get the idea." She waved her finger in the air. Leanne probably looked as sloppy as she felt. But at this point, did it matter? Who the hell cared?

"Oh, man. Can we get two more shots?" the guy called to the bartender. "Want another drink? My treat."

"Tequila. Chilled. Thanks," Leanne said, nodding her head.

The guy walked down toward her end of the bar. "Mind if I sit?"

"Please, go right ahead."

Two more shots appeared in front of them along with another tequila.

"What should we toast to?" he asked Leanne.

"Hmm. That's a good question. To…" Leanne was feeling pretty tipsy by now. She couldn't really think of what they could cheers to, seeing as they were both mending love wounds.

"Let's just say, 'things can only get better.'"

"Agreed." They clinked tiny cups and effortlessly threw them back.

The bartender took their glasses and tossed them away. "Hey guys, we're about to start closing up. We close at midnight."

Leanne looked for her phone to see the time. But she forgot she left it in her car. She had no reason to have it—and if Rob called her, she wouldn't have answered it anyway.

"11:45. I haven't been out this late in a long time," the guy with the dimple and torn bill said, reaching for his wallet. He threw three twenties on the bar. "Everything's on me. I hope things work out for you. No one deserves what you went through today. Good luck with everything."

Leanne smiled at him. "Thank you. And thank you for getting my mind off of things for a while. I needed it."

"You okay to get home?"

"Yes, I'll be okay. I don't live far from here."

"Okay good. Good night, ladies," he said to Leanne and the bartender.

"Good night," Leanne said. "Hey! What's your name?"

"I'm TJ," he said, sticking his hand out to shake hers.

"Goodnight, TJ."

ROB

The night before, Rob had invited Leanne to the marina for drinks while he prepped the boat for another day of fishing. At first, he was a little leery seeing that their rocky past stemmed from that very bar not even a year ago. However, they had had a few great evenings together recently. He felt comfortable enough in his and Leanne's relationship; it was strong enough to handle it.

Only one year ago, Leanne and Rob were very close to being divorced. The only thing that had really kept them together at the time was the boys. They didn't want to embarrass them any more than they already had.

It all started at the marina where Rob kept his boat, *The Other Woman*. Rob spent quite a few evenings a week at the marina. Whether he was shooting the breeze with other captains or talking fishing, Rob was at the marina. And when Rob was at the marina, that meant Rob spent the same amount of time at the bar. Where Summer worked. It wasn't something that Rob had planned. And he definitely wouldn't blame Leanne for the lack of attention he was getting at home; even though he knew it was in the back of his mind.

Rob had been going to the bar for years at Sunset Marina. He kept his boat there, fished there, and often slept on his boat there. He knew just about everyone. Summer was a bartender and he'd known her for some time now. Never once did the idea of having sex with her cross his mind. Until early last summer.

It was the beginning of the spring fishing season and he was pretty much the only one sitting at the bar. Summer was closing that evening. He ordered food and a few beers like he normally would. This particular night was nothing out of the ordinary. But something definitely changed when she brought over two shots of whiskey.

"No one likes to drink alone. Let me join you." They downed some strong drinks—first whiskey, and then bourbon. She was technically still on the clock and wasn't done stocking the bar. Rob watched as she leaned over the beer coolers. Her shorts barely covered her bottom half when she did. Then back to whiskey. Her breasts were pushed up, showing off cleavage to the point that Rob was becoming more interested as the liquor kept flowing.

"Would you be able to help me reach the top shelf over here? No one thinks about me when they put things away. They forget that I'm only 5'3"." She pointed to the top cabinet where extra liquor bottles were kept.

Rob chuckled. "Yep, no problem. It's gotta be hard to be you, huh?" he teased her.

"Funny," she replied, gently slapping his arm as he walked behind the bar, which was normally her territory.

He reached for the tequila bottles for her and handed them down one at a time. There was a slight spring breeze in the air. He could see her nipples through her shirt, and her breasts were even more pushed up now as she clutched the bottles.

"Let me help you so you don't drop them."

His hand grabbed two of the bottles and he brushed up against her chest on purpose to see her reaction.

"*Tsk tsk* now."

Rob just smiled and set the bottles on the bar. He leaned up against the coolers.

"Since you're back here, think you could help me get this case of beer out of the cooler? It's stuck all the way in the back." She slid the top of the cooler open and leaned in. Her ass looked better from this side of the bar. She looked back over her shoulder and coaxed him over. Rob looked around the bar making sure that no one else was around. He slowly walked over to her. Her back was still toward him. She pressed herself up against him, which was already on the verge of arousal. He grabbed her hips and ass, pushing himself against her. Wiggling her butt side to side, Summer teased him even more. She made a little giggling noise. He turned her around so he could grab her breasts and tease her right back. He knew what he was going to do was wrong, but he felt so neglected at home at this point, he didn't care.

The lights of the bar were dimmed by this time of night and there were no people on the docks. Summer began to unbutton his shorts and he began to do the same to her. She slid her shorts off—not that there was much there to begin with. Rob grabbed her by the ass and propped her up on the beer coolers. She played with him just before leading him into her. He enjoyed the feeling and thrusted her onto him as she wrapped her legs around his waist. Rob picked her up off the cooler and massaged her tightly as she moaned with pleasure. She leaned back, exposing even more cleavage that Rob was admiring just minutes before. He held onto her tightly as she pulled her shirt open, leading Rob's mouth in. He played with her breasts using his tongue and mouth while she tightly held onto his waist with her legs. Rob hadn't felt sex like this since before he was married...

Even though Rob knew it was wrong, this wasn't the only time that this had happened. He couldn't count on both of his hands the number of times that Summer had joined him on his boat after her closing shifts. It was never planned per se, but he did find himself sleeping on the boat a little more often than normal. Leanne was working so much anyway, she never questioned it.

The night that Leanne came to the boat and found them was out of the norm. Rob was staying on the boat because he was fishing in the WMO the next morning. He had ordered food from the bar and was having it delivered to the boat. He liked to be in early the night before fishing because he needed his rest and had to be up early the next morning. After getting back to the boat, he was relaxing and watched TV before his food would be arriving. During a commercial break of *Wicked Tuna*, he heard a knock on the door. It was his dinner all right, and his dessert. Summer came in with a take-out bag and closed the door behind her. The food was quickly forgotten once she pushed him down on the couch and unbuttoned his pants. Everything after that happened like a whirlwind. He hadn't heard Leanne come in. They had been caught. Summer took off and Rob was left to face his wife of twenty-some years alone. He had felt ashamed and embarrassed at his actions. He had broken his vows and let down his family. He would make everything right with Leanne, who he had vowed to love, even if he had to try every day for the rest of his life.

Rob had woken up super early today on purpose. He wanted to run out and get Leanne's coffee for her before she left the house. And he knew she was an early riser.

He heard her footsteps coming down the hall from the bedroom.

"Good morning, honey," Rob had greeted her.

"Morning. Why are you up so early? It's not like you."

"I wanted to run out and get your coffee for you. I know just how you like it. You've been working so hard and I wanted to let you know how proud of you I am."

"That's so sweet." She leaned, pecked him on the lips, and grabbed her piping hot cup. That first sip feeling was like a drug coursing through her veins. It was ecstasy.

"And while I was there, I figured I would grab some donuts for the boys. They both worked until after midnight last night. I heard Josh get in around 1 and Nathan came home around 12:30."

"How many donuts did you eat already?" she asked, smiling. Rob opened the box to survey the damage. "Three."

Katherine Ruskey

JULES

Today was one of Jules' off days, and she had a date! She could hardly sleep last night because she was looking forward to seeing what TJ had come up with.

She poured her morning coffee and sat outside on the deck facing the bay. Her phone vibrated.

> *Good morning! Sunshine emoji*
>
> *Hey there! Waving emoji*
>
> *Is it okay to pick you up around 10:30? You'll need to wear your bathing suit and bring whatever you might need for a day outside.*
>
> *Sounds great. See you then.*

Jules couldn't stop smiling. She thought about the gorgeous day that was about to unfold. *I wonder what we're doing today, she thought.* Just as she was about to go in for a refill, Kit appeared from the kitchen with two cups of hot coffee.

"Hey. I thought you'd be gone by this morning. Still doing your laundry?" she teased.

"Actually, no. I'm staying in town. There's a huge party tonight over on Teal Drive. Laney and I are going over."

"Who's house is it?" Jules tried not to sound like their mother.

"This kid Theo. You don't know him. I mean, I don't really know him, but Laney knows him, and that's how we knew about the party. They have this like huge house on the water with a waterfall in the back that goes into their huge pool. It looks like one of those houses you see on a reality show. Seriously." Kit was scrolling her Instagram and DMing her friends already this early. Her oversized Rolling Stones T-shirt and a messy bun made her feel old. *When did she become a grownup?*

"Well, you know not to drink and drive. I will come and get you wherever you are. No questions asked. And I will never tell Mom either."

"I know. But I'll be fine. I think Laney is going to drive us anyway. I mean it's like right down the road anyway." Sipping her coffee, her eyes never left her phone screen.

"I don't care how far it is. No drinking and driving. And that goes for Laney, too."

"I know, *Mom*."

"What do you have planned for the day?"

"Not sure yet. We'll probably just hang out at the beach or something. Maybe drive to Assateague and hang out there."

"That sounds fun. You didn't ask what I was doing today." Jules smiled at Kit.

"Huh? Oh yeah. What are you doing today?"

"Today is my date with TJ!"

This caught Kit's attention. "Wait, the dog ticket guy? He's taking you out again? *That's* why you've had that big grin on your face."

"Yep. He's picking me up at 10:30."

"Wait, what are you guys doing?"

"I'm not sure. All I said was that we had to be doing something outside. You know I can't stand to be inside on a sunny day."

"Well, you will tell me every detail when you come back, right? I'll be here later tonight before the party."

"Of course."

Kit stood up, grabbed the empty coffee cups, and disappeared. Jules looked at the time on her phone. 9:15. She had to start packing her bag: *sunscreen, sunglasses, two towels, a cooler of water, snacks, etc.*

Katherine Ruskey

start putting her bags into her new suitcases, she thinks, a polka dotted mask.

TJ AND MARLIN

TJ and Marlin woke up and had their morning routine. Coffee, Kibble, outside time. TJ was thrilled to be taking Jules out today. He had an entire day date lined up. Even Marlin had a bigger pep in his step than usual. He seemed just as excited.

Throwing on his favorite board shorts, Billabong T-shirt, and torn hat, he began to load everything into the back of the jeep. *Umbrella, two beach chairs, empty cooler, rakes, and mesh bag. Paddleboards and paddles strapped to the rack on top. And don't forget Marlin's tennis ball.*

The dynamic duo jumped into the Jeep to make one quick stop before they headed into Ocean City. They needed to stock the cooler full of lunch. Cold cuts and turkey subs, shrimp salad, coleslaw, BBQ chips, iced tea, sodas, and water. Once the cooler was filled to the max, they headed into town to start their much-anticipated day date.

Because it was a Wednesday morning, the traffic to get in wasn't bad at all. Traveling over the bridge, TJ could see the tide making its way out. *Perfect.* There was a smattering of boaters out in the bay, but not like a weekend. A few anglers were out trying their luck along the channel.

TJ drove along the bayside down Edgewater Avenue when the GPS notified him that he had arrived. The time on the clock read 10:25. *If you're not five minutes early, you're already late.*

He knocked on the front door and patiently waited... There was no answer. He knocked again. His heart was beginning to panic. *Did she change her mind? If she did, that was awful quick, and...* Just then, the door swung open.

"Hey! Sorry! I can't hear the door when I'm outside on the deck. Come on in." She turned and led the two of them and Marlin through the house.

"I was beginning to think you changed your mind when you didn't answer." He started to nervously laugh and slid his hands into his pockets.

"Of course not. I've been so curious about what we're doing today. I love surprises!" She walked through the open door that led onto the wide deck.

"Wow. What a great view you have here. You get to see every sunset Ocean City has," he said, leaning his elbows on the railing ledge.

"Yes. It's incredible. I have dinner out here most nights because of the view."

"I don't blame you. I would, too."

They both stood for a few minutes admiring the crystal clear blue sky reflecting on the bayside.

Taking a deep breath, TJ asked, "Well, are you ready to start this adventure? I have to confess that I can't get everything set up alone. I am going to have to recruit your help... I mean, if you don't mind."

Jules' eyes squinted. "Oh-kay." She giggled a little at the anticipation of the surprise.

"Let's get heading out. We're kind of on a time crunch per se—but not really."

"Now I am *extremely* curious about what we're doing."

TJ grabbed Jules' hand. "That's the point. Come on."

Of course opening the door for Jules, he then climbed in and drove them five minutes down the road. He parked the jeep at a friend's place which had access to a pier.

He got out of the Jeep and helped Jules out of the front seat. Marlin followed closely behind.

"We're going on a picnic."

"A picnic?" Jules looked around. Now she had questions.

"Yep. Out there." TJ pointed to the middle of Assawoman Bay.

"In the middle of the water?"

"Eh. Kind of. That's what I meant by we're kind of on a time crunch. Low tide is in about an hour and a half. By the time we get out there and I set everything up, the water will only be at our ankles and we can set the chairs up and have our date." TJ was mentally crossing his fingers and holding his breath at the same time hoping she would like this idea.

"What a fun picnic! I can't wait! And we're getting there by paddleboard?"

"Yep." He had already begun to unload the Jeep with all the things they needed.

Each of them carried a beach chair on their backs like a backpack. TJ's paddleboard was loaded up, the cooler on the front, and he had to straddle the umbrella, which lay in the middle. Jules took Marlin on the front of her board as Marlin had already made his choice—he picked Jules. Jules' beach bag was strapped to the back, and they took off.

"Have you been paddling before?"

"Tons of times! I'll race you." And she and Marlin took the lead.

The two launched their boards from the pier and carefully crossed the small channel, which was luckily not terribly crowded. TJ watched as Jules and Marlin glided across the water toward the sandbar, which was playing peek-a-boo with the bay. She was wearing cut-off jeans shorts with a solid pink bikini top which was covered by a white T-shirt that came off the shoulder.

"I was really surprised that you answered your text so early the other morning. It was super early but I just couldn't wait to talk to you," TJ confessed.

"I'm not usually one to sleep in. I have to be at the park early anyway. But sometimes when I am up that early, I just like to sit and read. I was up reading. And I was glad to see your text." She smiled coyly at him as she paddled.

"I was glad that I had off today to take you out here."

By now, the water was around shin-deep.

"Just a few more yards and we can set everything up." He looked down at the water trying to gauge the depth.

"Look, there's a horseshoe crab," Jules said pointing under the water. It was gliding under her board minding its own business.

"I have always been a little leery of them. They just look so odd, I guess. I mean, I know they're harmless."

"They are gorgeous. I walk down the beach sometimes picking them up and putting the ones that get stranded back in the water. Families are always so curious. When I get the opportunity to, I love giving a little talk on them to show kids how impressive they are. They don't sting or bite and they only use their tails to flip themselves over if they flip over on their shell."

"When you put it like that, I feel kind of silly." He laughed at himself. "How does this spot look? The waters around our ankles but—" he looked at his watch, "—it'll be even shallower soon."

"Looks like a great spot to me." They dismounted their paddleboards, Marlin included. TJ found his tennis ball first and threw it. "He will do this for hours if I let him."

Jules laughed at Marlin, who was now rolling all over on his back in the shallow waters of the sandbar like a pig in mud. TJ set the chairs up. He secured the paddleboards to the umbrella which was thrusted down in the sand so it wouldn't blow away. The cooler stayed sitting on top of the paddleboard.

Like DeJa'Vu, Marlin ran full speed toward Jules, soaking wet. Except for this time, he didn't stop, and plowed right into her, knocking her off her feet and into the water. She landed with a small splash and landed in water that barely got her shorts wet.

"Oh god! I am so sorry!" TJ ran over to help her up. She was laughing so hard that he couldn't grab a hold of her. Jules yanked his wrist hard and pulled him down into the water with her. He lost his balance and landed on his back next to Jules. Marlin continued to jump and splash like a kid in the bathtub in between the two humans. His heavy tail flung into their faces and they both tried to block the flinging water.

Jules picked herself up and lent a hand to TJ. "We just need to be more like Marlin! Let's go!" And with that, Jules took off running down the lengthy sandbar which was beginning to emerge from the water. Marlin chased after she and TJ chased after them both. She found the tennis ball and threw it far enough to where Marlin had to swim in about two feet of water. But he definitely didn't mind. Heaving his hands into the water, TJ made a sneak attack and dowsed Jules from the back.

"Ahhh! Oh, you are in trouble!" She turned around and flung a wave of water in TJ's direction. Marlin came prancing over the waves in between the two of them and dropped the ball. This time, TJ grabbed it and launched the ball in the other direction. TJ and Jules raced back and forth with Marlin for another fifteen minutes. By now, the sandbar was completely out of the water and they were walking on the wet sand.

"Do you like clamming?" TJ asked as they walked.

"I love it! My dad used to bring Kit and me out here all the time when we were little."

"I brought some rakes in the cooler. Want to catch some dinner?"

"Dinner, huh? You're getting a little confident about this date, don't you think?" Her smile was genuine and sweet. He walked over toward where Jules was standing. She smiled at him. He put his hands on the back of her waist and leaned in and kissed her. Time seemed to stand still. Their lips parted and the only thing he could do was stand there and look at her.

TJ broke the beautiful silence. "I like you. I like you a lot. I was so excited to see you today that I couldn't sleep last night. You're all I've been thinking about."

Tendrils of her wavy beach hair lightly blew in her face. He gently brushed them away.

"I wasn't able to sleep last night either. And yesterday felt like the longest day of my life waiting for today." They kissed again—this time, a little longer. Marlin trotted along the sandbar and pushed his way in, entangling himself in between their legs. He sat between them, dropped his ball, and waited patiently.

Hand in hand, they both began to walk back toward where they set up their picnic.

"Um. Where are the paddleboards?" Jules looked around left and right.

"I tied them to the umbrella."

"Oh my God! They're in the channel!" She let go of TJ's hand and they both began running. The water was getting deeper; first shin, and now knee-deep. They got to the edge of the channel where the sandbar would dip off and the water would be over seven feet deep. They both dove in and swam to grab the boards. With one arm, they each slowly doggie-paddled back to the sandbar. Jules pushed her board, finally sitting on top to catch her breath.

She busted out laughing. "If this is our official first date, what are you going to make me do on our second?" She laid back on the board and tried to catch her breath.

TJ took the rope of Jules' board along with his own and pulled her as she lay there.

"I guess you'll just have to wait and see." He looked back and winked at her. He tied the boards up, this time to the chairs. "I'm hungry. Let's eat."

"Yeah. I might need more energy for the rest of this date. Who knows what you two have up your sleeves." She plopped down in the beach chair under the umbrella.

TJ opened the cooler.

"We have cold cuts, turkey sub, shrimp salad, coleslaw, BBQ chips, iced tea, soda, water..."

"Wow, you thought of everything. I'd like the turkey sub, please. And an iced tea."

"Coming right up."

LEANNE

Leanne dressed and went to work. She had a feeling of major guilt-gut. Rob had been trying so hard recently to earn her trust back. He'd been extremely attentive around the house and trying to give her enough space to figure out how to make sense of their relationship.

Her phone pinged. Again. Again. And again. Danger.

I'd like to see a house this evening if possible.
I think I'm finding exactly what I'd like in this area.
Please let me know your availability.

She picked up her phone to respond. Then she thought twice. She needed to back up a little from this situation and think clearly. Placing the phone on the seat beside her, Leanne picked up her coffee. Guilt-gut.

She grabbed her phone. *I'll see what I can do.*

FINN

He had planned on driving back to Baltimore today to check in on the crew, but he wanted to spend the day with Whitney. After dinner, they'd gone back home and enjoyed some much-deserved relaxing time with one another.

When he woke up around 7, Whitney was already gone. She had to get her runs in. When it was this hot out, she woke up even earlier to beat the heat.

From the bedroom, he could hear the front door latch click closed.

Walking sleepily from the bedroom out to the living room, his hair in a tangled mess, he walked up behind Whit. Her headphones were still in her ears. From experience, he knew she couldn't hear a dang thing. She kept them up so loud.

He snuck up behind her while she was making her morning coffee and wrapped his arms around her. She jumped and laughed.

Pulling her earbuds out, she said, "You did it again. Good morning." He kissed her forehead and hugged her.

"Morning, love of my life. How was your run?"

"It was great! No one was out, and there was a beautiful breeze."

"Good. I'm glad you're happy." Still groggy, he reached for a coffee mug. "Are you interested in a lazy boat day/nap day today? We have nowhere to be and nothing to do. It's like our perfect kind of day."

"You read my mind."

WHITNEY

Her alarm went off at 5 a.m. It was nothing out of the ordinary in the middle of summer when temperatures reached 90 degrees before 11 a.m. She quietly changed in the bathroom trying not to disturb her sleeping fiancé. Not one to dote on her body, especially since her diagnosis, she caught a sideways glimpse of her breasts. She was more attuned with her body lately and was always looking for something wrong. However, today, the sideways glance she caught was pleasing—sexy even. Her breasts seemed to be extra perky and full today in her sports bra. Usually, she would be telling herself that her body was broken or bad. But today was different. Today, she thought, *Damn, get it, girl*! She was excited to show her boobs off in her bikini later. *I wonder if Finn will notice?*

TJ AND MARLIN

After their lunch picnic was cleaned up, Jules and TJ lay relaxing in the shade of their umbrella on the sandbar. Marlin preferred the sun and still walked around on the sand, digging holes and looking for crabs.

"So tell me about fishing the tournament. How are things going? Are you going to win it all this year?" She leaned her head to the side and looked over at him.

"Actually, it's going great this year. We're in second place now in the tuna category and third in the white marlin

But that could change today. Hopefully, it won't, but you really never know with fishing. It's a gamble every time you go out."

"Did you fish it last year?"

"Oh yeah. Last year was probably the worst year I could've had in the tournament." He shook his head thinking back on the chaos that had unfolded.

"That sounds like an interesting story. Tell me about it. Did you have a monster fish on and when you finally got it close to the boat, it ended up being an old boot or something?" She laughed a little.

He quickly blushed and his dimple showed. "Cute. Yeah, nothing like that though. That would've been the best-case scenario. Last year, I was in second place going into the last day of the tournament. I was in the lead with a huge marlin on board that would put me on the top. I was on cloud nine! I couldn't wait to get in and weigh her and take us to the top for that year."

"That doesn't sound like the worst fishing trip ever."

"Oh, it gets better. We get back and weigh her and she's 125 pounds!" TJ swung his arms out to show just how massive this fish was. "That's huge in this area for a white marlin. I think the state record is like 135 pounds. It took us way out in the lead. We were unstoppable."

"Again, sounds like a great day on the water."

"Well, rules state that when you win over a certain amount of money—because we're not talking about a few hundred bucks now—we're talking well over a million dollars. Anyway, when the money gets high like that, we're required to take a polygraph test. You know, to make sure we're not lying. Some people I guess have dropped lines in before the start time or didn't take their lines out at 3:30. But whatever, I knew I won fair and square so I had no problem taking one. So when I took the polygraph, they ask you all the questions...and the polygraph came back that I had lied about how I caught that big fish. All of that big money that I had thought that I had pocketed was ripped from my hands before I even got to touch it."

Jules was looking curiously now at TJ, genuinely intrigued. "Did you lie?"

"No! That's why it was such a crazy situation." His hands shot up like he was being held at gunpoint. "I was being perfectly honest and I threw a fit. I would never lie about anything like that. I mean, I would never lie about anything, period. But anyway. It would be the dumbest thing that any captain could do. So, they stripped me of all my honestly-earned first-place winnings. And so it was supposed to go to the second-place winner, who ended up in 'first'."

"So what happened?"

"I had to appeal that polygraph and then wait for another test to be available. I took the polygraph again two days later and passed with flying colors. They asked me the same exact questions as the first time. I have no idea what happened the first time. Maybe I was so amped up and my pulse was so fast because I was excited to win? I'm not sure. I've wracked my brain over and over trying to figure out what happened."

"So the guy in second place thought he was getting the big prize money? And then he got nothing?"

"Yes and no. I mean yes. He didn't get first place and the big money, but second place does get a pretty good earnings, too."

Just then, Marlin came splashing over, delivering his tennis ball, eager for someone to throw it. TJ chucked it far enough for him to be able to swim to it and back.

"Have you ever been fishing? Like deep-sea fishing."

"Fishing, yes. My dad used to take Kit and me when we were growing up. But ocean fishing, no. I've always wanted to try it but just never got around to it I guess."

"I would love to take you out one day. That's if you'd like to be held hostage on a boat with just Marlin and me for an eight-hour trip."

Her eyes widened at the thought. Teasingly, she replied, "As long as you don't make me swim after anything you forget to tie up. I'm not going to have to swim after the boat, will I?"

"Touche." TJ's face reddened a little.

"Well we're not fishing today, but we can clam. I brought the rakes and a mesh bag."

Before he could finish his next sentence, Jules had already grabbed the clam rakes and was walking toward an open spot of sand. She knelt down and began to dig using the small hand rakes that TJ had brought.

"I love clamming. It's so fun! Again, this is one of those things that takes me back. My dad brought my mom, Kit, and me out here all the time. Sometimes we would come by boat. Sometimes we would just jump off the pier and swim over. We'd get enough to eat and make clams casino. It's one of my favorites."

"Mine, too. It's cool to think that we can come out here and catch our own dinner."

"You catch fish! You do catch your dinner every day," she said laughing.

Click! Jules' rake caught on a hard round object under the sand. She used her rake to pull up from underneath. She held the clam up as if she were presenting a trophy to TJ.

"Got one!" she said proudly.

Click! TJ reached underwater. "Me, too." He showed off his clam and they threw them both in the bag. "Let's try to catch a dozen for dinner. We can make clams casino," he said.

"Dinner, huh? Are you staying for dinner?" She smiled and looked away.

"Only if I catch more clams than you."

TJ started to dig.

KIT

Kit and Laney drove in her two-door white Jeep Wrangler down Teal Drive. The sun was just going down but the fun was just beginning. Both girls wore their cutest bikinis barely covered by high-waisted jean shorts and crop tops.

Teal Drive was an exclusive area on the bay side tucked away from the lights and traffic of Coastal Highway. The cars in the driveways were a collection of BMWs, Audis, and Range Rovers. The houses, which stood at 2,500 square feet and above, were magnificent in size and held even more beauty with their waterfront views.

The house they were headed to belonged to Logan Wilson—well, his parents' house, really. They parked down the cul-de-sac, which by now looked like a Jeep dealership on Route 50. The front lawn looked like a 1980s movie where all of the kids' bikes were strewn about along the lawn—except these bikes held beach baskets on the front and half-empty seltzer cans leaning to one side of the colorful baskets.

The house was the biggest on the cul-de-sac and had a teal blue door—Teal Drive. The door stood in the center at the top of a grand staircase which led down to the left and right. To the left side of the house was a circular four-car garage that held Mrs. Wilson's white Ranger Rover and Mr. Wilson's fire engine red Porsche. Obviously, neither of them was home; hence the party. Laney had mentioned they were in Costa Rica.

"Who all do you know here besides Logan?" Kit asked Laney, who was checking her makeup in the side mirror of someone's red Wrangler.

"Oh, just Logan. We grew up together. But I am sure there will be plenty of guys to check out. Logan's a big surfer and has a lot of surfer friends." She wiggled her eyebrows at Kit. Laney was taller than Kit. Her long tan legs came up to what felt like Kit's belly button. Her family was from Kona so she had a beach vibe, exotic look. Gorgeous. Her jet black hair came down to the middle of her back and her tan looked like she sunbathed daily, whereas Kit's naturally highlighted brown hair was shoulder length and her tan came from a tanning bed, even in the summer. It was hard to compete for anyone's attention next to Laney.

"Whoa... This house is gorgeous!" Kit followed Laney up the stairs awing at the size.

"Yeah. They have a lot of money. But they're cool. Not snobby like a lot of rich people." The girls walked through the front door. Empty. The house was empty? Had Laney made a mistake?

"Everyone's out back." They walked through the immaculate house. Everything was decorated in shades of greys, whites, and no surprise, teals. Nothing was out of place. There was absolutely zero sign of any party happening. Until...

They walked through the everything-white kitchen and opened the back door. The pool which was lit by underwater globes changed all colors of the rainbow. Girls sat on the side, legs dangling in. Guys cannon-balled in to splash the girls. Another group was playing one-handed volleyball so they could still keep their Solo cups in hand.

Someone grabbed Laney around the shoulders from behind.

"Hey! Glad you made it!" A tall, tanned guy with broad shoulders hugged her friend. He was a little wobbly on his feet indicating that whatever was in his cup wasn't water.

"Hey, Logan! This is my friend, Kit. Kit, Logan. Logan, Kit." He bent down to hug Kit and welcome her.

"Nice to meet you. There's beer and liquor at the bar under the deck and at the bar over there by the waterfall." He pointed left, then right. "And bathrooms are over there in the pool house. No one inside."

"Got it." Kit nodded that she understood.

"The paddleboards are out on the pier and the kayaks are..." He looked around. "Someone must have them out. But they're there. And lastly, please follow me to the bar. Everyone that comes in must take a shot of my good friend, Jack."

The girls looked at each other and smiled. Tonight was going to be epic. He poured three shots into mini Solo cups and passed them around.

"To summer nights!" he exclaimed.

The girls echoed the sentiment and the three of them shot back their whiskey like it wasn't their first time.

After finding Laney a mango seltzer and Kit a watermelon, the two girls sat on the side of the pool. They were just about to get in when a beachball smacked Kit's can right out of her hand, landing in the pool. *Shit.*

A boy in Billabong trunks came rushing over, leaned down, and fished the can out of the pool.

"Hey, I'm really sorry. I didn't mean to do that." His hair was long and somewhat outgrown. His shoulders were broad and cut. He was adorable and hot all rolled into one.

"Oh, that's okay. No biggie."

"Let me go grab you a new one," the adorable hot boy said.

"I can go. Really." Kit was standing up, legs wet from the water. He reached down and helped her up.

"I'll walk over with you. I need a beer anyway."

Kit looked down at Laney.

"Go. I'll be fine. I'll find you later." She made a shooing motion with her hand.

The adorable boy walked with Kit over to the bar, this time by the waterfall. He grabbed another drink for Kit and a beer for himself.

"We should probably do a shot, too. I mean we walked all the way over here to the bar. We wouldn't want this trip to be wasted." He dangled the clear liquor bottle trying to convince her. Kit smiled and nodded. She thought he was really cute. He poured them each a shot of something clear. It didn't matter what it was. They were there to have fun. Back the cups went and an instant buzz into their heads.

"So, how do you know Logan?" he asked Kit, walking toward the pier. She followed suit.

"I really don't. My friend Laney," she pointed toward the pool, "she grew up with him, and Laney asked if I wanted to come tonight."

"How do you know him?"

"We were all friends in high school. All the guys here, we all just graduated this year." He took a sip of his ice-cold beer.

"Cool. I just finished my freshman year at Salisbury. Where are you going to college?" She secretly hoped for Salisbury even though she just met this kid three minutes ago. They reached the pier and sat along the edge and dangled their legs over.

"Salisbury, too." He cheers' her and they clinked cans.

"Major?" Kit asked.

"Sports medicine. You?"

"Communications. I'm not exactly sure what I want to do yet. But it seemed like a good start," she said as she took a sip of her drink.

"I'm Nathan, by the way."

"I'm Kit."

"Well, maybe we'll see each other on campus next year." He smiled and looked down at his feet. *Does he like me back?*

"Do you live down here or are you just on vacation?" *Please say here. Please say here,* she said to herself.

"I live here. My mom's a real estate agent and my dad does fishing charters."

"That's cool," she said out loud. But on the inside, she was doing backflips!

"And you?" he asked as she watched him take a chug of his beer. His Adam's apple danced up and down his throat.

"My sister actually lives here. I come in and visit. We have lunch or dinner. And I do my laundry. I actually live in Salisbury right off campus."

"That's cool." He paused a second. "Tell me something fun about yourself. Like a fun fact." He liked this girl. She was cute and relaxed. Nothing like other girls he's met his age.

A fun fact? Kit thought. It caught her off guard. She wasn't very interesting. Nothing really stood out about her. Kit had always considered herself a plain Jane. "I don't know. That's a hard one." She shrugged. "I grew up riding horses. I guess that's a fun fact. You're turn. What's a fun fact about you?"

Just as Nathan was about to tell Kit that he had a twin brother, he heard someone call out his name.

"Nathan! You and your girl want to go out?" The shouting was coming from Logan who was coming off of the floating pier. He had just ridden a three-seater jet ski and tied it up.

Nathan's face blushed a pinky hue. He looked over at Kit.

"He doesn't mean that. He's drunk."

Kit swung her legs back and forth. Her can was now empty and she had a nice relaxing buzz going. And she also didn't mind being 'his girl'.

"Do you want to go out on the jet ski with me?" he asked as he hopped up and reached his hand out for Kit to take.

Her logical side said *You don't even know this kid.* Her buzz said, *Cheers to summer nights!*

Walking down the pier, she got butterflies in her stomach. He hopped on the jet ski and swung back toward the pier. Reaching to hold on to his shoulders, Kit slid behind him and placed her hands around his waist. *No life jackets. It's fine. We won't be out long.*

"Just don't throw me off, okay?" Kit said.

"Never crossed my mind. I wouldn't want to hurt you." He twisted the throttle on the ski and they cruised down the canal out toward Assawoman Bay. The sun had just dipped under the horizon and the sky was as orange as a tangerine dipped in gold. The wind blew through Kit's hair.

"Faster?" he asked. Kit nodded and held her chin to his back. She tightened her grip and scooted in closer. She could smell the sunscreen on his neck.

The ski glided through the water. He did donuts in the channel. The bright lights of Fish Tales gleamed on the top of the bay. Their flags moved like slow jellyfish from the light breeze. He gunned the throttle out toward the covered sandbars. The high tide made them invisible to anyone other than a local. Careful not to run aground, he maneuvered around the bay using only the lights from waterfront condos.

The sky had gone from golden to pink and now navy blue. "We should probably get back. We can't see anything," Kit suggested.

The motor slowed a bit as Nathan coasted the jet ski toward the sandbar again. The water under them was probably three feet deep—two in some spots. They slid over the horseshoe crabs and the jellyfish, the minnows, and the perch. He yanked the key with his wrist and the motor stopped suddenly.

"What's wrong? Why are we stopped?" Kit looked around. She could see the lights of the waterfall and the tiki bar from where they were floating. But they were still far enough that no one was able to see them; especially in the dark. Nathan turned around on the long seat of the ski. They were face to face. Knee to knee.

He leaned in and kissed her. It was soft and pleasant. Not rushed and not forced. Kit kissed him back. And before she knew it, they were making out on the jet ski. Her legs were now on top of his and his hands were touching her butt. They floated up and down with the current. It was the most romantic thing Kit had ever done. It was also the most dangerous thing Kit had ever done.

Their moment of passion was interrupted by loud sirens and the sight of flashing red and blue lights. They looked at each other in shock, confused about what they should do.

Looking back and forth, she asked, "Do we go back? I left Laney at the party!"

"No, we don't go back." He started the engine of the jet ski.

"But what about the jet ski? It's going to look like we stole it!"

"I don't know but we need to find a place to tie it up and park it for the night. I can take it back in the morning before anyone wakes up."

"Where do we put a jet ski? It's not exactly something we can fit in our pocket." They drove through the dark bayside along the lines of piers and boats close enough to be able to see where they were going. They came into Harbour Island Marina slowly like bandits. That's how she felt. Still clinging tightly to Nathan, Kit wondered about Laney. *Was her friend looking for her?*

Just as they were tying up to the piling, Kit felt her phone vibrate in her pocket. She slipped it out, careful not to drop it. She saw that the text was from Laney.

OMG! Kit, where are you? Everyone ran and I couldn't find you!

I'm at Harbour Island Marina with Nathan. I'm fine. Are you?

Who's Nathan?
Yes! I'm fine.

How did you get there?

I'll call you later and explain. Are you okay to get home?

Yes. I'm at my car.

Are you sober enough to drive?

I'm good. Should I be worried about this Nathan kid?

No. I'll call you when I get home.

K

"Laney just texted and said everyone ran out. Parties over I guess." Nathan and Kit walked along the pier.

"Sorry about that. But I didn't want to get us in more trouble and take us back. I'll text Logan and tell him the skis at my house. Where do you live? I can take you home."

"The house is over on Edgewater Avenue."

"Oh yeah. That's close." He grabbed her hand and led her up the pier. They walked slowly up toward the parking lot admiring all the big boats. Kit loved looking at the names and how clever people would get. *Reckless Woman, Maggie Jo, Heels, and Reels.* Why are all boats named after women? She wondered...

They hopped in Nathan's car and slowly drove out of the complex and down Edgewater Avenue.

Kit pointed. "It's that one." She looked carefully. There was a blue Jeep in front of Jules' place. *Whose truck is that?*

Nathan turned off the car and walked Kit to the front door. He looked first at his feet, which were still bare.

"Sorry about all the commotion. But other than that, I had a fun time. Can I call you tomorrow? Maybe we could hang out at the beach or something."

"Yeah, sure. I'd like that." She Airdropped her number and he did the same.

He touched her hand and pulled her in close. His hands were in her back jeans pockets and hers on his chest, they kissed for a few minutes before her lips began to hurt. She pulled away and walked up the steps toward the door.

He began to back away, still watching Kit. "Good night. I'll text you tomorrow," he said and smiled at her.

"Good night," she smiled back. She opened the door and closed it behind her. *Cheers to summer nights.*

ROB AND LEANNE

That evening, Rob and Leanne had ended up being home together for the first time in weeks. Leanne walked into the kitchen after a long hot shower in sweats and a baggy T-shirt. Rob could see from the corner of his eye that she wasn't wearing a bra.

"Hey, sweetheart. How was your day?" he asked.

"Oh, it was good. Getting a lot accomplished. It's been a whirlwind around the office. There are so many clients coming in, it's hard to keep everyone straight." Leanne walked out to join Rob on the outside porch facing the bay. She sat in the empty chair that Rob had been staring at recently, glad that she was finally there to occupy it. She propped her feet up on the ottoman and sipped her Pinot Noir.

"What do you think about you and I going out and having a nice romantic dinner, just the two of us tonight? It's been far too long since we've spent some nice quality time together. We'll pick a nice quiet table in the back, no interruptions." He looked at her and reached out his hand to hold hers. She reached out and intertwined her fingers in his. His heart was aching for her. He wanted to have her tonight. And not just sex. He wanted her love, her attention, her gaze. How he missed her when she wasn't there. He was really trying here.

Leanne saw her husband, who she had been married for over 25 years, looking at her like she remembered him looking at her on their wedding day. She felt a twinge of guilt and remorse for a split second. But the feeling that was most overwhelming was how full her heart felt just holding her husband's hand. An emotional rollercoaster was an understatement.

"I would love that," she replied with a sigh. She tilted her head to the side. "I would really love that." Rob pulled Leanne carefully out of her chair toward him, careful not to spill her wine.

"Come here," he said in a low, gravelly tone.

She carefully set her glass on the side table and let Rob move her toward his lap. He cradled her, pulling her legs up across the arm of the chair. His strong arms supported her back as he held her close to his chest. He brushed her stray hairs out of her eyes and away from her lips. She gazed up at him as she smoothed down the side of his thin beard. Rob moved his hand up and down her legs, stopping to pay more attention to her lower half. When she was satisfied, he continued moving his hands upward under her baggy T-shirt toward her breasts. He cupped them gently in his right hand, still cradling her with his left hand. She let out a low moan of pleasure and leaned her head back a little more.

Rob moved his hand lower toward her waist, went a little further down past her navel, and massaged in between her legs before reaching where she wanted him to go. Leanne let him spend some time down there, rubbing for her pleasure. She was enjoying the warmth of his touch to the point where she couldn't take it anymore. She reached up, touched the back of his head, and led his lips to hers. They kissed passionately, their tongues entangled, hardly able to pause for breath. Rob's hands explored more purposefully now on Leanne's breasts under her shirt. He loved the way she felt in his arms. He squeezed her breasts, massaging her nipples, making his way back down with his hand as his wife was moaning much louder now than before. Leanne could feel him on the small of her back through his shorts. Rob continued to massage more eagerly now and his hands couldn't stop. He quickly stood up and carried his wife into their bedroom, still tangled in their intense kiss.

Rob and Leanne lay in bed, Rob behind her softly touching her, his leg on top of hers. Leanne's head lay on Rob's arm. She ran her fingers up and down his arms, the arms that just so easily carried her into their bedroom and had gently laid her down to make intense love to her.

"I love you," he whispered in her ear. "I've always loved you, and I always will."

Leanne turned over to face her husband. She kissed his lips tenderly and touched his bare chest. "I love you, too," she replied. They lay in bed for the next hour just holding each other, re-exploring what they'd been missing for the past few months. After another round of re-exploring their love for one another, Leanne looked up at Rob. "How about that dinner," she asked, smiling.

TJ AND MARLIN

TJ out-clammed Jules by one. Winning was winning! They cleaned up the sandbar picnic. The water was about five inches now and things would start to float away soon. They packed up the paddleboards, cooler, and clam rakes. TJ set the bag of clams he would be making Jules for dinner on top of her board.

"Just so you can see what winning looks like. You can hold the clams," he said with a wide smile.

"Oh. You're funny." She threw her arms up. "But you won fair and square. Now you get to cook me dinner." Her face was tanned and her blonde hair was pulled up. She took his breath away every time he looked at her.

"We may have this backward. Isn't the winner supposed to have dinner cooked for *them*?" he said. They were carefully paddling the boards across the channel. The water was choppier this afternoon due to an increase in the evening boat traffic.

"Not in this game. You set up the rules. I just went by them." Jules looked at her watch. It was around 3 p.m. and the sun was directly on top of the bay. It was a gorgeous day and she had not been disappointed by TJ's choice of dates.

The three of them made it across the channel, back to the pier, and unloaded everything. TJ drove Jules back home. He got out and opened the Jeep. They walked toward the front door.

"Well. What time will you be coming back to cook me dinner?" She smiled brightly at the thought of him coming back. Wisps of hair fell into her face.

TJ fixed the bill of his hat. "What time do you want me back?"

"How about we do dinner at 7? Is that too late? I know you have to fish in the morning."

"I'll be here at 7 on the dot." He kissed her on the lips and ran his hand down her arm.

"Don't be late."

As TJ drove off with Marlin in the back seat air drying in the summer heat, Jules' heart was slowly melting, and TJ was falling hard.

JULES

TJ out-clammed Jules. By one. She lost on purpose. She had caught probably a dozen more clams but secretly threw them back so TJ wouldn't see. *Shh*. Sorry, not sorry.

She dressed in cut-off jean shorts and an off-the-shoulder top that showed a peep of midriff. A knock came at the door at 6:59 in the evening.

Swinging the door open, she laughed. "Wow. That's impressive."

"I may have sat in my car for a few minutes so I wasn't too early." He and Marlin came through the door. TJ was holding the bag of clams, a grocery bag full of ingredients for clams casino, and an impressive bouquet of flowers in a mason jar from Assateague Island Farm.

Jules motioned her arms like a *Price is Right* model. "Here's the kitchen. I guess I will sit back and watch. Did you want a beer? Or an iced tea?" She took the flowers from him and placed them on the center of the table outside on the deck.

"Sure. Iced tea sounds good. I know I mentioned before, but I'm not a huge drinker. Never really was." Based on what she saw next, she knew he had obviously made this dish before. She watched him lay out everything in order of when he would use it. This is quite the opposite of her cooking style. She was more of a make-a-mess and clean-it-up-later cook. It was nice to watch. She poured them each a glass of iced tea.

She had already gotten a pot out for steaming and a baking sheet for the broiling for him. He really could just sit back and watch. Sitting down, she propped her long tan legs up on the stool.

"I'm not a big drinker either. I do enjoy an ice-cold margarita though."

"Good to know." He looked up from the sink as he cleaned their dinner.

The clams were delicious. TJ had made a Caesar salad to accompany the dish. They sat outside on the deck and dined, Marlin at their feet. Boats drifted north and south as they passed them. Some were fishing. Some were enjoying the hot breeze. And the sun looked like a peach in the sky. Summer sunsets got better as the summer progressed in Jules' opinion.

They cleaned up dinner and sat back out on the deck. Time seemed to fly when they were together but also stood still.

"I had a great time today on our day date turned into a night date. I think you had that planned all along," Jules said with a smile.

They had their legs propped up on the same chair, tiny grains of sand still stuck on their feet. "I'm not going to lie; it was not the plan, but I was hoping it would happen. I really enjoy your company."

"I'm glad we got to spend the entire day together." Jules skimmed her foot on TJ's. The two of them sat and relaxed. For the rest of the evening, they shared stories of themselves growing up—family parties, birthdays, school, sports. They talked about anything and everything.

Almost three hours later, the moon dangled overhead. As they held hands, TJ stood up.

"Dance with me?" He looked down at her with soft eyes.

Allowing TJ to assist her, she slowly stood up. He took her in his arms and they slow danced. The only music was the quiet lapping of the waves on the pilings below. She tilted her head up to allow him to kiss her. Just before their lips locked, they were interrupted by footsteps.

WHITNEY AND FINN

Their boat day consisted of cruising Assawoman Bay, a stop at De Lazy Lizard for their crab grilled cheese, and a great view of the bridge, followed by a lazy day boat nap in the shade of the boat's canvas cover. They ended their day together with the sunset, nice warm showers, and loaded nachos from Annabelle's. Both Finn and Whitney agreed that crawling into bed together after a day outside on the water was pure perfection.

Thursday

Category: White Marlin
1st Place: The Other Woman
2nd Place: No Limits
3rd Place: Big Distraction

Category: Blue Marlin
1st Place: Weekend Vibes
2nd Place: Salty Bitch
3rd Place: One and Only

Category: Tuna
1st Place: Weekend Vibes
2nd Place: Big Distraction
3rd Place: The Other Woman

FINN

It was a little after 9 in the morning on his second day of The White Marlin Tournament. He and his boat Week-end Vibes currently held 1st place. As Finn captained the boat further out into the deep blue Atlantic, he couldn't help but think about the previous months that he and Whit had been going through. Never did he think that having a baby would be this difficult. Months back and forth at the doctors, numerous medications, phone calls, appointments, fertility clinics, and the list goes on. But the crying and blame that Whitney put on herself are what really killed him. He would do anything to take that burden away from her.

Back in August of last year, they had received great news from Whitney's doctor. The IVF had worked and Whitney was pregnant. She was very early on. Six weeks. But six weeks of being pregnant was nothing short of a miracle for them after Whitney's cancer. They had gone out to a low-key dinner to celebrate that evening at their favorite pizza joint, Pizza Johns, followed by two chocolate snowballs. Having a family was a dream of theirs. But a few weeks later, it just seemed that it wasn't in the cards for them.

Whitney was on hour seven of a twelve-hour shift when she started having major abdominal cramping. It started out small at first. She thought that maybe it was the taco salad she had for lunch. But as the next hour went on, the cramping became more intense and even more rapid. She immediately called Dr. Maggio. She directed her to go home immediately and lay down. The cramping had become more constant as she drove herself home, something else to add to her terrifying situation. At one point, she thought she was going to have to pull over on the often busy Interstate 95; however, she didn't want to chance anything. She pressed on, gripping the steering wheel as sweat began to bead down her back. She grabbed her phone, trying to keep her eyes on the road too, texting Finn. 36 long minutes later, Whitney pulled into her and Finn's empty driveway that led up the side of their newly-renovated house.

As she rushed through the door and into the kitchen, she could feel some of the tightness begin to subside. She removed all of her clothes and ran a warm bath. As a nurse, she knew that she needed to relieve some stress, and this was a great way to begin. Laying in the claw foot bathtub that Finn had installed just for her, Whitney looked around. For such a romantic-looking bathroom with its elegant lighting, separate dual head shower, and his and her sinks, it held such heavy memories. It was in this very bathroom that she had taken over thirty pregnancy tests, all screaming that little red minus sign. Negative.

After her bath, Whitney dried off and wrapped herself in her white terrycloth robe, and laid down in bed to relax and take a nap.

An intense cramp woke Whitney up a few hours later.

"I'm here. I'm here," Finn said. When he arrived home, Whitney had already fallen asleep and was resting. In an attempt not to disturb her, Finn lay on the bedroom floor on Whitney's side of the bed.

"I need to go to the bathroom."

"Okay, I'll help you." He helped lift her off the bed and walked, holding her up, through the sliding barn doors that separated the two rooms.

And it was here on their bathroom floor where Whitney miscarried two hours after leaving work. Finn had rushed home as soon as Whit had called to tell him she was on her way home. It scared the hell out of him that she was one, driving herself, and two, about to miscarry their unborn child. Again.

Finn cradled Whitney on the cold floor of their cozy bathroom where they both cried.

Katherine Ruskey

LEANNE

Last night with Rob was unbelievable. It had been a long time since they had any time together with her working so many crazy hours and focusing on clients. She had planned on having a nice evening on the sofa working on some showings for the following day, but Rob had caught her off-guard. They hadn't had sex like that in months—maybe even years. She missed it. But she also knew what was waiting for her at the office and couldn't stop thinking about it.

That morning, Leanne went for her morning coffee on the way to work. She had four listings that she was scheduled to show today. Two before noon and two after.

The first listing was a bay front condo on 23rd. It was a newer development. Two bedrooms, one and a half baths. Boat slip included. Walking distance to Fish Tales, where one of the boys worked. Listed for around $370,000. The couple was impressed but still asked to see another condo later in the week.

The second was further down toward Bethany Beach. Single house. Bayfront. Five bedrooms, four and a half baths. In-ground swimming pool. Kayaks and paddleboards included. Hammock hanging in the shade under the above-ground deck. Listed at $869,000. The older couple that was looking decided that they absolutely loved it and wanted to put in a bid. They started at $825,000, which she told them was a little on the low side. But they didn't care and were hoping that they had luck on their side.

After going back to the office, Leanne worked on the paperwork for the couple's bid. She quickly heard back from the buyers who countered at $855,000. She spent the entire time she had allocated for lunch back and forth on the phone with the buyers and the sellers. After about two hours of back-and-forth phone tag, the sellers accepted a final offer of $845,000. With her commission, she would bring in roughly around $60,000.

She had spent so much time on her second showing for the day, that not only did she not have lunch, but she also had to call and reschedule her third showing for the day. That meant she had one more showing. She allotted the most time for this client on her schedule for today. She was hoping to get a little more insight into his style. She began getting butterflies just thinking about spending some time with him. She looked at her phone. 1:33. She was scheduled to meet him at 3 but decided to send a quick message.

Hey—I'm available now if you'd like to see the house sooner than later.
Sounds perfect. Where should I pick you up?

The thought of getting to spend even more time with him if they drove together was tempting. But she decided against it.

I'll send you the address and we can meet there around 2?

Her heart started beating faster as she could see the three dots on her phone screen indicating that he was texting back.

I look forward to seeing you.

Leanne went to the bathroom to freshen up her makeup and hair. Her dark brown hair hung slightly past her shoulders. She decided a low chignon would be more suitable. She pinned her hair up and applied a light perfume. She had an extra dress in her office as a backup. She changed dresses in her office behind closed doors. She took off her casual wrap dress and slung it into her work bag. She would need to remember to take it out later to wash it. The backup dress was hanging in her office closet. It was more formal than not with a plunging hanging neckline that showed just enough cleavage. It was dark navy with a zip-up back. It clung tighter to her body than other dresses she normally wore but she liked it for this occasion.

Leanne took one last look at herself in the mirror. *What are you doing?* she thought. *Oh, stop... Nothing's going to happen. I just want to make a good impression.* But was that really the case?

Leanne grabbed her purse and listing binder. She closed her office door and jetted out of the office. She hopped in her BMW and decided against putting the top down. *AC all the way,* she thought. The weather had been unbearably steamy and humid and she didn't want to risk smelling like a gym when she got there.

Her goal was to arrive at the small cottage before him. It wasn't professional to keep clients waiting. However, when she got there, there was already a car in the driveway. She parked next to the black Audi and started toward the front door. But he caught her eye down by the water's edge. His back was toward her so she could admire his broad shoulders. He stood over 6 feet tall with a tight athletic frame. His white button-up shirt was un-tucked over blue khaki shorts and he was adorning super casual brown flip-flops. His shirt sleeves were rolled up, slightly exposing a high-dollar Armani watch and no wedding ring. His light brown hair was slightly blowing in the light coastal breeze. He was younger than she was but not by much.

He turned around and smiled as he saw Leanne approaching.

"How are you liking the view?" she asked as he walked toward her. It was a bit tricky walking in the grass with her heels on, but she made it look graceful.

"I forgot all about the view as soon as I saw you in that dress." He approached her and kissed her softly on the cheek. She felt his hand brush the small of her back and it sent a sensation of tingles through her.

"Well thank you for the compliment. Are you ready to see the inside?" She was nervous. And rightfully so. What in the world was she thinking wearing this dress? It was way too revealing for what they were out here for.

"Well, I want to first talk about the outside. I love the curb appeal. It's simple, not too flashy. It's quaint. It looks like I could pull my boat through here right down to the water. I like that very much. Not a lot of upkeep on the outside. And you really listened when I said that I wanted privacy. There are no neighbors around. That's a real perk." As he finished his sentence, he looked Leanne up and down with his dark brown eyes, his hair still fluttering from the breeze.

Leanne blushed. He followed her toward the front door. She turned the key and walked across the threshold. Directly in front of her was an entire wall of 12-foot bay windows facing the waterfront. It was like you were outside while you were in the living room. Off to the left was a decent-sized living area. It was equipped with a larger fireplace and mantle off on the left side of the wall. To the right was a larger kitchen with granite white countertops with dark grey cabinets, stainless steel appliances, and four bar stools that stood around one side of the kitchen island.

Leanne led him into the living area so that he could admire the view. He walked into the kitchen and ran his hands across the smooth granite as he walked by. He moved slowly like he was taking it all in. He walked to the outside deck door that was directly in the middle of the bay window wall. He stood taking in the bay, the bay grasses, and the vast area that could possibly be his new "vacation house".

He turned around slowly. "Let's take a look upstairs at

the bedrooms." His smile was coy and dangerous—like he knew a secret that he wanted to tell but wasn't allowed. With his right hand, he gestured for Leanne to take the lead. She walked past him and just the proximity of their bodies, she felt another jolt of electricity go through her. She tried to focus and talk about the amenities that the house had to offer.

"The upstairs has the master bedroom with an attached full bath equipped with a shower with dual heads and a Jacuzzi tub. Again, you have the large bay windows that allow in the afternoon sun. You could watch the sun set from bed if you wanted. And across the hall, you have a smaller full bath and a smaller bedroom for guests. The house comes fully furnished so anything that you see in here comes with the house."

The master bedroom showed an exquisite king-sized bed with a large white headboard. The light and dark navy bedding and large pillows gave off the serene and quiet ambiance that Leanne loved as a real estate agent. The dressers matched the large shiplap-looking headboard and there were various beach nature scenes along the walls of the entire house. They walked the rest of the upstairs chatting about what he liked about the cottage.

"I want to take another look from the living room," he said.

"Take all the time that you need. I'm going to be in the kitchen if you have more questions." Leanne left the client upstairs standing in the large master bedroom. Her mind was racing about things that could happen so moving downstairs seemed a little safer. She walked into the stylish kitchen to calm her nerves.

A few minutes later as Leanne's heart was just starting to slow its rapid rhythm, she felt him. He had come up behind her and lightly touched the top of her right shoulder with his index finger. He softly slid it down toward her elbow. His other hand was gently rubbing the left side of her waist. She felt goosebumps starting from the inside out. She tilted her head to the left to expose her neck. He sweetly began to kiss the back of her neck, then moved toward her shoulder. His hands continued to caress her waist while his lips began to brush against the side of her neck. She was so glad that she put her hair up. He pressed himself closer up against her back as his hands went from her waist further down.

"This dress is too much for me to handle," he whispered in her ear. He nibbled the lobe of her ear as he said it. Her eyes were closed by now, taking in his cologne and the warmth of his arms around her. He tasted the crook of her neck once again sending chills up her body. He carefully turned her around so that she was facing him now. His hands were now along the outside of her thighs, sliding her dress up one slow inch at a time. She held onto his shoulders and felt the broad muscles that were about to envelop her. He continued his hands around her back toward her zipper. He slid it carefully down about halfway, just enough to slide her dress down off her shoulder. And then her bra strap. She wore her sexy lace bra today. After last night with Rob, she felt amazingly sexy and had picked it out from the back of her dresser drawer.

Down came her bra strap and in went his strong forceful hands. He grabbed her breast with a tantalizing force that made her gasp. With his other hand, he was still exploring under her dress. His lips were making their way around her neck and her collarbone. He kept going down further until his mouth reached her nipple. He gave a hard suck and teased her with his teeth a little. It made her gasp each time she felt his teeth but she never wanted it to stop.

His hands made their way down to her hips and he smoothly and carefully lifted her up onto the white granite kitchen counter. He slid her dress up and reached under with both hands. His lips never once stopped exploring her neck. Her body was on sensory overload. With both hands, he slowly slid her black lace thong down and off her ankles and around her heels, letting them fall to the beautifully-tiled kitchen floor. He grabbed her from behind and slid her closer to the edge of the counter. Her dress was now almost around her waist and he knelt down in front of her, taking his first taste. He took control for what felt eternally blissful before he came up for air to pay more attention to her top half. As he did so, he unbuckled his belt. She helped with little effort due to the paralyzing feeling that was jolting through her. Her heart was beating forcefully in her exposed chest. He looked her in the eyes as she unbuttoned his shirt halfway down to kiss on him. She grabbed his muscular shoulders, pulled him in closer, and allowed herself to enjoy him.

ROB

Rob was feeling extra lucky ever since he woke up that morning. He and Leanne had a spectacular evening the night before, and he intended on keeping the momentum going. After their seductive time in bed, Rob continued the romance by taking Leanne to dinner at Harrison's Harbor Watch overlooking the inlet. Leanne wore a remarkable little black dress that he hadn't seen before, and he even decided to slip on a nice button-up shirt. He opened the car door for her and held her hand as she stepped out. They walked hand in hand toward the restaurant. He opened the restaurant door for her and they were taken to their waiting table. He slid out her chair and placed an order for a delicious bottle of Sauvignon Blanc with which they toasted "to us."

Rob first ordered the crab dip—because it was Leanne's favorite—along with an order of premium black-label oysters. Maybe he'd take her home after this and he'd make love to her for the third time this evening.

"I want to make a second toast," he said. "To our life together. Wherever it takes us, wherever we are, I will always love you."

"Cheers," replied Leanne. They clinked glasses and dove into their appetizers.

"This food is even better than I remember," Leanne commented.

"It is really good." Rob forked a big glob of crab dip onto a cracker.

"Is that for me?" she joked.

"Of course it is; I always let you have the last bite." Leanne leaned across the table, mouth halfway open toward Rob. He teased her a bit first and brought the loaded cracker back toward him. She slapped at his hand just before he fed her the last bit of crab dip by hand.

"Can I get you anything else right now?" the waiter asked as he took the empty appetizer from their table. Rob could feel Leanne rubbing her foot along the inside of his leg, getting higher and higher the longer the waiter stood there. He cleared his throat loudly and adjusted himself.

"Ah—hhmm... No, thank you. We're doing just fine." He took a sip of his wine and smiled.

After their romantic dinner of fresh swordfish and Maryland lump crab cakes had concluded, Rob and Leanne got into his SUV and headed back toward home. Rob couldn't keep his hands off of Leanne as he rubbed the sides of her legs. He never wanted to let her go. They pulled off of Coastal Highway onto 14th street. He punched in the gate code and pulled into the gated condominium. He put the car in park and leaned over for another kiss. At first, it was soft and romantic but it quickly became passionate and hard. Leanne took charge and began to unbutton Rob's shirt as she kissed him passionately. She reached down and felt him getting excited.

"Let's get inside," she suggested. Rob got out first and came around to open Leanne's car door. He tapped her playfully as she maneuvered out of the car in that little black dress that showed some cleavage that Rob couldn't wait to get closer to once inside the house. Rob followed behind as they opened the front door. She led him into their place, undressing herself as she walked down the hall into their bedroom leaving a trail of heels...her little black dress. Rob took care of the rest as they stopped in the middle of the living room.

And just like Rob hoped, he had yet a third time with his wife, partially blaming it on the oysters at dinner.

• • •

Leanne nonchalantly walked out onto the patio naked and took a beach towel that was hanging on the railing to wrap herself in. She sat on a chair overlooking the bay, which was calm with a glitter of moonlight on top. Rob came out holding a martini and a beer. He offered his gorgeous wife the martini. She accepted and sipped. Her hair was hanging down below her shoulders, still a little tousled from earlier. He sat down in his matching chair and sipped his beer.

"I have to go to the boat tomorrow and get ready for another tournament day. I would love it if you'd join me. You can grab a martini at the bar, walk around, and then we can grab dinner together. I can't be out late because I have to be up early the next morning. What do you think?"

Leanne looked over at Rob. "You know how I feel about going down there."

"I know, but we won't stay long. We can just relax and grab a drink while I get the boat ready, and then we can grab dinner somewhere in West Ocean City. We can go over to Sello's for Italian or stay here and see one of the boys at Fishtales or Ropewalk." He was running his pointer finger along her arm. "Come on. It'll be nice to have you there. You might even be able to make some new connections for clients who are here from out of town." His finger shot up. "That actually reminds me. I am meeting someone at the boat tomorrow who's interested in fishing."

She paused and thought about it. As long as she didn't see *her*, Leanne would go.

"Okay. I'll come along. It's been a while, and I'd like to see what you've done with the boat." She leaned over and kissed him.

WHITNEY

Whitney woke up and ran. It wasn't her greatest yet not her worst run. She had a hard time getting into a groove today. Usually the day after a relaxing boat day she kills it—but today just wasn't the same. Feeling a little sluggish, she poured an extra cup of coffee once she got back home. She sat out on the balcony enjoying the quiet morning breeze.

As she scrolled Instagram, an advertisement caught her eye. Scrolling back up, she saw a familiar-looking face. It was a woman she had seen before. Her hair was long and brown. She was classy looking. Underneath the photo read: "Realtor: Delmarva." *How would I know a realtor down here?* She continued to scroll mindlessly when it dawned on her. She met her at the bar the other night at the boat! *We talked about martinis. What boat did she say her husband captained again...?* That was going to bother her now. She scrolled back up to see the photo again. Staring at the photo, she racked her brain to remember what the name of the boat was. After about a minute of thinking, Whitney's brain connected two and two. *The woman at the pool with the martini was the same woman she met at the bar!* Wow, what a small world. She and her husband were getting really cozy in the pool that day. She had seen them when she walked into the pool area. They were the only three in the place. And the martini glasses were kind of odd because who really drinks martinis at the pool?

Next time she sees her at the slip, she'll have to mention that she saw her.

Whitney had another free day to herself. Finn was out

fishing with the band again today. It was his second day of the tournament and he was in second place. *Salty Bitch* came in with a monster marlin yesterday and almost knocked him down a spot. He was still on top of the blue marlin category.

Making herself a favorite breakfast of hers—scrambled eggs and half of a bagel—she began to get a bit of a stomach-ache. The smell of the eggs, which normally smelled like heaven, was making her queasy. She barely reached the bathroom before vomiting her morning coffee into the toilet. Her head almost exploded. No.

Running back into the kitchen to turn the stove off, she tried to remember when she had her last period. She opened her phone and tapped on the calendar app. She wasn't late, and she hadn't missed her last period either. Whitney was on top of this stuff. How was this possible? She had opted to stop birth control when she found out about her cervical cancer. It didn't make sense to add another medication into the mix. The possibility of getting pregnant while going through treatment was rare. And most of the time they used protection, just in case. But there were occasions when they didn't have one or "forgot".

With a head full of mixed emotions, she walked a couple of blocks to the nearest convenience store. The aisle was all too familiar. She picked up three different brands to make sure. On the way home, her steps began to quicken. Her heart was beating faster, almost as if a butterfly were caught in her chest. The excitement of a positive test was beginning to take flight. However, there was always that worry of a positive test in the back of her mind, too.

Here she was again. The same old song and dance. There she sat, again, in the awkward position to pee on the stick three different times. The pregnancy tests were lined up neatly on the sink all in a row. She paced back and forth not knowing whether she wanted to see the results. One minute. Two minutes. Three minutes. Each test had a different wait time. She decided to wait for them all to be finished at one time.

Her heartbeat was rapid. She touched her stomach under her belly button. Whitney had set a mental timer. The clock had read 10:10. The test with the longest time was four minutes. 10:14. Slowly walking back into the bathroom, she held her breath.

Tears welled up in her eyes making it difficult to see— yet clear as day, she saw the results. *Positive... Positive... Positive.* Whitney sat down on the floor laughing. She felt on high. She felt scared. She felt terrified. She felt relieved. Whitney would call the doctor today and get their first available appointment. She would take every precaution she could.

After taking a picture of the three positive tests, Whitney cleaned them up and disposed of them. She wanted to find the best time to tell Finn. Maybe this weekend? She wouldn't have an appointment by then, but three positive tests were a tell-all. She walked back into the kitchen to make breakfast— obviously not eggs. So instead she opted for watermelon and her bagel instead. It might be time to start eating a little more. She made the second half of her bagel, loaded it up with cream cheese with chives, and savored every bite.

The day was hers to do as she pleased. But relaxing at the pool would be challenging knowing that she has this newly-found secret. What would keep her mind busy? She threw on her favorite green sundress and headed north. She would spend some much-needed time at her favorite bookstore. *Bethany Beach Books—I'm coming for ya!*

JULES

It was hard to sleep again last night. Being with TJ on the date was a dream. He was cute and funny. And he could really cook!

Jules had woken up earlier than normal. She couldn't stop thinking about him. She decided to surprise him at the dock before he set off on his second fishing day. It was early, yes, but this tiny gesture would show how much she liked him.

Throwing on cutoffs and an Aerosmith T-shirt, she stopped for two coffees and drove toward Sunset Marina.

TJ AND MARLIN

This morning was the same as any other fishing day. Except he had gotten minimal sleep and was surprisingly not tired. Being with Jules felt right, and even though he was on four to five hours of sleep and had a full day of fishing ahead of him, he woke up before his alarm and already had a pep in his step as he popped out of bed.

Marlin was out. Coffee was brewing. Kibble was served. He was in third on the leaderboard but knew it was only temporary. Today was the day. Luck was on his side! After yesterday, he was on the fast track to success.

Driving to the marina, the air had a cool morning feel. It seemed less humid, which would be a nice break. TJ and Marlin parked the Jeep and walked toward the boat. From afar, he could see the majesty of its size and the beauty of the teak. *Big Distraction* ran across her stern in beautiful lettering. *Ocean City, Maryland* just underneath. He loved this little ocean town.

As he approached the boat, something strange caught his eye. The door looked like it was slightly slid open. He looked at his phone. 4:11. Kyle *wouldn't be here this early...would he?* Walking closer, he could see that the inside lights were still off. So no, it wasn't Kyle. None of the rods or tackle was set up either. Definitely wasn't Kyle.

Stepping on board, he used his phone to slide and tap his flashlight on. He carefully slid the door open and shone the flashlight in. Nothing seemed out of place or off. He walked in and flipped on the lights of the living area. His eyes opened wide. Was he seeing what he was really seeing? The body of a woman lay like a ragdoll in the main living area.

"Jesus!" he yelled. He ran over to the limp-looking body. He couldn't see her face. Rolling her over on her back, her face was now upright.

"What the hell, Mallory! How the hell did you get in here?" She smelled putrid. It was the vomit on the front of her shirt. He could smell the alcohol seeping from her pores. He shook her awake and tried to move her.

He suddenly remembered how she got in. TJ had never changed the code lock on the door of the boat. She must have still had it in her phone or memorized it. *Idiot. Mental note: change the code.* Mallory began to stir. Her moaning indicated how terrible she felt. That much alcohol will do that to you. She tried sitting up. He got a bottle of water from the refrigerator.

"Here. Drink this." He stood away from her, looking disgusted.

"My head." Her hair was matted and stuck to her face.

"You need to leave. I have clients coming on board. And not to mention, I need to clean up the puke you left. Get off my boat."

"Geez. I thought you'd be happier to see me." Trying to stand up, her skirt got stuck over her hip.

"Seriously? No underwear? You're unbelievable. I'll be changing the code on the lock so forget the one you have. This is completely inappropriate and I should call the police! I'm infuriated. Get off. Now."

Mallory smoothed her skirt and brushed her hair off of her face. She got a whiff of herself and felt a little embarrassed. "You just blew it. You had your chance to get back with me. But with the way you're acting, it'll never happen now. I came down here to surprise you. You're a dick." Her words were slurred and sloppy. She found her sandals and headed for the door. Almost falling on her way out, she stumbled onto the deck of the boat. TJ was hoping that Kyle wasn't outside. It would send an extremely wrong message.

He began the gross job of cleaning up what Mallory left behind. *Nasty.* After spraying what felt like an ungodly amount of bleach, he walked outside.

Mallory had sat down on the fighting chair and had fallen back asleep. Now he was pissed. He hoisted her up, placing his arms under hers. Her legs barely held her own weight. He climbed up and stood on the side of the boat, trying to steady her on the pier, careful that she didn't fall overboard. Mallory managed to stand on her own. She seemed a little more steady than when he found her. He wasn't a malicious person, but right now he could care less how she was going to get home.

Placing his hands on her shoulders from behind, he walked her toward the parking lot. Her feet stopped moving and she turned her body around to face his. She placed her hand on the back of his head and pulled him in for one last kiss.

JULES

Walking down the pier with two cups of hot coffee, Jules looked for the name *Big Distraction*. TJ had kind of explained during their date yesterday where the boat was located in Sunset Marina. There were hardly any people out. She had thought because of the popularity of the tournament, the dock would be peppered with fishermen.

Further down the pier, she could see shadows of a woman carrying her own sandals with a man following her from behind. As she got closer, she saw the woman lean into the man for a kiss. Just then, the moon reflected just right on the stern of the boat they had just come off of. She could make out the words *Big Distraction*. She stopped in her tracks. The man was wearing a baseball hat. Looking to her right, a dog walked around the deck of the boat. Her heart imploded.

TJ AND MARLIN

"Seriously. Get the hell out of here!" TJ grabbed Mallory by the shoulders and leaned away. An audible gasp from a few boats down broke the quiet on the pier. TJ looked over—and there was Jules.

"Jules?" TJ pushed Mallory out of the way and ran toward Jules. He watched as she set down two to-go cups down on the *Salty Bitch*'s dockbox and begin to walk away. He ran past and caught up to her.

"Hey! What are you doing here? That wasn't what it looked like. Let me explain." He was trying to get her to stop walking so fast.

"That's okay," she said calmly, trying to swallow the lump in her throat. "I don't want you to explain anything. I don't want to talk to you anymore." She climbed into her car and slammed the door. Tears began to stream down her face as she started the car and drove out of the parking lot.TJ was calling her phone. She let it go. Her chest was tight and her heart actually ached.

"TJ and Marlin" lit up on the screen of her phone again. She let it go. A text popped up. Delete. She didn't even want to read it. Jules knew she deserved better, and she didn't have time to put herself through this.

She drove back to Edgewater Avenue, climbed into bed, and tried to forget anything ever happened.

The outgoing calls next to Jules' name showed the number 9. Nine times he had tried to call her. All before having guests show up for another day of fishing. An entire screen of text messages all said "delivered"—but not one response. And the worst thing was that his communication would be cut off once they hit a certain number of miles out to sea. He felt defeated. Like a crab in a trap with no way out.

He walked back to the boat not knowing what else there was for him to do. He took off his hat and chucked it on the fighting chair. Marlin went over to sniff. Kyle came out of the cabin.

"Hey man. You all right? Where were you?" Kyle asked, setting the rods in the holders.

"Nothing. I was down..." he pointed back. Climbing on board, he picked up his hat and placed it snugly back on his head. It was his security blanket.

"Did you go out last night?" He was untangling the line on a reel.

TJ shook his head. "No. Not out. I mean, I was out. But not at a bar. Do I look that rough?"

"No man. I was just wondering why there was puke all over the bathroom inside."

"Son of a..." he trailed his thoughts. "I'll go clean it."

"I already took care of it." He didn't take his eyes off the spool. "I thought it was from you, and I knew we had people coming on at 5, so..."

"Man, I appreciate it. I'm sorry you had to deal with that." He patted Kyle on the back and shook his head. He began to climb to the bridge and get himself together. Halfway up the ladder, he stopped and looked down. "Remind me to change the code on the door before we leave tonight."

"Will do."

FINN

Finn and the band took off around 5:20 a.m.

"Nice of you to show up." Alex was already busting on Luke for being late.

Luke climbed aboard shaking his head. "Sorry guys. Emmi had us up all night long with a fever. I was up from 2 to 3:30. I tried to give Amanda some rest because I knew she would be with them all day by herself."

"Is she going to be okay alone with them and Emmi being sick?" Finn asked, genuinely concerned.

"Yeah, I think so. I asked if she wanted me to cancel and stay with her. But she insisted on me coming."

"I'll text Whit and let her know. Maybe she can relieve Amanda for a little sometime today." Finn pulled his phone from the dash.

Morning honey! I hope you had a good run! Luke said he was up all night with Emmi. She's got a fever. Would you check in with Amanda sometime? She might need some help. Thanks so much! Love you! See you soon. Kissy face emoji

The handsome foursome untied *Weekend Vibes* and they coasted off the dock. A little later than they expected, but when you have a family, priorities change. And Finn looked forward to the day when he was able to say, "Sorry, my son has a baseball tournament" or "I was up all night with my daughter because she wasn't feeling well." They would be incredible parents. One day. Eventually.

Finn and the band had a chill ride out. None of them

were particularly chatty—they were just there enjoying each other's company on a fishing trip. A few hours later on the ledge of Baltimore Canyon, the rods were in and the depth finder showed monstrous potential!

Trolling south at a few hundred fathoms, something rammed the rod on the back right side of the boat!

Alex, the rebel, snagged it from the holder and began pumping. The other band members each grabbed a rod and began to reel, getting the lines out of the way. Finn navigated the boat to help Alex. Today was different from the other day. Monday they were yelling and cheering each other on. Today's sound was more mellow—like a well-oiled machine.

"Keep it coming, man," Trevor encouraged. "Watch for it. Watch for it." A mountainous splash disturbed the top of the indigo water. "There she is!" He pointed out the back right of the boat. Finn fine-tuned the steering to keep the line at the back of the boat.

Alex stood with his feet planted firmly on the boat deck, his arms consistently reeling. She was about 100 yards out and he had a lot more work to do to get her on board.

"Damn, she's heavy! I like them big girls! Come on, Momma! Come to Daddy." The beads of sweat started to crawl down his temples. He wiped them away with his shoulder.

"Come on baby. Come on!" *Pump. Pump. Pump.* The splash came again about 50 yards from the boat. "That's it. Come on over." Alex coaxed the fish near with that sexy talk.

Trevor snagged the gaff from the holder and stood on standby at the back. The monstrous fish was so heavy the rod looked like it was bent in half.

"Here she is! Here she is! Bring her over here! Over here!" Trevor directed Alex. Luke watched from behind.

Finn yelled from up top, "Do it now! Use the gaff!"

Trevor slammed the gaff into the front right area of the mega blue marlin that Alex just brought in. Luke wrapped the rope around the tail. It took all three men to drag her on board. Alex laid on top of the fish and gave it a big old kiss. "That's right, Momma. Come to Daddy! Wooo!"

Just as they were packing her in ice, the tip of the one rod they left in took on another hit!

"Grab it!" Luke lunged for the rod. He grabbed it and began reeling. The deck floor was soaked from the first fish and he almost fell. Steadying himself, he tried to plant his feet but the deck felt like an ice skating rink. Luke slid, toppling forward, not wanting to let go of the rod.

"WHOA! WHOA! WHOA!" Alex scooped his friend by the waist and pushed him near the fighting chair. "Sit down!" Luke obeyed. His arms and shoulders worked in sync to lure the line in with the reel. After a few minutes of hard pumping, he began to fatigue.

"What are you doing? Keep reeling!" Finn was screaming from behind the wheel of the boat. He had to look backward to make sure he didn't run over the fishing line.

"Guys, I'm so tired. I don't think I can get this one in." The lack of sleep was catching up to him—and the fish was winning.

"Guys! Wake him up!" Finn was not going to lose this fish because his friend didn't sleep last night. Dads don't sleep. They're programmed to fight through exhaustion.

Alex reached overboard with a bucket. He struggled to pull the full one up. Lifting it over the back of his friend's head, he doused Luke in a bucket of cool ocean water. Luke's eyes shot open with the shock of the cold. He swished his hair out of his face with a quick swoop of his head and belly-laughed so hard, it was now the laughing that prevented him from reeling.

"Whoa! That'll wake you up!" He grabbed the rod with purpose now. "Here fishy, fishy, fishy," he wooed.

"Yeah, boys! That's how you do it!" From the wheel, Finn roared loudly.

Reel. Pump. Reel. Pump... Rope.

Bringing in another marlin, this time a white, *Weekend Vibes* was most definitely vibing. With a 753-pound blue marlin on board and now a 1-pound white marlin, they were on their way to the top.

Finn took a break from the helm and passed it over to Trevor. Luke was still sleep-deprived and Alex was busy eating. Finn climbed down and grabbed himself a sub and a beer from the cooler. As he made his way from inside the cabin, the outrigger hit fast and hard!

"Damn! Here we go, boys!" He dropped his lunch and ran over. Grabbing the rod, he began to reel and quickly passed it over to Alex. He ran up the ladder, two steps at a time. Trevor slid down the railings skipping them all, landing with a thud.

Jamming the boat in reverse, Finn watched Alex and the line. Trevor and Luke followed their orders of reeling in the other rods that were in the way. This time, slow and steady was the name of the game. This one didn't want to be rushed. She had succumbed to the idea of being captured, but she was making them work on her clock.

An hour later, she made her debut on the back of *Weekend Vibes* coming in at 85-pounds, lifting the band a tad higher on that podium.

"We're doing it, boys!" High fives from Trevor all around.

Chomping away at the bit, *Weekend Vibes* carried in an incredible number of fish. Two blue marlins: 753 pounds and 408 pounds, three white marlins: 91 pounds, 85 pounds, and 100 pounds, and 7 mahi.

The band was back together! A reunion tour, if you would.

TJ AND MARLIN

Even after last year's false polygraph test, today was the hardest day of fishing that TJ had ever had. Monty's crew had come to play hard today, and TJ was just not in the right mindset.

Leaving the docks on time was a challenge. TJ was distracted. Luckily, Kyle was there to keep him straight. Riding out directly east today was different for TJ. He wanted to try something new. Maybe this would keep him more motivated. He wouldn't be able to talk to Jules for the next eight hours at least, and each minute of not being able to explain everything was killing him inside.

Monty took notice of TJ's mood.

"Something troubling you today, Captain?" He sat next to TJ as they trolled new territory.

"I am a bit distracted today. I'm sorry. Nothing that I can't get through though." He stared along the horizon, the boat drifting over the rolling waves.

"Does it have to do with a lady perhaps?"

TJ nodded, still staring off. "But I don't want to trouble you with my problems. We're here to fish."

"Yes. I appreciate that. But we have the time." He took a lengthy taste of his beer. "I myself was your age once. I know I don't really look like it. But if there's anything that I've learned in my years, it is that if it's meant to be in the long run, it will be. Simple as that. I know it's cliche and sounds juvenile. But it's true."

Looking over at Monty, TJ asked, "Has something ever gotten screwed up so badly that it passed the point of no return?"

"Oh yes. A few times, actually. When I was just out of high school, I had a girlfriend. Her name was Ada. We were young. I was going to ask her to marry me. I bought a ring. The diamond was maybe the size of a pencil point. Back then I didn't have a lot of money. But before I got the chance to propose to her, I was drafted into the military and I decided not to propose."

TJ wanted to interject and ask why someone would choose not to propose to the love of their life. But he didn't want to interrupt.

Monty continued. "My father told me that I was a fool if I thought that a girl like that would wait around for me while I was off, possibly getting myself killed. He talked me out of it. I spent four years touring overseas. Ada and I wrote letters back and forth for two years. She was, in fact, waiting for me. But as the third year of my tour began, her letters came less often and when they did, they were brief. In her final letter to me, she wrote that she had fallen in love with a man named Bill. And they were engaged. She apologized. She wrote that she still loved me, but she couldn't wait around any longer. She wanted to start a family and felt that her time was running out." He looked over and TJ with sad eyes.

"Wow. Did you ever see her again?"

Monty cleared his throat. "I did. But it was too late. She passed away of brain cancer at the age of 42. The last time that I saw her, she was lying in a casket wearing the beautiful set of pearl earrings that she never took out. And no wedding ring. I had found out only weeks before, that she had gotten a divorce several years earlier, just after giving birth to her third daughter. I had kept that engagement ring all those years tucked away. I couldn't fathom getting rid of it. It was meant for Ada and only Ada.

"I cautiously approached her daughters at the funeral parlor and explained who I was. I told them about the ring and asked them to take it. I wanted them to have it. Susanna, her eldest daughter's eyes welled up when I told them our story. She walked away briefly and returned with an old box. She handed the box over to me. Inside the box were all of the letters that I had written to her from my years in the military. And underneath the letters laid a tattered photo of me in my uniform from so many years ago. On the back in her pristine cursive handwriting, I read: 'The love of my life.' To be honest, at that point I could hardly contain my emotions. Her middle daughter sat and consoled me. She asked if I would stay and be a pallbearer. Their father was no longer in the picture. He had run off with some other woman and left them all high and dry. Of course I stayed. I loved her."

TJ was speechless. At one point he almost forgot he was driving the boat.

"The next day at the funeral, I sat with the girls in the front row. No one questioned who I was, and even if they did, I didn't care. Right before I walked up to say my final piece, Susanna had placed something in my hand.

"The ring," TJ stated.

"The ring. I took it from the box. I slid it on Ada's left ring finger. I kissed the top of her hand and gently placed it back. The lid to the casket closed."

TJ didn't know what to say.

"I'm not sure if that's the answer you were looking for. The short piece of advice would be to do what you feel is right." He quickly interjected. "Don't get me wrong. I love my wife and my life now. And even she doesn't know that story. But I often think about what my life would be like had I not taken my father's advice."

TJ stood driving the boat, mindlessly driving along the ledge. TJ and Monty didn't say anything for a few minutes. They didn't need to.

The zip of the line being taken by a fish snapped them both back to reality. Monty slapped TJ on the shoulder. "Chin up! We got a fish on!"

Walt was in the fighting chair by the time Monty climbed down. The fish was an easy reel. It didn't put up much of a fight. By the time they got her near the boat, she wasn't large enough to take her in. They released her and Kyle reset all the rigs and lines. It was a sign of hope that there were fish in the area. Maybe even more of a sign that TJ would push through this issue with Jules.

The guys were downstairs sipping their scotches neat. They laughed and talked about what the 'good ol' days' looked like. Except for Brendon. He just sat around and listened. The fishing was steady. Nothing large to speak of and lots of fish were released. They definitely wouldn't be making any moves up on the leaderboard in the marlin category. They had a handful of tuna on board with a couple of mahi. Maybe they could make the cut in those categories. They discussed how they were going to cook it when they got back home to New York.

Two bottles of scotch were emptied by the time 3:30 hit. They were all ready for a nap on the ride home. Kyle pulled the lines up and gave TJ the go-ahead. TJ turned the boat west and headed back toward Sunset Marina. He drove the boat faster than normal. He wanted to get close enough to be able to text Jules and ask if he could meet her. If she didn't answer, he would go over to her house and knock on the door.

When the boat was a few minutes from the Ocean City buoy, TJ slid his phone up. He opened the text thread with Jules. No responses. His heart shattered all over again.

JULES

Jules' day at work dragged. It was miserable. It was hot and she had no motivation to be there. But she trudged through and made it home around 5. She didn't feel like cooking. Jules opened her phone and texted Kit.

Walking tacos?
I'll get the bikes! And I need to talk to you!
Same.

Kit got the bikes and propped them up on their kickstands outside. This was kind of a girl's tradition. They loved walking tacos from Fishtales—but they loved riding their bikes there even more to get them. The afternoon air was becoming surprisingly cool. The sun hung just above the bay. It was going to be another beautiful sunset in Ocean City.

"Ready to go?" Kit yelled out, the front door slamming behind her. "Wait until I tell you what happened last night!"

"Wait until I tell *you* what happened this morning. But you go first." Jules loved that she and Kit were able to talk openly about relationships and guys. It was nice to know she had a confidant.

Jules grabbed her keys and threw them into the front of the basket on her bike. She purposely left her phone inside. Jules and Kit hopped on their beach bikes and headed down Edgewater to St. Louis Avenue.

"So, what's your news, Kitten?" She had given Kit that nickname when she was born. Kit had been a tiny baby weighing in around three pounds. Her parents tried to teach her to be gentle like she was holding a kitten. Ever since then, Kit was 'Kitten'.

Kit laughed and took a deep breath. "I met this boy last night at a party on Teal Drive. His name is Nathan, and he is so cute! We hung out all night. Until the party was over, which was early because the cops showed up."

"Oooo. That's not good. I mean the cops part. But the new boy you met sounds nice."

"He's kind of surfer-like. He's tall. But everyone's taller than me."

Jules nodded her head. "That is true."

"He has brown hair and he's really tan. Oh! And he's starting Salisbury in the Fall!" Kit was grinning ear to ear talking about her latest crush.

"Does he work? Where does he live?" Jules wanted the basic info.

"He lives down here. And I'm not sure where he works. I didn't ask."

"What else did you find out about him?"

"We didn't do a ton of talking..." Kit's voice trailed off. Her face blushed and she smiled innocently at Jules.

She didn't blame Kit for going out and having a good time. As long as she was smart about what she did, she approved. Kit had a good head on her shoulders.

"What about your news? What happened with that guy, TJ? Are you going to see him again?"

"Um. Absolutely not. We had this incredible date on Wednesday. He took me clamming at the sandbar."

"That's cool. Like we did with Dad growing up."

"Yes. He packed a picnic lunch and Marlin sat on my board on the ride over and back. We had so much fun! Then we had a clamming competition."

"You crushed him."

"I lost on purpose because I wanted to have dinner with

him that night, too. I really liked him. He made clams casino for me and we talked all night on the deck."

"When I got home, he was still here. That's why I'm confused about why you don't want to see him."

"I had such a wonderful time with him last night. I couldn't even sleep. So I decided to grab two cups of coffee and wish him good luck before he went out to fish this morning."

"Okay..." They cut through the church parking lot on 17th street.

"When I got to the dock, I started looking for the name *Big Distraction*. And right as I spotted it, I saw TJ kissing a girl that he had just walked off his boat."

"Dang," was all that could escape Kit's mouth. "Are you sure it was him?" Her eyebrows scrunched together.

"Yep. He ran after me when he saw me. I guess I caught him off-guard. He probably never thought that I would ever come down to the boat. So why not have a girl over to sleep with him."

"I'm sorry. Now I feel bad for talking about my good news."

The two girls peddled their bikes down the back roads to Fishtales and locked them up on the fence. Jules grabbed her keys and hung them from her wrist.

"Crap. I forgot my wallet." Jules stopped in her tracks.

"It's fine. I got it." Kit held hers up.

Kit and Jules walked and checked in with the bouncer. They weren't drinking so they didn't need wristbands. The two girls walked past the long line of vacationers waiting for a table. On the overhead intercom, a young girl's voice echoed, *"Cooper, party of four—your table is now available."*

Jules and Kit walked up to the outside bar closest to the water. They each ordered a walking taco and a water. The girls sat at the bar discussing what Jules should do.

"Well, I think you should hear him out. What if it's not

what you think?" Kit said while taking a sip of water.

"It was pretty clear what was happening. He left my house and went to meet up with another girl on his boat."

"From all of the other stuff you've told me, it doesn't sound like something he'd do. You ticketed the guy and he still wanted to take you out."

A young barback with tousled brown hair came and delivered their walking tacos. Kit's mouth dropped. She grabbed Jules' leg, digging her nails into her tan skin.

"Thank you," Jules said to the barback. "Ow! What is wrong with you?" She swatted Kit's hand away.

"Jules!" Kit leaned into her sister's ear. "That's him! That's Nathan. The guy from the party."

"He's cute. Why didn't you say hi?"

"He looked right at me. Why didn't he recognize me?"

"Next time he comes over, say hi to him. What's the worst that can happen?"

"Um. Lots of stuff can go wrong!" Kit almost lost her appetite, but there was a delicious walking taco in front of her that she wasn't going to let go to waste. *But why didn't he say hi to me?* she thought to herself.

"Are you sure it's him?" Jules loaded salsa into her taco bag.

"Seriously? My tongue was down his throat. I remember what he looks like."

"I don't need gory details. Maybe it just looks like him." Jules flagged down one of the bartenders.

"Excuse me." The bartender walked over slinging his bar rag over his shoulder.

"The bar back that just delivered our food—what's his name? He looked familiar."

"That's Josh," the bartender replied, half paying attention as he listened to another customer's drink order.

"Thanks." She turned to Kit. "See. It's not him. You said his name was Nathan. That guy's name is Josh."

"I'm telling you. That is *him*." Kit finished her taco and sipped her water. "I need to ask him before we leave. It'll kill me if I don't ask now. Why would he tell me the wrong name?"

"Weirder things have happened," Jules said sarcastically, enjoying her food.

Jules looked around for her wallet.

"Oh my God, I forgot my wallet." She ran her fingers through her hair knowing that she was distracted before she left.

"We already went over this. It's no biggie. Here." Kit threw Jules her wallet as she finished her drink.

"I'll pay you back. I just wasn't thinking straight when we left the house." Jules took Kit's credit card from her wallet. Kit was now on her phone, probably texting Laney. The bartender collected the little black checkbook and swiped the card in one quick motion. It was obviously not his first time. He delivered the book back and thanked the girls for coming in. Kit signed and left a gracious tip.

"Ready?" Jules asked Kit, swiveling off of her bar stool.

"There he is. He's coming back over here." Kit shooed Jules away. "I'll meet you by the bikes."

Jules got it. No one wants their older sister hanging around when they're talking to a boy they like. She left Kit at the bar and walked along the pier. The pirate ship was busy with kids climbing up and down. Some sat getting their faces painted just inside the gate. She loved seeing families spending time on vacation. She always loved when her parents and Kit come into town for a week. They all stay at her house. It was like when they were little. Their mom would make French toast and bacon, brew fresh coffee, and make a cinnamon-y coffee cake to accompany it. They played board games and made dinner together. They went out to dinner one night of the week and they discussed which restaurant to go to all week long. It was already August and they hadn't said when they were coming in. She'd call them tomorrow.

Kit leaned on the bar waiting for "Josh" to come back over. He delivered a basket of Thai shrimp and crab dip to the couple to her left. He looked up and smiled at her.

"Hi! I didn't know you work here." She fiddled with her phone in her hand. "Remember we met at Logan's party the other night? We rode the jet ski."

"Yeah! That was an awesome party. Too bad it got busted."

"I had a really fun time with you on the jet ski."

"Wow." He dragged both hands through his hair. "I rode the jet ski? I was so wasted that night, I don't remember hardly anything."

Feeling a bit embarrassed, Kit could feel her face getting more red. *He doesn't even remember kissing me or holding my hand.* She could feel her throat begin to tighten as she tried not to cry in the middle of the bar.

"Well, it was good to see you." Kit turned to walk away. She could faintly hear him yell something behind her. It sounded like, "What's your name?" A single tear slid down from the corner of her eye and down her cheek. She felt stupid. *He doesn't even know who I am.* And to top it off, she was now crying while walking through a crowded bar in front of a bunch of strangers.

Kit finally made her way through the maze of people and reached the bikes where Jules was waiting. Jules' face turned from happy to concerned as soon as she saw Kit's tears.

"Oh my God, Kit. What's wrong? What happened? Why are you crying?"

Kit began to hiccup.

"He doesn't even remember anything from the party that night. Not us riding the jet ski. Not holding my hand. Not kissing me. None of it. I feel so stupid. He even asked me what my name was just now." *Hiccup!*

Jules' heart broke for her little sister. Falling for a boy wasn't easy; especially when he just completely tramples your heart. "Whether they mean it or not, boys suck sometimes." She reached over and took her sister in a hug. She smoothed her brown hair down and rocked back and forth. "We just wear our hearts on our sleeves. I think we need a break from boys. Come on. Let's get home for some ice cream and watch *Pretty Woman*."

Kit sniffed and caught her breath. They unlocked their bikes and began the peddle back home.

Jokingly, Jules said, "You don't think that there's two of them, do you?"

"Huh?"

"Like twins." She laughed and shrugged.

"Yeah, right. What are the odds of that?"

LEANNE

After Leanne's exciting morning, she ran home to change and head to Sunset Marina. Harbor Island was buzzing with excitement over the weigh-ins. Rob had been knocked into 3rd place—but there was still time for him to get back up. He was fishing today, and then his final day was tomorrow. Fingers crossed.

She showered and dressed in a flowy navy blue sundress. Her hair was curled and her make-up looked perfect. *Was she trying to make a point to someone?*

Josh was working at Fish Tales and Nathan at Ropewalk tonight. Both boys loved making their own money. She had to admit, it was really nice.

She checked her phone. 5:10. This was the earliest she had been home in weeks. Getting in her car, Leanne felt...nervous. Why was she nervous? She had been to Sunset several times during the past twenty years. There was no reason to be nervous...but something inside her couldn't shake the feeling.

It took a little bit longer to drive over there from Harbor Island. The summer traffic was heavy as to be expected, in addition to the tournament traffic. Finally finding a parking place when she arrived, she put her car into park, climbed out, and texted Rob as she walked toward the boat slip.

I'm here. Walking down now.
Oh good! See you soon.

Leanne wanted a martini but she didn't want to stop at the bar. If Summer was working, she may do something that she would regret. She bypassed the bar and headed straight for *The Other Woman*. It was almost as if the boat was playing a sick joke on her. But Leanne had her own secret. So there.

Walking toward the boat, Leanne saw from afar that Rob had someone on the boat with him. He mentioned yesterday that someone would be meeting him regarding a charter. Maybe she should wait. By the time she got close enough to see, her heart felt like it had actually stopped in her chest. It was too late to turn back now. Rob had already seen her.

"There she is now." He pointed toward Leanne.

The man on Rob's boat turned around. He smiled.

"Dean, this is my wife, Leanne. Leanne, this is Dean."

Danger! Danger! Danger!

He extended his hand to Leanne. "Pleasure."

She couldn't breathe.

"Nice to meet you." He held her hand just a second too long for her liking. It was one thing when they were wrapped in the sheets of an ocean blue bedroom or having a secret rendezvous with martinis—but this! This was...dangerous! What the hell was he doing there?

"Leanne is the best real estate agent on the Delmarva." He held out his hand to help her on board. She left her sandals on the dock.

"Oh stop," she said, slightly blushing from the compliment, or perhaps the nerves rattling inside her body. She wasn't sure.

"Dean was just telling me he's looking to buy a place down here. I gave him your card." He was the doting husband, trying to be supportive; especially since she was here at the dock. It had been a long time since she had been there. And for good reason.

Leanna was sitting on the side of the boat, legs crossed away from Dean. She needed to chill out before she gave herself away. "I'd love to help you find a place. Give me a call sometime and we can talk about what you'd like me to do to you—*for* you." She stood up. *Get away fast.* "I think I'm going to walk up to the bar and get a drink."

"Yeah, I think I'm going to walk up, too," replied the client.

"How are the martinis here?"

"Boy, you are with the right person. Leanne is a martini connoisseur." Rob laughed. "I knew you two would hit it off. Honey, will you bring me back a beer? You can put everything on my tab."

Dean stepped off of *The Other Woman*. He extended his hand to Leanne.

"Need some help?" he asked, smiling at her.

She looked at him stiffly. Rob was behind her so he wasn't able to see her facial expression.

"Thanks," she said, and she slipped her sandals back on.

"I'll be right back," she called over her shoulder to her husband. As she walked toward the bar with the guy who had given her an incredible amount of pleasure just hours ago, she wracked her brain.

"Two martinis, please." He turned to Leanne. "And what does your husband drink?" He turned and winked at her.

"What the hell are you doing here?" She leaned into the side of his face so he could hear. She hoped that her voice didn't carry with all of the other patrons around who could be listening.

He leaned on the bar. The bartender shook two martinis and handed them over. "What should I order your husband to drink?" He handed Leanne one of the glasses.

"Two Bail Money IPAs," she called to the bartender. *They may need some bail money if this thing implodes tonight.*

Dean threw a fifty on the counter and left holding martinis and the two cans for Rob.

"I was thinking that while I'm in town, I might as well get some much-needed R and R. And why not do a little fishing."

"First of all, The White Marlin Open isn't 'a little fishing.' Secondly, why on his boat? There are hundreds of others to pick from." Her martini was half gone and they weren't even back to the boat yet. She should've ordered two.

"It's fun this way, don't you think?" He eyed Leanne all the way down.

Her heart was in her chest and she was sure she was going to have an aneurysm before the night's end.

They returned back to the boat. Dean handed the two cans off to Rob. He cracked them open.

"So, Dean, when are you thinking about doing some fishing? The tournament is over Saturday. We could set something up for early next week."

"That might work. I need to check my schedule." He leaned in closer to Rob. "I've been seeing someone recently and she's been taking up a lot of my spare time if you know what I mean." A huge grin spread across his face.

Rob was jealous. Here was this incredibly handsome guy with more money than he knew what to do with. He was probably seeing someone half his age. Probably having sex three and four times a day. And then here he was. His wife had finally just had sex with him after months of practically begging.

Rob nodded his head discreetly at Dean. "Understood." He cheered his beer with Dean's martini.

"Well, I should be heading off. I know you're trying to get everything ready for tomorrow. Can I get anyone another drink before I leave?" Dean asked.

"We're good," Leanne snapped back quickly. "But thank you."

"Dean, we'll be in touch!" Rob shook Dean's hand—the hand that rubbed his wife's leg just hours before.

"Thanks, Rob. Leanne, I have your card. You'll be hearing from me." He shot her another wink when Rob was not looking.

"I look forward to it." But it was quite the opposite. She dreaded it and felt worried. *If he and Rob went out fishing for the day, what the heck would they talk about for that many hours? Would he just spill his guts and tell Rob everything? Every meeting? Every drink?* She couldn't allow this to happen.

"Nice guy," Rob said and he sat next to Leanne. "We had an interesting conversation before you got here."

Oh, God. Did he tell Rob? What was interesting? Her mind was racing a million miles an hour. And then...

"Hey, Boss!" Kevin was coming down the pier with his wife and daughters. "Mind if I bring the girls on to show them the big boat?" Kevin's youngest daughter was perched on top of his shoulders and his youngest held on to his wife Lori's hand.

Waving his arm over, Rob shouted, "Come on in! Hi girls! Look how big the boat is. Daddy gets to work on this. Isn't it big?" Rob reached over and lifted Siri, Kevin's oldest, onto the boat, then helped Lori step on. "You guys remember my wife, Leanne."

"Yes, it's so nice to see you. I see your pictures all over the place. Real estate, right?" Lori frequently read the papers.

"Yes. That's me. Good to see you again." She knelt down to Kevin's youngest, Sunny. Trying to escape Rob, Leanne asked the girls, "Would you girls like a popsicle?" That's one thing she knew that Rob kept on board in case anyone got seasick. She walked inside and retrieved two popsicles from the freezer.

Leanne walked back and handed the girls the treats. She then got off the boat. "I'm going to get another drink. Does anyone want something?"

"No thanks, honey," Rob said.

"We're good, thank you." Kevin and Lori were sitting on the boat with their family. It was a beautiful summer picture. *Sigh. If I'm going to be here, I'm going to need a stronger martini.*

Leanne made her way through the throngs of people. Because the tournament's last day of fishing was tomorrow, the docks and bars were insanely crowded. There were definitely not going to be any seats at the bar. The crowd was a sea of Pure Lure, HUK, and WMO shirts. She wiggled her way to the front.

"Martini, please. Extra olives." The man nodded his head and then immediately after, begin pouring her drink. She watched him shake the two silver cups together. It was a beautiful sight. He poured, garnished, and delivered.

"Do you have a tab open?" he asked her.

"Yes, Hennesey. Rob Hennesey."

A girl's voice came from the side of the bar. "Hey again." It was the same girl from the other night. Leanne had run off and left the girl in the dust when she looked across the bar and saw her client.

"Yes, I remember. How are you?"

"Doing good." Just then, Finn came up behind the two ladies.

"Hi, honey!" Whitney pecked him on the cheek.

"Hey, Finn!" Leanne reached over and gave Finn a hug. "It's been a long time! I saw you're doing well at the scales."

Whitney interjected, looking back and forth at the two of them. "How do you two know each other?"

"Leanne is Rob's wife. Remember? I worked with Rob on *The Other Woman*."

Whitney felt silly. "Of course! I am so sorry I didn't put two and two together the other day when we were here."

"That's okay. I wasn't thinking straight either. I've been working so much, I don't even know which way is up half the time."

"It was so good to see you, Finn. Make sure you stop over and see Rob."

"I'll stop by. See ya!"

Leanne walked away with her martini and Finn slipped

into her spot next to the bar. Whitney was confused now.

"Rob is her husband? The one you worked for?" She tilted her head.

"Yeah, why?" Finn ordered a beer from the bartender.

"Well. When I was at the pool the other day, I knew I saw her—it just didn't register until now. I went to lay at the pool and when I walked in, there was a couple there. They were all over each other. And they were making martinis. I took a nap and when I woke up, they were gone, but their martini glasses were there."

"It couldn't have been her." He took a swig from the bottle.

"I know it was her. How many people drink martinis at the pool? ...and she was drinking one just now."

FINN

Finn knew it was none of his business, but he and Rob had gotten close in the years that he worked for him. Should he say something? Was Whitney wrong? Was Leanne cheating on Rob?

ROB

Rob really enjoyed having Leanne in the middle of all the excitement of the tournament. She looked great in her little blue dress. And he loved her obsession with martinis.

He finished prepping the boat and was all set for his last day of fishing. The weather had shifted and there were chances of pop-up thunderstorms throughout the day. But it was nothing he hadn't come across before.

He would be sleeping on the boat for the last night. He also was determined to make sure he kept this great momentum going with Leanne. Maybe he would switch things up and stay at home tonight...Well, maybe.

"I'm all wrapped up here. Are you ready for dinner? Where do you want to go?"

They hadn't seen the boys in a long time, so Leanne asked to eat at Ropewalk on 82nd. They had to drive separately since it wouldn't make sense to make Leanne drive all the way back out to the boat and then home.

Nathan was busy bussing tables and didn't see his parents walk in. It gave Rob and Leanne such pride to see their kids beginning to flourish in the real world.

They ordered bada bing shrimp and crab cake egg rolls to start. Rob ordered the scallops with orzo pasta, and Leanne ordered the Atlantic salmon and vegetables.

Rob cleared his throat. "Did you know that Dean has like three other houses? One in the Hamptons, one in Key West, and the other..."

"Catalina," Leanne chimed in as she took a bite of her

dinner. *Shit. Shit. Shit.*

"That's it." They munched on their appetizers. "How did you know? Did you guys already start real estate talk at the bar? I told you that coming down to the pier would open up doors to new clients." She was getting squirmy, he noticed.

Trying to smooth any wrinkles in her story, Leanne began, "Yep. He told me what he was looking for and the types of properties he already had. So now I have some type of lead and can start looking for some places to show him." She swallowed her piece of egg roll hard. "There's Nathan!" She waved him over, happy to change the subject.

"Hey, I didn't see you guys come in. I thought you'd be at the boat tonight, Dad."

"Well, we wanted to come to see you and have dinner. And I thought about staying home tonight with Mom since I haven't seen her in a while." They both stopped what they were doing and looked at Rob, shocked. The awkward silence was strange. They looked at Rob questionably

"But tomorrow is a fishing day. You always sleep on the boat the night before. Mom said you do some type of fish dance or chant?" Leanne laughed out loud.

"I used to tell the boys that when they were growing up."

Rob laughed at the idea. I guess it did seem something like that. He sat back and crossed his arms.

"What are your plans tonight after work?" He knew it was summer and their fun started in the late hours of the evening, once everyone else in town's night settled down.

"I'm not sure yet. I met this girl the other night and I texted her to see if she wanted to hang out—but I haven't heard back from her." Someone caught his attention from the other side of the room. "Hey, I have to go. I'll see you guys later."

It took every ounce of control from Leanne to not kiss him on the cheek before he left. He wasn't a baby anymore. But he would always be her baby.

NATHAN

Hey, it's Nathan from the party.
I was curious if you wanted to hang
out tnt. I get off work at 10.
(7:21 pm)

Hey didn't know if you saw my
text. I'm off soon and thought I'd
see if you wanted to meet up.
(8:45 pm)

Nathan placed his phone back in his pocket. He wondered why he didn't get a response. He really liked Kit and wanted to see her again. Feeling a little down, he went to bus table 86.

KIT

Jules and Kit got home after their bike ride and tacos. They slipped into comfy clothes and vegged out on the couch. *Pretty Woman* was playing on the DVR when Kit felt her phone vibrate. Searching inside the blankets, Kit found it. It was a random number she hadn't saved. She swiped up. Her eyes squinted in disbelief.

"Oh my God! Seriously? That kid Nathan Josh texted me and asked me to hang out. Right after I left the bar crying? What an asshole!" She threw her phone back into the blankets.

"At least he's persistent. That's what these boys have going for them today. I've gotten a ton of texts from TJ, too."

She turned to her sister. "But I don't think TJ lied to you. I think it's something else. There's more to that story there."

Jules shrugged. "I doubt it." Jules had on her comfiest Quiet Storm hoodie that was over ten years old. It was an old trusty. She was hugging a large container of Fisher's Popcorn. Their caramel popcorn had always been a comfort food for her.

"But this guy, Nathan Josh, why would he lie about who he is? I don't have time for that."

"Now I think there's more to *that* story. You should text him back," Jules said, popping a piece of caramel popcorn into her mouth.

"No thank you."

TJ AND MARLIN

TJ was now close enough to land that he had cell service. About an hour out of Harbour Island Marina, TJ needed to get to the scales, but hightail it to Jules' house. He wasn't going to go down without explaining what had happened.

The boat parade through the inlet was one of TJ's favorite parts of the marlin tournament. People lined up at the inlet, parked their cars, set up tents, and cheered as captains and anglers came in. Boats were decorated with flags of caught fish right side up and upside down for releases—blue marlin, white marlin, tuna, wahoo, dolphin, and shark. *Big Distraction* proudly flew several flags as TJ made his way along the jetty. Parents whistled, kids waved, and dogs sat watching, wanting to jump in and enjoy the fun, too.

The scales were busy. They had to wait for a little outside the marina for the boats in front to weigh in their catches. When it was finally their turn, TJ maneuvered *Big Distraction* along the pier. Tank, the weigh master, came over to get the first fish hooked up.

Over the intercom, the emcee announced, "*And here we have Big Distraction out of Ocean City, Maryland captained by TJ Moxley and Marlin the Dock Dog.*" Marlin had an official title at the tournament as well.

The emcee continued. "*We've got a couple of tuna on board! Let's see if they can make some moves on the leaderboard.*" The angler on this first tuna was Walt Jones out of Manhattan, New York. The weighmaster slowly lifted the round tuna for weighing. The cameraman zoomed in on the scale and on the big screen TJ could see '96.5' flashing!

"*And we got a 96-and-a-half-pound tuna here from Big Distraction!*" The crowd clapped and cheered. The next tuna was then handed off the boat and hung to weigh.

"*And we've got an 81-pounder off of Big Distraction. And the angler was Brendon Smith from Manhattan, New York as well. Come on over guys and get that picture for us.*"

TJ handed off four dolphins coming in at 37, 32, 28, and 26 pounds. The anglers, Kyle, TJ—and of course—Marlin all stood around the slew of fish from the boat today. It was a good day looking from the outside. TJ was glad he was able to put some fish on the boat and keep them in the winning column... But he needed to get back to Sunset to drop off the boat before heading over to Jules.

ROB

Who was he kidding? His family was right. He drove back to Sunset Marina to sleep on the boat. As he drove over the Ocean City bridge back to West OC, he could see the most brilliant nighttime sky. The colors were deep purple and pink, with streams of navy blue running through. Ocean City did have some of the best sunsets he'd ever seen.

Traffic was light but Rob drove distracted. He couldn't help but think about the conversation that he and Dean had before Leanne arrived. Rob began to think of Summer. *I wonder if she's closing the bar?*

About five minutes out of the Sunset, he picked up his phone.

You working the bar tonight?

Yes sir.

See you soon.

(smiley face emoji with tongue out)

Rob slid onto a bar stool at Teasers. Without a word, a beer appeared in front of him along with two shots of whiskey. They threw back the shots. Two more were delivered a few minutes later. And then again. And then again. Rob remembered stumbling out of the bar toward the parking lot for something. He felt a hand on his back. When he turned around, there she was. All five feet of her. They made out like teenagers on prom night up against the side of his truck. He knew people were walking by, but he was so intoxicated that he didn't care to hide.

That led to her coming back to the boat. It was like De-Ja'Vu—except this time, his wife didn't interrupt. He passed out in bed and didn't wake up until the next morning.

WHITNEY

Whitney was pregnant, and she wanted a special way to tell Finn. She didn't want to make it super grand because of everything they'd been through. But she did want to make it special.

After Finn and *Weekend Vibes* bolted up the leaderboard for their monstrous blue and white marlins, Finn and Whitney had a few drinks with the band. Whitney got ice water with lime that looked like a gin and tonic. The boys celebrated with shots. Whitney said she was driving, and no one knew any different. It was their last day of fishing and they were on top of the world!

It was getting late. They paid their tab and decided to leave. Walking out of the marina, Finn held Whitney's hand. He leaned down and kissed the top of her fingers. He was the best husband and would make an incredible father. They decided to drive home together and get Finn's car in the morning.

Approaching Whitney's car, Finn could see the silhouettes of a couple a few feet away. It was a man and a woman. She was much shorter than the man. The man looked familiar, but Finn had a few beers in him so he couldn't be sure. They seemed to be awfully entangled with one another like teenagers. As they got closer, Finn's vision became crystal clear. It was Rob Hennesey and Summer, the bartender. Whitney was wrong. Rob was the one cheating on Leanne. He couldn't believe it. Whitney looked up at Finn with wide eyes.

"Is that...?"

Finn cut her off. "Yep."

TJ AND MARLIN

TJ got the boat situated in the slip. Sunset Marina was packed. Only one more day of fishing and people were out and about, drinking and dancing. Except TJ. He and Marlin were on their way out of the marina. Marlin jumped in the back of the Jeep ready to go.

TJ slid his phone open and called Jules. The phone rang a few times. He put the car in gear and took off, headed toward her house.

Her voicemail came on. *"This is Jules. Leave a message."*

"Hey, Jules. It's me. I'm on my way over. I need to talk to you. I'll be there in about half an hour." He hung the phone up as he passed Eagle's Landing golf course.

The weather had gone from the hinges of hell to a much cooler breeze. TJ turned the heat on. A few raindrops had begun to pepper his windshield. The radar had shown pop-up showers beginning later this evening, but I guess they had changed their mind.

The jeep drove past the line at Dumsers, then the pavilion of Hooper's Crab House. He turned right toward downtown then made an immediate right heading toward MR Ducks. The rain began to come down more steadily. TJ and Marlin now had water dripping from their faces. He drove with purpose toward Jules. He didn't care if he made an ass of himself. He needed her to know the truth.

He pulled up just feet from her front door. He ran up and knocked on the door. Marlin, now soaked, stood at TJ's heels.

Jules and Kit had fallen asleep on the couch. A loud knocking woke them both up.

Rubbing her eyes, Jules said, "You stay here. Don't move." She rushed toward the door and cracked it open to see who it was.

"Jules! Don't close the door! I need to talk to you. Please, don't close the door." She saw TJ standing on the steps trying to talk to Jules. Kit had walked down the hall and could hear TJ's pleas. She liked him. He was trying.

"I don't have anything to say to you," Jules spoke through the crack of the door.

"You don't have to say anything then. Just listen to what I have to say." The rain was steady now and TJ was getting soaked trying to explain to Jules what she saw.

"I had the most amazing time with you this week. And then when we got to spend the entire day together yesterday... it was the best I'd ever had with someone. And then I got to cook dinner for you; it was like we were together. And I loved every second of it."

Jules was leaning up against the wall. She still had the door cracked and was able to see rain dripping from TJ's hat. Kit stood farther down the hall but heard every word TJ was saying. Her heart ached for him. She wanted someone to love her this much.

"Look, when I left you on Wednesday, it actually hurt my heart. I just want to be around you all of the time. I don't care what we're doing. We could be watching the sunset or cleaning the dishes from dinner. As long as I'm near you. That's what I want." He leaned his head up against the doorframe. His eyes had a glimmer of tears welling up. He tried to hold them back.

"And what you saw the other morning at the pier? I couldn't sleep at all Wednesday night because I kept thinking about you. I was up early and headed to the boat. When I got there, the door to the boat was open. I walked in, and that girl you saw, was passed out drunk. Her name is Mallory and we dated off and on for a while last year. She must have remembered the code to get in. I had bumped into her when I was out at lunch the other day. She bought me a drink and had it sent over. It's not something that I was pursuing. I went surfing later that day and she followed me to the beach. I want nothing to do with her. I was trying to get her off the boat. She was a sloppy mess. I am being completely honest with you." The rain relentlessly pelted down on TJ and Marlin. TJ paused a moment before he said, "Jules. I am completely and utterly in love with you."

Jules had tears in her eyes. He said he loved her. Any animosity she held toward him quickly dissipated into the torrential downpour. Her heart was exploding on the inside.

He stood there waiting—hoping that Jules would open the door. TJ gave all he had to her. He had nothing to hide.

Jules backed away from the door and hesitated a moment—and opened it the rest of the way. She stood there facing TJ. She stepped out into the rain toward him. He pulled her in and kissed her. They stood holding each other, both now soaking wet. Jules' tears washed away with the rain.

Kit was speechless as she watched Jules and TJ's relationship unfold right in front of her. It was like watching *The Notebook* in real life. She wiped her own tears on her sleeve.

Friday

Category: White Marlin
1st Place: Weekend Vibes
2nd Place: The Other Woman
3rd Place: Big Distraction

Category: Blue Marlin
1st Place: Weekend Vibes
2nd Place: Salty Bitch
3rd Place: One and Only

Category: Tuna
1st Place: Big Distraction
2nd Place: Weekend Vibes
3rd Place: The Other Woman

ROB

Rob woke up on the boat Friday morning. It was pouring. Spotty showers were expected, but last-minute Mother Nature had different plans. It was their last day of fishing and he didn't want to opt-out.

Making his coffee, he grabbed some medicine to get rid of the pounding headache.

He wasn't sure what he was feeling this morning. Guilt, pleasure, pain? Emotionally, he was torn. Rob wanted to be with Leanne and his family. On the other hand, he should have some type of remorse. But he had none. He was almost numb to any of it now.

"Morning, Boss." Kevin came on board. Rob wasn't even dressed yet. Rob had been too distracted by his thoughts that time had gotten away from him.

"You doing okay? You're looking a little rough this morning." Kevin sipped on his sweet iced tea.

Rob was out of it. He went to stand up and get himself together. "Yeah. Just stayed out too late last night. I'm getting dressed now."

Kevin sensed that there was more but didn't press. He slid into his waders and slicker. It was going to be a wet day but there were still fish to catch.

Bill and his family showed up at five on the dot. The weather was dreary but the family had all the energy in the world to tackle just one last day on the open ocean.

"Last day guys," Rob said as they climbed aboard. "It's going to be rough but we got some fish to catch. You ready?"

"Let's do this!" Bill and his family were all decked out in their rain gear and ready to go.

"To the canyons!" Rob announced. Lines were off and out they went.

TJ AND MARLIN

TJ had gotten only a few hours of sleep. But it was well worth it. He had put everything out on the line last night. Jules obviously didn't want anything to do with him when he had first arrived. But after pouring his heart out and explaining everything, she fell into his arms. They kissed in the rain. It was like an old romantic movie you see on TV. They sat up all night long together talking, Jules laying in TJ's arms on the couch. He didn't leave her house until about 1 a.m., giving him only four hours of sleep.

He knew today would be hard with the lack of sleep in addition to the unexpected change in the weather, but he felt one hundred percent better than yesterday. He and Jules were together and he couldn't be happier. Everything was cleared up and they could now move on with their relationship.

TJ and Marlin got to the boat a little later than normal, around 4:35. Kyle was already there. Everything was in place and there was nothing that was going to stop them! TJ was going to get them back on top of the leaderboard—no ifs, ands, or buts.

Monty and his crew climbed on board not a minute too late. All of the men were excited at the prospect of getting back on top, and their enthusiasm showed. It was their last day of fishing, and they were going to make it count.

FINN

Finn slept in. It was Friday and it was pouring. He was on cloud nine at the top of the leaderboard. Late last night, he saw the weather forecast and decided to opt-out of fishing today. Not to be cocky, but he was winning by a lot. Finn was also mending a headache from all the fun he and the band had last night celebrating their monster billfish. Young at heart but not when it came to drinking anymore.

He rolled over and was shocked that Whitney was still in bed. She never slept past seven. Slowly waking up and walking to the kitchen, he went to make his gorgeous girl coffee in bed.

Finn walked back in with two mugs. One black and one with cream and sugar. He set them both on her nightstand. Her hair was tousled and messy. She wore no makeup. She took it off every night to avoid wrinkles later in life she said. She was the most beautiful woman he'd ever laid eyes on. She was more beautiful today than the first day he met her. He sat on the side of the bed watching her sleep. He would do anything for her.

With the money from the tournament, they would be able to start the adoption process they had been talking about for a while now. If that's the road they needed to take to become parents, that's what they would do.

Whitney began to stir. He brushed her hair out of her face.

"Good morning, beautiful." She stretched and smiled back.

"I smell coffee," she said sleepily.

"I made you coffee in bed."

"Mmm. Thank you." She slowly sat up against the headboard and took a sip of the deliciously dark drink he had handed her. "I want a French Cruller. From Laytons." She looked over her coffee mug at Finn.

He laughed and kissed her on the forehead. "I'll be back in a few minutes." Finn threw on some gym clothes and headed out for donuts.

JULES

Jules made her and Kit breakfast—bacon and egg sandwiches, their dad's recipe. The secret was a little bit of mayo on the toasted bread.

Kit made them coffee and walked it to the table.

"So last night was..." Kit stopped.

"Unbelievable. I didn't want it to end."

"I told you there was something more to the story."

"Yes, you did. I'm sorry I didn't listen to you." Jules sipped her coffee.

Kit smiled. "I'm really happy for you two. I want a guy to tell me how much he loves me like TJ did to you last night. He stood in the rain for you! That's love." She took a huge bite of her egg sandwich.

"It was romantic."

"Where is he today?"

"Today's his last day fishing in the tournament. I'm going to go to the pier later for the weigh-ins. You should come with me."

"Sure. I have nothing else to do." She talked with a mouthful of eggs.

"That's the spirit."

TJ AND MARLIN

Three hours southeast at the canyons, *Big Distraction* was rocking and rolling over the gigantic waves that were brought in with the rain. Four to five-foot waves lifted the boat up and down with each passing swell. Brendon had been in the cabin throwing up since they left the Ocean City buoy. He asked if he wanted to turn back and drop him off—not ideal, but he's been there before. Sea sickness is a monster of its own. Brendon had passed. He wanted to finish the tournament strong, even if it meant hurling over the side of the boat every few minutes.

Kyle was kicking ass on the deck. Lines were out and baited.

"Let's go now!" TJ was at the wheel. Monty and Walt stood holding on to the rails waiting for some big ones to hit! All of the men looked like the guy on the fish stick box.

After a few minutes of trolling south, the left spreader hit!

Zzzz!

"Fish on, baby!" Kyle yelled at TJ. "Let's go! Let's go!"

Monty ran over and grabbed the rod. She was pulling hard and running with the line. TJ followed her patterns at the same time trying to keep the waves at bay.

The wind was picking up speed and the rain was coming in sideways, pelting Monty and Kyle in the face.

"Come on baby! Come on in here! We got this!" Monty was pumping hard and fast. His adrenaline was taking over. Harder and harder! *Pump! Pump! Pump!*

Brendon staggered to the doorway to watch as Walt was bringing in the fish. The rod was bent over like Brendon was hurling over the side of the boat. Kyle stood nearby in his bright orange waders and rain jacket. The wind had knocked his hood back and his face was soaked and dripping.

TJ was up top. Rain was being blocked by the plastic windows that he had snapped on earlier that day. Even though they were buttoned tight, the wind still snuck in gusts of rain, getting TJ damp.

It was hard to see over the chop of the waves, but TJ saw a flash of the fish thrash from the back of the boat.

"Yeah, baby! Straight back! Keep it coming in! She's a big one!" The fish wasn't cooperating with the waves and the boat had to go straight into the waves—an unfavorable situation for the boat. Still, TJ needed to keep everyone safe on board.

"Watch out! Hold on!" Kyle grabbed the fighting chair to stabilize himself as a wave smashed over the back of the boat. Monty lost his footing for a second but damn it, he would not let go of that rod.

Still grinding it in, Kyle saw the thin body of the gigantic fish coming in on the right side of the boat where Brendon was hurling.

"Move man! Get to the other side!" Kyle yelled and shoved him back.

Monty followed with the rod as Kyle leaned over trying to grab the bill. The monster thrashed back and forth. The boat fell rapidly up and down the swell of the waves. Rain was coming down in buckets! Kyle grabbed the bill. It took all of his might and balance to drag the monster over the side. The fish slipped and fought back. She wasn't going down without a fight! The massive marlin had to have been over five hundred pounds. And with the pouring rain, it made it even more dangerous leaning over to get her in. Kyle took a final yank, planting both feet firmly on the deck. Brendon was even able to catch a second wind and help heave the fish in. The boat swayed right with the added poundage on deck.

The guys went wild! TJ jumped up and down! Kyle was pumping with adrenaline. Even Brendon had more color on his face as he momentarily stopped throwing up. Monty and his crew yelled and screamed over top of the million-dollar blue marlin. This was one of the biggest marlins TJ had ever seen!

"Hell yeah, boys! Let's keep it up!"

Just then TJ heard a "May Day" call on channel 16. He turned the volume up so he could hear it over the wind and rain...

"The Other Woman! The Other Woman! To Coast Guard, Coast Guard. Other Woman, Other Woman, Coast Guard, Over."

"This is The Other Woman, Other Woman. I've lost steering capabilities and I'm taking on water. Over."

Radio Screech. "Coast Guard, Other Woman, Roger Captain. How many people are on board and can you give me a GPS position? Over."

"This is The Other Woman to Coast Guard. There are eight people on board. The coordinates are at 37.45 North and 78.483 West. Over."

"Coast Guard to Other Woman, I need the vessel length and make. Over."

"Other Woman to Coast Guard. It's a 61' Buddy Davis, white and blue. Over."

"Coast Guard to Other Woman, Can you tell me exactly what's happening out there? Over."

"Other Woman to Coast Guard, We've lost steering capabilities and we're getting tossed around like a toy out here. We're gonna need some help getting back in. Over."

"OKAY. Captain. I've got a 61' Buddy Davis, white and blue, 8 people on board with no steering, coordinates are 37.45 North and 78.483 West. I'm going to need everyone on board to get their life jackets on and stand by. We have a Coast Guard boat about 20 minutes South coming up for you. Over."

"Coast Guard, this is The Other Woman. Life jackets are on."

"Coast Guard to Other Woman. Go ahead and switch over to channel 22. Over."

"Other Woman to Coast Guard. Channel 22. Over."

That was Rob calling in for the Coast Guard to help. He looked at the coordinates Rob called over the radio. He was just North of him and could be there before the Coast Guard.

"Kyle! Get everything in! A boat called in a 'May Day' and we're going over! Hurry up!"

Their big fish celebration was cut short but with good reason. It was a known code that when any boat called in a May Day, all hands were on deck to help. Literally. Kyle, Monty, and even Brendon began to reel in all lines as quickly as they could. Depending on how much water Rob's boat was taking in, you never really know how much time you have before things got even more dangerous.

TJ charged South toward Rob's coordinates. He yelled down to the guys to look out for *The Other Woman* and anyone in the water. He didn't know how serious things were. He switched the radio to channel 22 to listen in.

Silence.

TJ picked up the radio.

"Big Distraction to Other Woman. I'm about five minutes North of you. We're on our way to assist. Over."

"Other Woman to Big Distraction. Copy."

The rain was getting lighter but the wind was still howling. The radar had not shown these conditions earlier in the day. The waves were 5-6 feet and the chop was rough. Three minutes away but with the weather beating against them, it was hard to get a direct route.

Kyle hung on tight down on the deck looking out for anything in the water. Brendon was standing straight up for the first time all day. He looked like he was feeling better. Adrenaline does that to you. The other men stood watching the waves ahead, waiting for any sign of *The Other Woman*.

Kyle used binoculars to help him see through the rain. A small boat just off their starboard caught his eye. "Over there, TJ!" He climbed up toward TJ and pointed off their bow.

TJ turned the boat facing toward *The Other Woman*. They didn't see anyone in the water, but he needed to be careful just in case.

"Big Distraction to Other Woman. We can see you off our bow. Is anyone in the water? Over."

"Negative. Everyone is on the deck wearing their life vests. Over."

"We'll get as close as we can. But the water is too rough to pull up on your port side."

"Coast Guard to Other Woman. Be careful transferring people boat the boat. This ocean—she's not very friendly today. . Over."

"Copy."

Rob could see TJ's boat approaching from their stern. They had made great timing and Rob couldn't be more grateful for the assistance.

TJ got as close to Rob's boat as possible without hitting. It was a tricky task with the ocean as unorganized as it was. TJ stayed behind the wheel to keep the boats from smashing together. He wasn't sure how to get one person from their boat to the other without getting them into the water. He saw seven people hanging onto the railings of the Buddy Davis.

"I don't want to but let me try to pull up alongside them!" He was yelling down at the group of guys below. He could see Rob on the bridge of his boat, helpless with no steering.

TJ pulled along their port side. The two boats bobbed erratically back and forth with the movement of the waves.

"Try to get one of them off. Throw them that rope and

pull them over. See if they can jump. Don't lose your grip on them," TJ yelled from the bridge! Rain began to pick back up. Kyle tossed the rope over to Kevin. Brendon stood near Kyle in case he was needed.

One of the younger ladies on the boat grabbed the rope but no one knew exactly what they were supposed to do. The boats bobbed dramatically and it was hard to get any footing.

"Hey! What about putting that rope up there through the ladder? Then they could swing over. They don't have to drop into the water!" Brendon shouted into the rain as he pointed up, trying to help.

"That might actually work." He slapped Brendon on the back. "Let go of that rope! I'm going to pull it back over!" Kyle was yelling over to *The Other Woman* as rain needled him in the face. The rope sloshed through the waves as Kyle quickly pulled it up toward their boat.

Kyle gave the rope to Brendon. He climbed up the bridge and stuck the rope through the ladder on top. He gave the end to Kevin and threw it over to the group wearing life vests. The same lady grabbed the rope and wobbled as she tried to climb up the side of the boat. She slipped once but someone was behind her and helped her stand.

She grabbed the rope tightly and jumped like a tree swing flying over and landing in Brendon's arms! He grabbed her and helped her to the deck. The other men were there to take her to the other side. Kyle threw the rope back over to the group. Another lady about the same age grabbed the rope. The men wearing life vests lifted her onto the side, trying to keep their balance at the same time. She mimicked the first woman and swung over. Brendon was there to catch her and help lift her down.

This time, an older woman came to the side of the boat. She was having a hard time standing. She was very petite and small. She couldn't have weighed more than 100 pounds. TJ had caught fish quadruple her size. The three men on *The*

Other Woman tried to reassure her she would be fine. Just as she was about to swing, the boat lurched up and a massive wave came over the side, knocking her off her feet. As the boat came down off the wave, her tiny body was tossed overboard and into the ocean right in between the two sterns.

"Man overboard! Man overboard!" This time it was Kevin that was yelling! Sharon Wallace was now getting tossed around like a rag doll in danger of being sandwiched and smashed in between *Big Distraction* and *The Other Woman*.

Kyle rushed to toss a life ring to her. Sharon scrambled to grab the ring. Linking her arms in the middle of the ring, she yelled, "I've got it! I've got it! Hurry up!"

Kyle yanked her toward the side of the boat. Brendon, leaning over the side of the boat, grabbed her by the life vest. Kyle grabbed at her legs to lift her whole body in. Sharon was on board. She was scared and in shock. But she was on. Her two daughters-in-law came to scoop her up and embrace her tightly. There were four people left on the helpless boat, not including Rob. The Coast Guard would be here soon.

Bill Wallace's sons forced him to go next. He caught the rope from Kyle. Brendon stood back a little bracing for the arrival of the gigantic man about to plunge from *The Other Woman*. Bill stood up and hurled himself over, hanging onto the rope with white knuckles. He gracefully landed on his side. He scrambled to Sharon and the girls. Walt's sons were left. The rest of the family was safely on board *Big Distraction* thanks to TJ, Kyle, and his anglers. Even though the sea was uncooperative, TJ was able to steer as smoothly as possible without hitting Rob's boat.

Adam grabbed the rope. He held onto his brother's shoulders to stabilize himself. His foot slipped off the side. He instinctively let go of the rope to catch himself. Just as he was getting ready to fall overboard, Kevin grabbed ahold of his arm. He was hanging on to him by his wrist. He was slipping! His arm was wet and his body was sloshing with the chaotic waves. Kyle threw the rope back over to them. Adam was able to grab the rope with his other hand.

"I got the rope! Let me go!" Kevin obeyed. Adam had a death grip on the lifeline. Kyle and Brendon pulled nonstop until they could touch his vest and hoist him up.

A boat approached. It was The Coast Guard. The strong and sturdy vessel slowly bobbed over the waves unbothered by the erratic movement of the ocean. *The Other Woman* and *Big Distraction* were now close enough that they were almost touching. Bill's youngest son jumped from the side of one boat to the other, landing on his knees. He got up and went to hug his family.

"The Other Woman to Coast Guard. I've got two people on board, myself and my first mate. All other anglers are now safely on Big Distraction. Thank you, Captain Moxley. Over."

"Coast Guard to Big Distraction. Are you okay to head back into the docks with all passengers aboard? Over."

"We are good over here. I'm going to move out of the way and let you help. Over."

"Thank you, Captain. Please start heading back in. Let us know where you're heading to. Other Woman, let's get you hooked in the front here so we can tow you back in. Over."

TJ, Kyle, and the others huddled near one another watching as *The Other Woman* was hooked up to the Coast Guard to be towed in. The rain was ironically subsiding, even though it would've helped more about fifteen minutes ago.

"Big Distraction to Coast Guard. We're heading into Harbor Island Marina. Over."

"We will give them the heads up. Safe travels, Big Distraction. And thank you for the assistance. Over."

LEANNE

Word was all over the radio about the distressed boat signal from Rob Hennesey. Shock rang over several marinas. Rob was as seasoned a captain as they came. People were shocked.

Someone from the Coast Guard had called Leanne and let her know of her husband's distress call.

Leanne's phone rang a strange number. She answered. "Hello?"

"Is this Mrs. Leanne Hennesey?" the caller asked.

"Yes, this is her."

"Mrs. Hennesey, this is Andrew calling from the Coast Guard."

She cut him off. "The Coast Guard? Is everything okay? Is Rob okay?"

"Yes, ma'am. Your husband sent in a distress call. His boat lost steering and was taking water over the stern because of the rough conditions. All of his anglers are safely on another boat. And he and his first mate are being towed in as we speak. It'll take them a few hours. They were out pretty far. But the good news is no one was hurt and everyone is accounted for and on their way back towards Ocean City. ."

"Oh my God!" Leanne fell back onto the couch. "Thank you! If you talk to him, let him know we're on our way to the marina and we will see him when he gets there!" She hung up the phone and called the boys immediately.

ROB

He felt like his life was this way and that. Thursday he was with Leanne. Last night he ended up with Summer. And now, he has put an entire family in danger. He needed to get his life together.

The Other Woman was being towed by the Coast Guard while he sat, powerless. He owed a lot to TJ and *Big Distraction*. If TJ hadn't come along, the situation could have gotten a lot worse.

They were about two hours from Harbour Island Marina and the weather had changed from six-foot waves down to two feet. The sun had come out and the clouds painted the most gorgeous sunset out in front of the bow.

It was an oxymoron. Being towed into the pink and red sunset felt what? Unfair? Contradictory? Lucky? How can this beautiful sunset be happening right after he just had the worst day of his life on the water? His crew of fishermen had to be rescued from his boat. Yet here he was witnessing that tequila sunrise color in the sky.

My luck is going to run out sooner or later. You need to do something before things blow up in your face. Maybe the weather opening back up was a sign that even though his life was a mess right now, just maybe he would make it out of this storm he called life.

JULES

It was around noon on Friday. Jules was dressed in her rain slicker and boots. Driving the cart around the campground, she heard her phone ping a text. Even though he was too far out of range for texting, she still hoped it was TJ. It was Kit.

She opened the text to a link. The title was "White Marlin Open Rescue." Clicking the link, a spotty swaying video appeared. From what she could see, it was of two boats, one with several people on board wearing bright orange life preservers. The transom of the boat read *Big Distraction*. The raindrops stuck to the lens of the camera phone making it hard to read the other boat's name. The waves slammed into the other boat making large splashes onto the deck. It looked as though people were swinging from one boat onto the other. Both boats were bobbing erratically from the rough sea. The wind was pushing the rain sideways.

Oh my God! That's TJ's boat!

That's what I thought. There was some type of distress call and he was the first to be able to arrive. It says six people were rescued from that other boat before the Coast Guard arrived.

We're going to the marina! Be home by 4! You're coming with me. I need some emotional support!

JULIE

TJ AND MARLIN

Big Distraction was about thirty minutes from the marina. The Coast Guard was expecting them at the scales at Harbour Island, then to the dock at Sunset Marina. The evening was turning out to be some of the most beautiful weather he's seen. He wanted to send Jules a text and let her know what was happening.

Hey! We are heading to the scales at Harbour Island and then back to Sunset. We had a big day and had to rescue some anglers that were on another boat that was in distress. If you want to come to the marina, let me know and I'll look out for you. I'd love it if you came.

OMG! It's all over the internet and social media! TJ, are you guys okay? The weather looked so dangerous!

Everyone is safe. I'm safe.

We'll see you at Sunset! I'm so glad you're okay! See you soon.

• • •

Approaching the Ocean City buoy, TJ called down, "Hey guys! We have to hit the scales before we get to Sunset. Are you guys okay to come with us?"

"Of course! We'll go anywhere you need us to," Bill yelled up to TJ. "I see you got a big one on. Let's get her to the scales!"

TJ steered *Big Distraction* through the inlet. He joined in the boat parade with the other marlin week anglers. The sun was setting and TJ could hear whistles and clapping from the shore. He loved this part of the day. It felt great to be a part of something as big as The White Marlin Open.

People chanted from the inlet, "TJ! TJ! TJ!" He looked over and *Big Distraction* was getting a standing ovation from everyone lined up. Boats in front of him and behind him blasted their horns in celebration. What TJ did was nothing heroic; it was an unspoken captain's code. They looked out for one another, no matter the cost.

TJ blasted *Big Distraction*'s horn a few times in gratitude. Cheers erupted even louder from the crowd on land. Everyone on board waved back to the people, kids, dads, moms, and dogs. They felt like rockstars.

The Route 50 bridge was opened for them as they rounded the bend in front of Frog Bar. People were sitting, enjoying the view, and waving. Cruising passed the Angler, the open bridge, then Da Lazy Lizard, boats anchored up at the sandbar watched as boats brought in million-dollar fish, listening to the emcee on the live stream coverage.

TJ and his large crew edged near Harbour Island Marina. Making a right into the canal, the crew on board heard...

"And coming in now, the big story of the day! It's TJ Moxley on Big Distraction and his crew with the addition of the anglers from The Other Woman!"

The applause was roaring from the crowd. Whistles and whoops were echoing from one side of the pier to the other. TJ pulled up alongside the scale. Dock hands threw Kyle lines to tie up. TJ came down the ladder. He gave the dockhands his information and registration.

"And what do we have coming in today, Captain?" The announcer came over with the cameraman for those viewing online.

"We've got a big marlin on board. She put up a good fight. And we got her in just in time. I can't wait to see what she weighs." Kyle uncovered the large fish as the cameraman stood with his toes on the edge of the pier.

Gasps and noises were coming from the enthusiastic fans. More clapping and more whistles followed. TJ's group of anglers smiled at the unveiling.

As TJ was being interviewed, the dock hands and Tank, the weigh master, were busy measuring length and girth to ensure it was the minimal length to qualify.

Tank yelled up, "It's a qualifying fish! Let's get her on the scale!" Again cheering.

It took seven men: Tank, Brendon, TJ, Kyle, Bill, and his two sons to maneuver the fish. The dock hand secured the fish's tail with the rope and hook. The strain of the scale began to crank. Oohs and aahs from the crowd began to get louder as the magnificent fish was slowly lifted from the boat and its grand weight came off the pier. The scale bounced numbers up and down. The bill of the fish finally came off the dock. She hung like the gorgeous trophy fish she was. A marvelous blue marlin. Everyone's eyes bore into the face of the digital scale...

"1,136 pounds!" Tank announced.

The emcee repeated it into the microphone for all of Harbour Town Marina to hear. "*We've got a 1,136-pound blue marlin from Big Distraction! This breaks a new state record and White Marlin Tournament record by one pound!*" The crowd erupted into cheers and claps!

TJ, Kyle, and the other men of *Big Distraction* jumped up and down hugging and slapping hands!

"Yahoooo!" Brendon yelled, picking TJ up in a bear hug. Monty and Walt clapped along with the crowd. The Wallace family, who was still on board *Big Distraction*, celebrated as well. They hugged and high-fived each other, including TJ's anglers. They were celebrating not only a big win for *Big Distraction*, but a huge thank you for the heroic acts of the anglers to get them off of *The Other Woman* safely.

Katherine Ruskey

The dock hands got the chalkboard ready.
Fish: Blue Marlin
Weight: 1,136 pounds
Angler: Monty
Boat: Big Distraction
Date: August 12, 2022

TJ, Marlin, Kyle, and the rest of the anglers gathered around the enormous fish. They were like movie stars. People were whooping and hollering, whistling and clapping! It was a great day for *Big Distraction*.

ROB

The Coast Guard towed *The Other Woman* all the way back to Sunset Marina. He and Kevin arrived at the slip around 8 o'clock.

Leanne and the boys were at the dock waiting. Kevin's wife was there, too. She had left the girls with a sitter.

He got off the boat feeling battered and worn out. Leanne ran over to him and hugged him. His boys were right on her tail.

"Oh, God, Rob. Are you okay? The Coast Guard called and all they would tell me was you're being towed in. What happened?"

"I'm fine. Just feel like a dog with its tail between its legs. We had a fish on, white marlin, and she was taking us in all directions. She was right out of the transom and the boat kept taking on waves over the back. Then all of a sudden, the steering went out. I had no way to direct us. The waves were brutal and the weather picked up so fast. It was a freak accident. It wasn't something that I could have prevented."

"Dad, we're glad you're okay." Nathan stood close by with Josh at his side.

"Where are all of the people from your charter?" Josh asked.

"They're over at Harbour Side Marina on TJ Moxley's boat. He heard the distress call on the radio and was able to get to us before the Coast Guard. He and his guys got the anglers from our boat onto his and brought them in."

"TJ? He's the captain of *Big Distraction*, right?" Nathan got his phone from his pocket.

"Yeah." Rob sat on the dock box.

"There are pictures of him all over the marlin social media page. They just weighed in a blue marlin at 1,136 pounds! A state and tournament record!" He held the screen up so Rob could see it. Rob glanced at the screen, feeling frankly—depressed.

"He deserves it. Good guy. Even better captain. And I appreciate what he did for me today. Glad he got some recognition." Rob felt tired and beat up. He needed to figure out what went wrong with the boat today—but he just wasn't up to it. Luckily, today was the last fishing day. He wouldn't need his boat for another few days. At least he had luck on his side with that. It's been a while.

People were starting to crowd the piers. He could hear the band playing *Uptown Girl* on the platform. Tunas were being filleted and bagged up. Boats were being shammied and wiped, spit-shined and polished. Sandals and flip-flops lay forgotten on the docks as everyone climbed onto their respective boats for cocktails, fishing tales, and laughs. People were buzzed and feeling great.

Leanne was walking back from the bar with a martini and a beer. She climbed on board, handing the beer to Rob.

"Here, you need this. I'm sorry you went through this today. Is there anything that I can do?" She knew nothing about boats or how they worked. Leanne knew the answer to her question before she even finished.

He took a huge gulp and sighed.

He wanted to be honest with Leanne. She deserved better than this.

KIT

After about twenty minutes of looking for parking, which seemed impossible during the tournament, they were finally walking toward Sunset Marina. Trucks and Jeeps slowly drove by doing the same thing Jules and Kit had just done.

Walking through the throngs of people on the piers, trying not to fall overboard, Jules went toward the slip she had seen TJ at just a day ago.

"Kit?" The girls had heard a voice coming from aboard a parked vessel. They turned around. It was Nathan Josh, the barback from the Fish Tales. He was standing there next to another boy, who looked identical to him. Kit froze.

"What are you doing down here? I've been trying to text you." He climbed off the boat and onto the dock. "But you never texted me back. Did I do something wrong?" People tried to squeeze by them, holding their aluminum cans and plastic solo cups.

"Nathan?" Kit was still in shock.

"Yeah. It's me. From the party. We went out on the jet ski—and did other stuff..." He lowered his voice as he leaned in a little closer to speak the latter.

"You have a twin brother?" She pointed over toward the boat.

"Yep. That's my brother, Josh." Josh waved. He was with a girl with blonde hair wearing cut-offs, a crop top, and no shoes.

"Does he work at Fish Tales?" Kit looked up at the sky. The sun had already set and the sky was a deep purple-blue.

"Yeah, do you know him?"

Kit was so embarrassed. "I, um... I actually bumped into him there. My sister and I went to dinner and I thought it was you. So I went to talk to him and he had no idea who I was. He told me his name was Josh...and I thought it was you blowing me off." She looked at Nathan's hair curling out from under his hat. "I am embarrassed." She slid her hands into the back pockets of her jeans shorts.

"Wow. I had no idea. I started to tell you that I had a brother at the party, but that's when we went out on the jet ski and the cops and all of that happened. I didn't get a chance to finish. I'm sorry. It's my fault."

"It was a misunderstanding." Kit shook her head and looked up at Nathan.

"I'm really glad that's cleared up. I really wanted to see you again." He smiled.

She smiled back. "Yeah, me too. What are you doing down here? Do you know the owners of that boat you're on?"

Nathan laughed out loud. "Yeah. I kind of know him. He's my dad. And really the main reason I'm here is because my mom called me in a panic. My dad's boat had taken on water and lost steering. He called a distress signal to the Coast Guard. He needed to be towed in from the canyons. He's lucky nothing worse happened. Another boat came over and helped get the people off—"

Kit cut him off. "TJ's boat! That's why I'm here. My sister and TJ are kind of seeing each other. He texted her about everything and then I showed her the video. She panicked, and that's how I ended up here. My sister is around here somewhere. I think she walked over to TJ's slip. But I don't know which slip is his."

"No way! Small world. We owe a lot to him for helping my dad. His boat's down there." Nathan pointed toward the right just passed the stage where the band was now singing *Purple Rain*.

"I'll walk with you."

Nathan and Kit walked toward *Big Distraction*'s slip. It was overly crowded due to the rescue and the record-breaking fish they just weighed. However, TJ and Jules were nowhere to be seen.

JULES

Jules made her way down to TJ's slip. A crowd had congregated around his boat. He apparently had just weighed in a big fish and everyone wanted to talk to him. She excused her way through the crowd nearing the boat. TJ spotted her in between the throngs of people. He got off the boat and went over to her.

"I am so glad to see you." He kissed her on the lips Holding her hand, he led her through the bodies and helped her onto the boat.

"Let's walk inside for a second." He opened the door of the cabin. The cool air conditioner felt good as it wrapped around her ankles, then her arms, then her face.

"What is happening out there?" Jules looked around the immaculate inside of the boat. It was one hundred times as gorgeous as her house and even more spacious.

"We just brought in and weighed a blue marlin that was 1,136 pounds! One pound over the state record."

"Wow! That's great! But what happened with the other boat you texted about? Something about the Coast Guard?"

"That's another reason there are so many people here. We heard a distress call from another boat, *The Other Woman*. We were closer than the Coast Guard so we went to help out. The weather got nasty real fast. We helped get the people off that boat and into ours. The Coast Guard got there just as we got the last person off. Rob, the captain, and his first mate stayed on their boat and were towed into their slip."

"That sounds so dangerous. I'm glad you're home safe."

TJ pulled her close and kissed her on the lips. "Come on.

Let's go celebrate!"

He grabbed two chilled glasses and a bottle of champagne from the freezer.

They walked back out on the deck. She spotted Kit on the pier. With Kit was a boy that looked to be Nathan Josh. She tilted her head to the side in question toward her sister. Kit motioned to check her phone. She immediately did.

This is Nathan. He has a twin brother, Josh, who works at Fish Tales. Laughing emoji.

Twins, huh? Who would have thought? Dancing twins emoji.

TJ AND MARLIN

Later that evening, TJ walked down the dock to *The Other Woman* to see Rob. Jules decided to hang out on the boat for a little while and people-watch. Nathan and Kit took a walk around the marina to look at the boats.

TJ found Rob sitting on the deck of the boat. Rob stood up.

"Hey. I can't thank you enough for what you did for us out there." Rob shook TJ's hand.

"Anyone would have done it. We look out for one another." Marlin was right at TJ's side wagging his tail.

"And I hear congratulations are in order. A new record for that marlin! I'm happy for you."

"Yeah, we had just gotten her on board when I heard you on the radio. We took off right as we brought her in."

"Well deserved. Great job."

"Thanks," TJ added, "I just came down to make sure you were okay."

"Besides a bruised ego, I'll make it." He rubbed his hands on his cheeks and felt the few-day-old stubble. "The Wallace family was safe. They left to go home and rest. It was a long day for them. I'm happy they're safe."

The men shook hands and said their goodbyes. TJ walked away with Marlin at his ankles. They were ready to celebrate their new state and tournament record with Jules.

ROB

After the excitement of the last tournament day had settled, Rob asked Leanne to come inside the cabin. He needed to get everything off his chest.

They sat on the sofa. Leanne rested one hand on his upper leg while the other hand acted as a resting place for her, what—third martini?

"Leanne, I wanted to talk about something." Her eyes were so brightly colored against her smooth tanned skin.

"Is everything all right?" She set her drink down on the coffee table and really looked at him.

Inside, his heart ached with the confessions he wanted to tell about Summer. About last night. He began to speak.

"I love you so much. And when I was out there today and I had no control over what was happening, do you know what I thought about? You. Not the boys, not our home, not our past—but our future. I want to start over. I want us back. I'll do anything to make this, us, better again. I miss you. I miss us."

Leanne's eyes began to mist. She could feel the tears sitting inside the bottom lids of her eyes. She wanted it, too. But were they too far gone at this point? She squeezed Rob's hand. No words came from her mouth.

"I don't know how I let our marriage get this far gone. I promise from now on to be a better husband, more attentive, and focus on mending our relationship."

Leanne reached over and kissed Rob. Her arms wrapped around his neck. Small tears trickled down her face. Her heart ached for him. Even after being married for so long, seeing him at one of his lowest moments still pulled on her heart-strings. She did love him.

She didn't need to say anything. He knew that their marriage wasn't a fully sunken ship. They would work together and mend what was broken and strengthen what still stood strong above the water.

There had been no mention of Summer. Rob had said what he wanted, even if he didn't fully unload the whole story. He even kept to himself the fact that he knew Leanne had been sleeping with her client, Dean. Regardless, he was done with the back and forth. He wanted his wife back.

ROB

After the excitement of the last tournament day had settled, Rob asked Leanne to come inside the cabin. He needed to get everything off his chest.

They sat on the sofa. Leanne rested one hand on his upper leg while the other hand acted as a resting place for her, what—third martini?

"Leanne, I wanted to talk about something." Her eyes were so brightly colored against her smooth tanned skin.

"Is everything all right?" She set her drink down on the coffee table and really looked at him.

Inside, his heart ached with the confessions he wanted to tell about Summer. About last night. He began to speak.

"I love you so much. And when I was out there today and I had no control over what was happening, do you know what I thought about? You. Not the boys, not our home, not our past—but our future. I want to start over. I want us back. I'll do anything to make this, us, better again. I miss you. I miss us."

Leanne's eyes began to mist. She could feel the tears sitting inside the bottom lids of her eyes. She wanted it, too. But were they too far gone at this point? She squeezed Rob's hand. No words came from her mouth.

"I don't know how I let our marriage get this far gone. I promise from now on to be a better husband, more attentive, and focus on mending our relationship."

Leanne reached over and kissed Rob. Her arms wrapped around his neck. Small tears trickled down her face. Her heart ached for him. Even after being married for so long, seeing him at one of his lowest moments still pulled on her heart-strings. She did love him.

She didn't need to say anything. He knew that their marriage wasn't a fully sunken ship. They would work together and mend what was broken and strengthen what still stood strong above the water.

There had been no mention of Summer. Rob had said what he wanted, even if he didn't fully unload the whole story. He even kept to himself the fact that he knew Leanne had been sleeping with her client, Dean. Regardless, he was done with the back and forth. He wanted his wife back.

Saturday

Category: White Marlin
1st : Weekend Vibes
2nd Place: The Other Woman
3rd Place: Big Distraction

Category: Blue Marlin
1st Place: Big Distraction
2nd Place: Weekend Vibes
3rd Place: Salty Bitch

Category: Tuna
1st Place: Big Distraction
2nd Place: Weekend Vibes
3rd Place: The Other Woman

TJ AND MARLIN

TJ woke up on Saturday morning a little later than usual. The crackling of bacon was coming from the kitchen and the smell of freshly brewed coffee lingered in the air. Marlin was nowhere to be seen. Getting out of bed, he found his clothes and walked sleepy-eyed into the living room.

Jules was in her pajamas cooking breakfast. Marlin was basking in the morning sun on the deck. He watched as small boats puttered out from their docks and tried their luck at some early morning fishing.

He walked over to Jules and put his hands around her waist from behind and kissed her neck. "How did I get so lucky to find you?"

She turned around and leaned on the counter. Kissing him on the lips, he pulled her in closer.

"Good morning! Coffee is in the pot. Bacon is cooking—and Marlin is enjoying his view." She pointed outside onto the deck. Marlin was taking in the new morning over Assawoman Bay. It wasn't his normal view, but he could get used to it.

TJ poured himself a cup of coffee. He walked outside onto the deck to greet Marlin. The tide was going out and there was a slight breeze. Sitting on the Adirondack chair, he took his first sip of liquid energy. Jules came out and sat on the matching chair right next to his. He held his hand out and she met him halfway. TJ held Jules' hand and didn't intend on ever letting go.

FINN

Saturday evening was the final event of The White Marlin Open. The drinks were flowing and tan lines from anglers' sunglasses were out on display.

Finn and Whitney were there with the band along with their wives and kids. Hundreds of people flowed into the hotel's event room.

Families were there with their kids. Whitney looked around thinking that this time next year, they could have a family of their own. She smiled at the thought.

The emcee announced that the awards ceremony would begin in just a few moments. People began to find a place to settle.

The banquet room was decorated in blues and whites. Tall tables were scattered around the room, royal blue tablecloths draped and cinched at the bottom. A large ice sculpture of a white marlin arched in the center of the room was lit up from underneath.

"*I'd like to welcome everyone to the final day of the White Marlin Open! It's always an exciting time to come to Ocean City, and this year proved to be no different!*" Applause and whistles roared around the grand room.

"*Just to recap, over 500 boats participated in this year's tournament making it the largest payout that the White Marlin Open has ever seen.*" More cheers and whistles! "And in addition to that, over ten million dollars in prize money!" The crowd went crazy!

The emcee stood up on stage and tapped the microphone. He held the results of the tournament in his hands on a small white piece of paper. Off to the side of the stage, trophies and plaques were lined up ready to be celebrated. "*Without further ado, I'd like to start our evening with one boat that cannot go unrecognized. I would like Captain TJ Moxley of Big Distraction to come on up with his mate and anglers. TJ and his crew showed the meaning of real sportsmanship and heroism. Our goal out here at the White Marlin Open is to catch fish, but our number one priority is keeping everyone safe while we're doing it. And Captain, you certainly showed that it's not every man for himself but we're all in this together.*" TJ and his crew received a standing ovation from the other anglers. Jules took pictures on her phone and had to wipe away a tear.

"*We have a special plaque for you and your crew. But someone else would like to present it to you.*"

Rob Hennesey walked up toward the front of the crowd. He shook the emcee's hand and then gave TJ a hug. He presented TJ with a Captain's award, shaped like a marlin. The entire group stood in front of the room full of fishermen. Claps and cheers were deafening as they all stood posing for a photo.

"*Thank you, gentlemen.*" TJ and fellow anglers returned to their families. The guys walked off stage and back to their families.

The emcee continued. "*This year, we were able to donate over ten thousand pounds of fish to the local food bank. It's because of you and your generous donations that this was able to happen.*" Applause continued.

"*And now the moment you've been waiting for. In first place in the dolphin category, we've got Captain Shannon on The Salty Bitch and their 37-pound dolphin. These ladies are coming in winning $20,000!*" The ladies of *The Salty Bitch* came up hugging each other. The room cheered and hollered for the only all-girls team in the entire White Marlin Open. These incredible ladies posed for their pictures with their enormous check.

"Next up is the shark category. In first place with a 140-pound shark, from Duck, North Carolina, Captain Cooper S., and their 140-pound shark were worth $145,000!" The captain and anglers from *One and Only* came up to accept their winnings, high-fiving, and whistling! Before posing for their pictures, Cooper called his five grandchildren, who were all under six, to join them for the celebration. The kids all yelled "Cheese!" and practically stole the show.

"All right! Next, we have the wahoo category. The minimum weight for a wahoo was 40 pounds and coming in just over that at 41 pounds was Island Girl and captain Scott C. And that 41-pound wahoo brought in a good chunk of money at $52,000. The Island Girl crew was thrilled to come up and accept their check." The crowd chanted, *"Wahoo! Wahoo! Wahoo!"* They left the stage fist-bumping everyone in their path.

"It's tuna time—and what an exciting category this was this year! We had tuna at the scales every night this week and each one of them was more impressive than the last. With that being said...in first place, coming in just shy of the state record at 234 pounds is TJ Moxley of Big Distraction!" Everyone cheered a little louder because of what they had already done for Rob Hennessey. TJ and the guys came up to accept their check for $1.1 million. They hooped and hollered and high-fived everyone in their paths! TJ loved watching the celebrations of the other boats but the feeling of being the one celebrating is even better. Accepting this check gave him a jolt of energy. He leaned down to pick up Marlin, who was donned out in his fancy marlin bandana specifically bought for the ceremony. The men all posed for their photo holding the enormous check in front of them.

"We saved the last two categories for last—and you all know what they are." More applause and whistles. *"The White Marlin Open has been around for almost fifty years. And we set yet another record this year. With an incredible weight of 1,136 pounds, breaking the tournament and state record...put*

your hands together yet again for our blue marlin category winner—TJ Moxley, and his anglers on Big Distraction! The guys will be bringing home a whopping $1.5 million!"

The guys walked up again, all grinning ear to ear. They shook hands with the emcee. Brendon had brought up a bottle of champagne. As they posed for their photos, Brendon shook the bottle. Twisting off the cork cage, he placed his hands on the cork and aimed high, *Pop! Cheers! Applause!* Champagne flowed out. He took a swig right from the bottle and passed it on to the next guy. Each fellow took a slug of the sweet, chilled champagne. Off the stage, cups were filled and laughs were exchanged.

"And last but not least, the one thing we've all been waiting for—the white marlin category! This year's tournament brought in 517 white marlins!" Applause and cheers. *"Every day you guys brought in the excitement to the scales. We love watching the boats coming in flying those marlin flags with pride."* Applause.

"Without further ado, let's get down to it. With a thick 1,001 pound white marlin, worth $3.6 million, we have Captain Finn Donahough on Weekend Vibes!" The entire room exploded with applause, hoots and hollers, loud whistling, and yelling! Finn and the band came to the front to accept their gargantuan check. Whitney, the wives, and their children all cheered for their husbands and dads. Finn and the band got their pictures taken with the enormous amount of money. They waved their families up to get pictures with them.

Whitney picked up Emmi and walked up toward the guys. Luke stood with Amanda, Trevor put his arm around a very pregnant Deanna. Alex picked up his son, AJ and Molly picked up their daughter, Juniper. Whitney went alongside Finn and placed her arm around his waist.

"I am so proud of you!" Finn leaned over and kissed her. Whitney looked at their group of friends, their kids, and the incredible amount of love that was there. She placed her hand on her stomach.

Everyone held the large check, which was written out to *Weekend Vibes* in very fancy cursive handwriting. Finn gently tickled Whitney's side. She knew that there would be no better time than right now.

She leaned in to whisper in Finn's ear.

The photographer was waiting for everyone to get situated.

"I have a secret." Finn grinned from ear to ear. Looking at her, he thought she'd never looked more beautiful. "What is it?" he asked curiously.

Whitney smiled ear to ear. "I'm pregnant!" Finn's emotions burst through like a marlin breaching the water! He pulled her close and kissed her hard. Whitney felt herself being lifted off the ground. He held her up for the photo in an elated state of emotion. "Yee-ha!" he yelled out!

Out in the audience, TJ sat with his arm around Jules as they enjoyed the site of the celebrations of another week-long tournament and the feeling of new love. Marlin sat on the floor, leaning against Jules' leg enjoying some ear pets. Kit was at the next table sitting closely beside Nathan. Their fingers were intertwined. Directly on the other side of Nathan was an identical-looking Josh. No wonder Kit was confused. Kit and Jules caught each other's sight and smiled.

At that same table, Rob stood behind Leanne, who was sitting with legs crossed, sipping a martini—extra olives. One of his hands was on her shoulder while the other held onto a beer. He intended on standing behind Leanne for the rest of his life, making sure to make her the happiest woman on the earth. Last night on the boat, they decided no more shenanigans and that they needed couples therapy. They start Monday—pending that no house showing comes up.

It took a while, but the family and crew of *Weekend Vibes* finally got in position. The photographer announced, "Okay, guys! Everyone say 'Marlin Week'!" Whitney and Finn's hands flew up in excitement! Finn couldn't think of a better way to end this incredible tournament.

And altogether, they yelled, *"Marlin Week!" Click!*

About the Author

Katherine Ruskey grew up coming "down the ocean" and quickly fell in love with the fun and charming town of Ocean City. Her favorite parts of beach life are the quiet morning runs along the boardwalk, the midday beach naps and books, and relishing in the breathtaking colors of the bayside sunsets. (A bucket of Thrashers french fries comes in as a top five favorite- but only if there is extra vinegar!) Marlin Week is Katherine's debut novel.

Children's Book Titles
by Katherine Ruskey

The A B Seas of Ocean City, Maryland

Elfcation

Inside Out Jammies

How to Plant a Jellybean

Let's Have a Parade

Elfis

About the Artist

Artist Carey Chen's love of the ocean, not only comes across in his artwork, but in his passion for sportfishing. Chen, a long time fisherman, spends most of his days out on the open sea where inspiration for his art runs as deep as the canyons. His attention to detail and artistic memory add to the brilliantly colored classic pieces that come to life. Whether the soft stripes of a thrashing marlin, the ombre blues and greens of a mahi, or the gleam of rays of sun reflecting off the crest of ocean waves, Chen captures the brilliance and beauty of the vast yet delicate details of elegant ocean life.

The Billfish Foundation

Founded in 1986, The Billfish Foundation set off on a mission to conserve billfish on a global platform. Since its initial tagging program, which began over 30 years ago, it has grown to be the largest international tagging program in the world. The Billfish Foundation has set itself apart from others by focusing not only on tagging but has expanded to habitat management and protection, conservation of species, and billfish database development. For more information on The Billfish Foundation, please visit www.billfish.org.

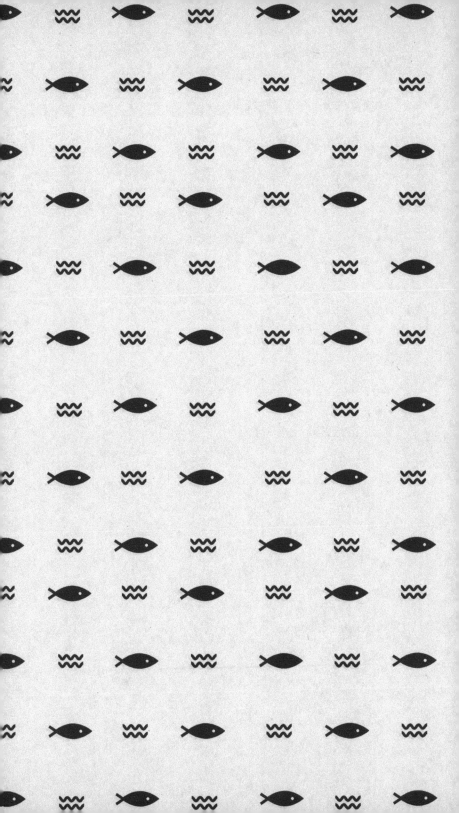

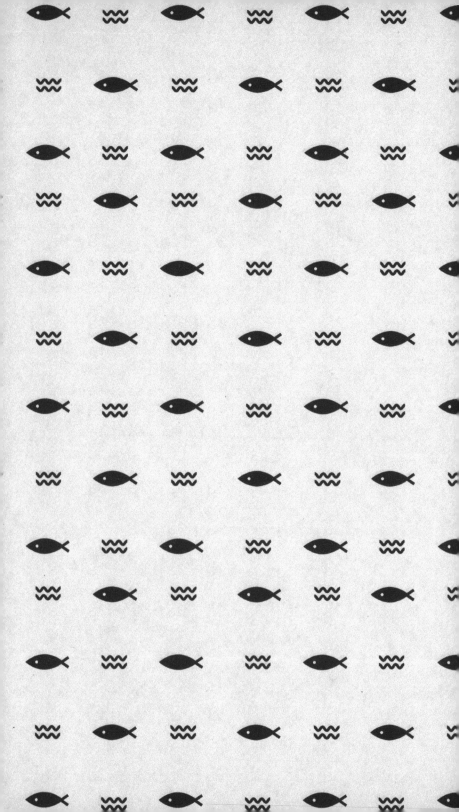

CPSIA information can be obtained
at www.ICGtesting.com
Printed in the USA
BVHW051838111222
653984BV00025B/559